SHIFTING BORDERS

JESSIE KWAK

RAZORGIRL
PRESS

Published by Razorgirl Press.

First U.S. Edition: November 2015

Cover design by EK Cover Design

Originally published as part of the *Four Windows: Seattle* periodical, September 2014

To Lacey, Love you, sis.

Chapter One

PATRICIA RAMOS-WAITES PICKED her way through the brackish puddles that passed for a sidewalk in this part of town. Reflected streetlight traced oily slicks in the pitted gravel, and a faint mist gathered on her cheeks and fogged her glasses. The neon sign announcing Oh Pho cast an orange hue in the premature evening gloom, but through the windows—papered with peeling, handwritten specials—the restaurant looked empty.

No, not empty. Her sister sat at a table near the door, shredding the label of her Tsingtao. Patricia waved, and Valeria scowled. Fantastic.

"Two small number sixes," Valeria said to the waitress before rising to kiss Patricia. They were alone in the restaurant, no surprise for a Monday night. Oh Pho's regular clientele of commercial truck drivers and warehouse workers had gone home for the evening, and it was too far from the artists' lofts and shops in Georgetown's main strip to attract the few people who actually lived down here.

"I saw two of your buses go by already," said Valeria. "You said you'd be here by five thirty."

Patricia wedged her stuffed backpack into the plastic booth opposite her sister, then slid in beside it. "Work was fine today, thanks for asking," she said. "We've been short-staffed this week, so things are extra busy. How are you doing, Val?" She searched her sister's face for cracks there—it had only been two weeks since the funeral, and though Patricia had called daily, Valeria had been putting her off.

She'd be putting her off today, as well. "Jesus, Pati," Valeria sighed. "Don't be a bitch. You're just never late."

"I can't make the buses run on time."

"But you can call."

So this was how it was going to go. "It's five forty-five, Val."

"Yeah. And I've got places to be."

"Then don't let me keep you waiting," Patricia snapped—and instantly regretted it, but didn't apologize. Just another snipe-fest between sisters, she thought.

The waitress returned before any more friendly fire could be loosed, two massive bowls of soup balanced on her tray. Valeria set to plucking out her slices of beef while they were still pink, draping them over the side of her bowl. Patricia used her chopsticks to plunge her beef deeper into the boiling broth.

"I need a favor from you tonight, Pati," Valeria said, shredding basil leaves into her soup without making eye contact. Patricia watched her with a sinking feeling, taking in her sister's black clothes, the black gloves lying on the table, the faint scent of pungent herbs rising above the anise aroma of the pho.

Nighttime favors were bad news.

"I have to help Ava with her science project," Patricia said automatically. She reached for the Sriracha, but hesitated when she saw the nozzle's tip: crusted over and black. Jalapeños would be— Patricia sighed. Would have been fine. Valeria had dumped them all into her bowl and was busy doctoring her soup into a nuclear accident of gloppy brown plum sauce and safety-orange Sriracha. Chile oil formed a greasy slick across the top.

"It's important." Valeria finally looked up. "It's Marco."

Patricia's heart broke for her sister. "Oh, Val." She reached across the table, took Valeria's cold hand in hers. The nails were ragged, chewed to the nub, like when they were girls. They were painted a *café con leche* color which nearly matched her own skin. A subdued tone. Everything about Valeria had been more subdued since Marco's accident.

And then the hand was gone. Valeria went back to her soup, not meeting Patricia's gaze.

"What is it?" Patricia asked, suspicious.

"I need to see him again."

"Val, you can't."

"Please, Pati."

"Do you have a permit? A court order? Because how will I explain to my kids that their tia has to go to jail over an illegal resurrection?" Patricia took a deep breath. "Val, I'm so sorry. I'm so sorry he's gone."

"Wouldn't you have brought Joe back if you could have?"

That stab, unfair and unexpected, sliced neatly through six years of emotional scar tissue. "Joe is in heaven," Patricia said quietly. "Why would I bring him back from that?"

"What if you knew he wanted to come?"

"You can't speak to the dead in their graves."

"You can if they want to be spoken to." Valeria met Patricia's gaze, eyes fierce and tear-bright, smoky eye makeup smudged around the lids. The restaurant's neon sign called out the reddish tones in her dark hair, but her curls hung limp, and her lips were chapped under the silver gloss she wore. "When I go out to his grave, I can sense him, just a little bit. He's waiting there. He wants me."

"But do you have the legal paperwork?" Patricia stabbed at her soup with her chopsticks. Legally, a few ghosts were allowed to come back, mostly to help solve unsolvable cases or clear up disputes over wills. Illegally... Patricia didn't want to know. Valeria had been selling her body for years to a local Mexican resurrectionist, acting as a host for the spirits he brought back. Valeria claimed that they only worked the lucrative court contracts, but Patricia knew her sister better than that.

Valeria hesitated, and Patricia could see her practicing the lie. But then she sighed. "No. I don't. This is entirely for me."

"And what do you think I can do?"

"Patricia, is it a crime to bring back the man I love? When he wants to be with me?"

"You said you were done with the illegal stuff. I'm not bailing you out of jail again." Patricia struggled to get a grip on a slippery piece of tendon, but her hand was shaking too badly to hold the chopsticks steady. Droplets of broth spattered the table when the morsel hit the soup's surface. "I don't know how you think I can help."

"I just need an extra pair of hands," Valeria said. "We'll be careful. No one will ever know."

Patricia sighed. "What about your Mexican guy?"

"Lucho's a businessman. He won't do a resurrection for free, and I can't pay him."

A chill traced itself down Patricia's spine. "So you're going to—"

"I've done it before. I'm not just hosting for him now—he's taken me on as an apprentice. I've done the last few resurrections on my own."

"Val." Patricia almost reached to take her sister's hand again. "Come over tonight. Adrian's at an away game, Ava's got her science project to keep her busy, and I think I might even have a bottle of wine somewhere. You can stay over."

"I can't. It has to be tonight." Valeria slurped a quick spoonful of broth, coughed on the chile sauces.

In the kitchen, the waitress and the cook were talking loudly in Vietnamese, pots banging as they cleaned up from the day. Calling this Monday night a bust, Patricia thought. Ready to go home to their own families just as soon as the Ramos sisters finished their meal. Patricia was suddenly very tired. "He's dead, Val," she said after a moment. "He won't be the Marco you loved."

"You haven't seen them, the way people are when they're reunited. The spooks are just as thrilled as the clients. I've made so many people happy, Pati. When do I get to be happy?"

"Val, this is stupid. You have to move on."

"Yeah, like you did? You still wear Joe's goddamn ring, Pati." She dug into her purse, and threw a ten-dollar bill on the table. "Forget it. Forget I ever asked you anything."

"Valeria, wait." Patricia grabbed her wrist, and Valeria didn't try to pull away. "Promise me..."

"Promise you what?"

Promise me you won't disappear without a trace this time, Patricia wanted to say, but that would only spark a fight she didn't have the energy for. "Promise you'll talk to me before you do anything rash."

Valeria pulled away. "I *am* fucking talking to you, Pati." She shrugged her purse over her shoulder and slammed the door as she left.

The bus, when it came, was nearly thirty minutes late and tailed closely by another bus of the same number. Patricia had given up on carrying a schedule.

Condensation from the crush of damp bodies fogged the windows. Smiley faces and tags and obscene words written in reverse were drawn in fingertip on the glass, their artists long disembarked.

Patricia was emptied by grief. She'd been soaked up and wrung dry so many times in the past two weeks that she could feel the very fibers of her psyche wearing through.

She grieved some for herself—she would miss smiling, joking Marco— but the largest measure of her grief was for her sister. Marco had brought Valeria back.

Ever since the first tattooed gangbanger Valeria had brought home to upset their parents, Patricia's sister had cultivated a sampler of horrible men— from the grunge wannabe drummer who never paid rent and stole her credit cards on the way out to the rich college kid who'd left her with an expensive cocaine habit. One had landed her in jail after he robbed an old woman and left Valeria's cell phone there by accident—not that Patricia entirely believed her sister's pleas of innocence. One had, thankfully, not landed her in jail after convincing her to ferry marijuana down from Canada. Valeria could be an idiot sometimes.

Their mother, Maryam, blamed the boyfriends for talking Valeria into these escapades, but Patricia wasn't so sure Valeria needed much convincing. Once she came up with a crazy idea, she'd do it no matter who it hurt—and no matter if she could talk anyone else into going along.

Over time, Patricia came to recognize the signs that something truly bad was about to happen. Valeria would show up unexpectedly to drop off some prized possession—a photo album of their parents in Nicaragua, or a gift Patricia had given her when they were girls. Right after Gabe had started high school, Valeria had given Patricia their grandmother's opal ring. "Just wanted to make sure you had it," she'd said before disappearing from contact, only to show up six months later with her hair dyed black, her eyes bruised and sunken, and a court date for fraud.

Marco had mellowed her out. He was a New Jersey transplant who'd come out to Seattle for a weekend visit and never went back, and he'd wax lyrical for hours about the scenery, the closeness of the mountains, the relaxed attitudes of the people. When he needed to blow off steam, he didn't take it out on Valeria or black out on Everclear—he'd just take whichever sports car he was working on for a drive around the Sound, or up the empty roads around Mount Rainier.

Maybe Valeria was getting older, maybe her semilegal resurrection work with Lucho gave her just enough of a thrill, but she seemed to have settled down. She'd had a steady-ish gig that probably wouldn't land her in jail, and a steadfast boyfriend who wouldn't land her in the hospital.

For nearly three years there'd been no more late-night phone calls asking for a ride back from Ellensburg or bail money. No cryptic texts saying she was in trouble, followed by months of radio silence. No random off-loading of her mementos just before she went on a truly wild bender. No more cocaine. No more pills. Just cold Tecates and the occasional joint with Marco.

Patricia prayed that this new Valeria was strong enough to withstand his loss.

Ava was in front of the television when Patricia walked in the door, a pair of scissors in one hand and a sheet of aluminum foil in the other. Bits of foil drifted like snow around her feet. Patricia leaned over the couch to kiss the top of her head. "You're supposed to be doing homework, Ava-bean."

"I am." Ava held up a lopsided star, brushing foil scraps off her arm to sift into the seat cushions. "It's for my project."

She was gluing the stars to the poster board in front of her, creating a glittering panorama around the printouts of Mars facts and a labeled diagram of the Mars rover *Curiosity*. Any normal kid would have stopped with the poster board, but Ava had also made up a scale model of *Curiosity*—displayed in a shoebox diorama of the Martian landscape—and had written a short story wherein the rover discovers gentle aliens who hope it has come in peace.

On the television, forensic scientists discussed motives while dissecting a murder victim. "I don't think this is appropriate for you, kiddo," Patricia said. "You know I don't want you to watch TV when I'm not around. You can put in one of your movies if you're done with your homework."

Ava shrugged, one skinny shoulder jerking toward her ear. "When is Mama Ramos coming home?" she asked, picking up the scissors.

Mama Ramos was what Marco had called Patricia and Valeria's mother, Maryam. His voice took on an Italian cadence when he said it: "I'll do the dishes, Mama Ramos," he'd say. "This is men's work here. Adrian! Front and center." And they'd be up to their elbows in soapsuds, talking about the beater car Adrian was fixing up.

Patricia's parents were settling beautifully into the snowbird lifestyle, ferrying their motor home between Albuquerque and Seattle with the seasons. They'd come up for the funeral, but hadn't stayed in Seattle's rainy November gloom for long. "They'll fly back up for Christmas," Patricia said. "I'll call her to make sure." She leaned to kiss her daughter's cheek, and caught a glimpse of blue hanging around her neck. Lapis lazuli, a polished teardrop on a delicate gold chain.

Valeria's necklace.

A chill ran up Patricia's spine. "Where did you get that?"

"Tía Valeria gave it to me."

"Did she say why?"

Ava shrugged again. "Because I liked it. She wanted me to have it."

"Did she give you anything else?"

"She gave Adrian T?o Marco's flask. She said it was his grandfather's."

"His flask? Really, your *tia* sometimes."

Ava nodded sagely and set to gluing another foil star into the crowded poster-board sky.

"Promise me you won't wear that at school, Ava-bean," Patricia said, dialing Valeria. "It's expensive."

"Can I wear it to church?"

"Of course."

Valeria wasn't picking up. The ringtone echoed into infinity—Valeria had never set up a voice mail account, said that she wouldn't listen to them anyway. Patricia hung up. *I'll do it*, she texted.

A second later her phone vibrated. *11:30.*

Dammit. *Pick me up.*

K. Wear black.

K.

Patricia slipped her phone back into her pocket, felt the familiar snag of her wedding ring on the edge of the fabric. She'd had a chance to say good-bye to Joe, to say her last "I love you," to give him one last kiss. Joe had had the chance to tell Ava to make him proud, Adrian to keep his head on straight, Gabe to keep on painting.

Joe had died a slow death, hooked up to IVs and monitors. Marco was gone in the blink of an eye, the slip of a tire. The fiery tumble of a sports car.

Didn't Valeria and Marco deserve the chance at last words?

Chapter Two

Forest Lawn Cemetery was a ten-minute drive from Patricia's house in White Center—less, the way Valeria was driving. "Slow down," Patricia hissed, gripping the door handle with all her strength. "If you get pulled over, I don't know how you'll explain that." She gestured at the duffel bag in the back seat. She had only a vague idea of what it contained, but it smelled sweet and foul as rotting fruit. "What's the hurry? He's not going anywhere."

Valeria's jaw tightened. "No hurry," she said, but she glanced once more in the rearview mirror, and the speedometer crept slightly higher.

They parked a few blocks away, where no one would remark on an extra car, and stepped past the heavy chain that blocked the cemetery's driveway. The earlier mist had shifted to a light rain, which was already soaking through the black Highline Pirates hoodie Patricia's oldest son had left at home. Her only rain jacket was baby blue, and had been summarily vetoed by Valeria.

Rows of flat headstones tufted the well-manicured lawn, following the gentle contours of the hills. Trim Japanese maples dotted the grounds, and a few oaks stretched dark silhouettes against the low clouds. Persistent clouds meant Patricia hadn't seen the moon for over a week, but the city lights infused the fog with the faintest of glows, illuminating their way. Barely.

Marco's grave was in the northeast corner—far from the road, Patricia saw with relief—tucked near the strip of wild brambled forest that covered the ridge's steep eastern shoulder. A waist-high fence separated the civilized dead from the disordered urban forest, and overhanging branches afforded Valeria and her just enough cover from the rain. The toes of her sneakers squelched in sodden fresh turf.

Patricia shivered, realizing she was standing on Marco's grave. She stepped aside.

Valeria's duffel bag clinked as she set it down. She stooped to brush the leaves and grass clippings off the stone:

Marco Caruso
Forever in our hearts.

"Who will Marco be when you bring him back?" Patricia whispered, and Valeria stiffened but did not answer.

Valeria's face glowed in the flame of her lighter; her jaw was set, her eyes flashing steel. She lit a pair of candles on the headstone, then a propane camping stove. She shook a pair of coals onto a grate over the flame. "Stop looking over your shoulder. You're making me nervous."

"I thought the cops were cracking down on illegal resurrections."

"The cops around here have drug deals to watch for. They're not out patrolling the cemeteries."

Strain as she might, Patricia couldn't see the gate over the rise of the hill—still, she felt exposed and nervous. Valeria looked up from her careful arrangement of . . . bones?

"It's fine, Pati. I've done this dozens of times. Hold this." Valeria handed over the flask of vile-smelling liquid, and Patricia held it at arm's length. She tried to force herself to relax.

The candles on the headstone sputtered as fat raindrops splashed down through the branches. It was never any use to talk sense into Valeria when she had a plan. When they were kids, she'd nearly drowned after breaking into a neighbor's swimming pool in Managua—Patricia had refused to go with her, and Valeria had snuck away to go on her own.

Their father had been angry with them both, but it was Patricia who'd gotten the spanking for not watching out for her little sister. Granted, Valeria had been in the emergency room, but the injustice still smarted.

Patricia had seen that same determined look in Valeria's eye tonight. "What do you need me to do?" she asked, afraid of the answer.

"I'll do all the ritual, don't worry about that. I just need you to hand me things when I need them, and to break the circle if anything goes wrong."

"Scalpel, stat," Patricia said, trying to laugh. She coughed nervously instead.

"Normally the resurrectionist summons a spirit into a host, but I've been reading about modifications to the spell that let a resurrectionist call the spirit directly into herself."

"Reading?"

"I've done the original spell before, and the variation isn't tricky. You're here just because if anything goes wrong, I'll need you to break the circle. Here." Valeria dumped the now-lit coals into a censer like they used in Catholic churches; she handed it to Patricia with a pair of tongs and a baggie full of sweet-smelling herbs. "If anything goes wrong, just dump the herbs onto the coals, erase part of the circle with your foot, and put a coal in each of my hands."

"Val—"

"Nothing's going to go wrong. But if it does, you just dump the herbs, break the circle—"

"And put a burning coal into each of your bare hands," Patricia said. She swallowed.

"Right. And keep an eye out."

"For the security guard?"

"Sure." Valeria swung her gaze over the cemetery, searching. When she seemed satisfied that they were alone, she lay down over the grave, her head resting just below the stone. She began to whisper, in Spanish oddly accented from years forgetting their native tongue and then relearning it at the hands of her Mexican resurrectionist. She seemed tense at first, hands clenched on her belly, but as she spoke she slowly relaxed, drawing her palms down over her hips, smoothing her dress in a way that seemed both self-conscious and sensual.

Water began to seep up out of the fresh turf, darkening Valeria's dress, cradling her hips like ghostly fingers.

Valeria's voice faded to silence, though her lips still moved. Patricia leaned closer, trying to make out the words. The salt ring glimmered a brief moment, then went dull once more. A faint play of light flashed over the wall of foliage beyond the edge of the cemetery.

Patricia looked up, startled.

Valeria's hands clutched the grass, fingers worming their way into the fresh soil, her back arching, shoulders writhing against the headstone.

The light came again, stronger.

It could be the headlights of a car, maybe, someone turning down a residential street? The foliage above them lit up again. Flashlight.

Patricia's mouth went dry.

"Valeria," she whispered, but her sister didn't seem to hear. "Valeria."

A breeze stirred the grass inside the salt circle, toyed with the ends of Valeria's hair. The air around Patricia was still.

The beam of light came again, stronger now. The police. Patricia's mind whirled, but there was no excuse that could explain away what they were so obviously doing. Oh, Lord, her job, her kids. Her church. "Valeria!"

Her sister moaned.

Patricia glanced back over her shoulder and caught a glimpse of a small group in the distance. Rough voices, laughter muffled by the fog. A hint of cigarette smoke drifted on the breeze before them.

Not the police.

"Valeria, we have to go." Patricia hesitated, her foot poised over the line to erase it. What would breaking the circle right now do to her sister?

As if in response to the thought, Valeria's body arched violently away from the ground, her face screwed into a silent scream. A trickle of black blood seeped from one nostril, and when she opened her eyes, the whites were colored an unholy pink.

Patricia fumbled for the brazier. She dashed her foot across the salt line, feeling a hurricane force of wind tear into her as she did. Her hair whipped across her eyes. She grabbed for Valeria's hand, plucked a fiery coal from the censer.

The stench of burned flesh stung her nostrils as she dropped the first coal into Valeria's hand—her sister gasped, flinging it away to hiss in the wet grass.

"Can't take him," Valeria whispered. "I almost—"

"Hey, hey, what you doing?" A shout came from behind them. "Ramos?"

The men were running, now. Glowing butt of a cigarette flicked into the grass, silhouette of a handgun against the fog.

Patricia grabbed Valeria's hands, tugging desperately against her sister's dead weight. "No, no no no," Valeria gasped. Her body arched again, wrenching violently as her heels dug into the fresh turf above Marco's grave. She screamed, piercing the night.

Patricia pulled once more with all her might, dragging her sister's writhing body past the salt line.

She gasped as an ice-cold wind rushed through her, then searing heat; her body suddenly felt too tight.

Too tight, yet surprisingly strong. She yanked her sister to her feet and half carried, half dragged her toward the cover of dense brush at the edge of the cemetery.

A gunshot rang out. Bark splintered off the oak above them. Someone let off a stream of curses. "Don't kill her, pendejo!"

Patricia boosted Valeria over the fence, then vaulted it herself, tumbling into a clutching Oregon grape that clawed at her baggy sweatshirt. She grabbed Valeria's arm, propelling her through the underbrush like a reluctant toddler, heedless of blackberry thorns and slapping wet ferns, sliding ever downward through the sloping underbrush.

Now running, now tumbling, until Patricia's shins hit the trunk of a fallen tree and she dropped, stifling a cry. She wriggled her way between the tree and the sodden earth, hugging her sister tight to her, hand clamped over Valeria's mouth.

Valeria shook uncontrollably, but whether from fear or cold—or from the spell—Patricia couldn't tell.

The crashing pursuit continued a few minutes longer, the men calling to each other, the beams of their flashlights streaking terrifyingly close to where the Ramos sisters lay. After a long while, the sounds faded to silence.

Patricia stayed still, unsure if they had actually left; the chorus of rushing blood in her ears and her sister's ragged breath muffled all other sounds. A stone dug into her ribs. When she could bear it no more, she lifted her weight onto just one shoulder, shifting so her hand could brush away the stone.

A twig snapped. Less than ten feet away.

She froze, her heart pounding.

"Val. Valium, baby." The man who had shouted earlier was wheezing now, his voice raspy from liquor and smoke. "I know you're in here somewhere. I know you can hear me, and you know what I want. I'm gonna send one of my boys to see you tomorrow. Call me in the morning, we talk, and I'll send Charles. But sweetheart, you think you're smart, you try to lay low? I'll send Javier."

He waited, as though expecting a response, but damned if Patricia was going to give him one. Valeria's breath came ragged and hot under Patricia's hand.

After what seemed like eternity, Patricia heard him clamber, swearing, back through the underbrush.

Patricia gripped her sister tight a while longer, her cheek wet with Valeria's tears, Valeria's fingers curled in her hair, her own fingers digging into the thin wet fabric of Valeria's dress. Valeria was shivering, flighty tremors that slowly grew into sobs.

The rich black earth reeked of decay, the slick mat of waterlogged leaves beneath them rotting back into soil. Something crawled over Patricia's hand. It had started to rain in earnest now, gathering in the leaves, dripping in fat drops onto Patricia's back.

"We should go," Patricia said finally, but she couldn't make herself move. She should be afraid, she should feel cold, but the only sensation Patricia was aware of was joy, elation at finding herself in Valeria's arms. :val, valvalval:

Something stirred deep within her, its attention pulsing toward Valeria. She stroked her sister's back, brushed her lips against her cheek.

"I failed, Pati," Valeria said after a long moment. "There's no second chance. He's gone forever."

Patricia kissed her sister's forehead, tucking a strand of hair behind her ear. Warm, vital blood rushed in her veins. "It's OK, babe," she heard herself say. "I'm here."

A pressure, like the pulsing ache of an anxiety attack, began in Patricia's chest, like her rib cage was too tight, her lungs carved of stone. She forced herself to take deep breaths, pushing against the pain.

"They wanted Marco," she heard Valeria say. "And they probably got him."

"What?" The pressure inside her chest swirled, fluttering against her ribs. A wave of clammy heat broke over her, and she tugged at the throat of her hoodie, trying to breathe. Nausea, throbbing head, hot flashes. Patricia ticked off the symptoms, trying to remember if she'd hit her head. She pushed Valeria away and scrambled out from beneath the fallen tree, just in time to revisit her earlier meal of pho.

Patricia wiped her lips on the sleeve of the now-filthy hoodie. *Sorry, Gabe.*

"You OK, Pati?"

Valeria's voice swam to her as though through water. "Who were they?" Patricia asked, and Valeria started to answer, in that hedging way she had when she was trying to lie without lying. Patricia couldn't make out her words —they sounded muddled, echoey, and Patricia fought down her rising panic. *I think I have a concussion*, she tried to tell her sister, but her lips wouldn't move. *I think . . .* And the pressure—the presence?—in Patricia's chest stopped fluttering. It shifted, just ever so slightly.

:who?:

"I'm Patricia," she whispered. "Who are you?"

Valeria stopped midsentence. "Pati? Oh, shit. Pati?"

Patricia could feel her sister's hands on her face, hear her frantic voice, but all she could focus on was the swirling voice in her head. *:whowhowho?:* The world went black.

Chapter Three

LIGHT, PALE AND grey, glowed through a stranger's lace curtains. Patricia slapped her hand out for her glasses on the nightstand—her nightstand?—and squinted as the ceiling came into view. Low and dingy, the gold-flecked acoustic ceiling tiles were watermarked in a half-familiar pattern near the wall. She swung her legs off the bed and was surprised to feel carpet. Her carpet?

"I'm home," she whispered, but the feeling of disorientation remained. A door should be there beside the dresser. Where had the door gone? Her heart began to race—but no, there was the door, across from the foot of the bed. Where it had always been. "Get yourself together, Pati."

She stood, dizzy, her vision distorted as though with a new glasses prescription. The floor seemed slightly too close, and she stumbled over the unfamiliar carpet, catching herself on the edge of the bed. Her stomach churned.

She made it to the bathroom, collapsed on the cracked and water-warped linoleum with her back against the door.

"Pati?" The hollow core door shuddered as someone—Valeria?—tried the handle. "Pati, let me in."

Her throat ached to answer, but it was as though she'd forgotten how to use her vocal cords. :*val?*:

Patricia's head felt crowded, split in two, ravaged by a cyclone of half-formed thoughts she couldn't quite make out. :*val its*: Bile rose in her throat, and Patricia lunged for the toilet, her bare knees screaming in agony as she knelt on a knife-edged crack in the linoleum. She vomited, then clutched herself before the toilet, waiting for the nausea to pass.

Slowly, pieces began to fill in. Why was Valeria here? Oh, Lord, what had happened last night?

"Pati?" The doorjamb splintered as Valeria threw her weight against the door.

When Patricia was reasonably sure she wasn't going to throw up again, she pulled herself up, gripping the bathroom counter. She looked terrible, mascara smudged over sallow cheeks. It was the ghoulish mask of an old woman playing out a party girl's hangover.

She rinsed her mouth, then clawed her fingers through the wavy tangles of her reddish-black hair, capturing it in a ponytail. She started to turn away, but something caused her to turn back. She examined her own face with new eyes.

:not val who?:

"I'm Patricia," she said, unsure of who—or why—she was answering.

:ah... :

The presence felt satisfied, slightly less panicked. She felt a sudden chill. "Marco?" A hopeful stirring response. "Marco, is that you?"

The doorjamb splintered and broke, and the door's cheap veneer cracked into pieces. Valeria tumbled in afterward, and at the sight of her, the presence inside Patricia leapt. Blood rushed to her head, and another wave of nausea hit her like a fist. She lunged for the toilet. She hadn't thrown up like this since... Since those dark drunken nights after Joe had died.

Valeria knelt behind her, stroking her hair, rubbing her back. "Marco, it's OK," she said. "Calm down. Everything will be all right. Marco. Can you hear me?"

Patricia whimpered, not of her own will.

"You remember my sister, Pati, right? You're with her. You'll be OK. We'll take good care of you. Don't worry about trying to tell me anything yet—we've got time, babe. Just be cool right now."

Patricia spat and wiped her mouth with a wad of toilet paper. "What time is it?"

"I already called the clinic and told them you're not coming in. I told them you've got that thing, that flu that's going around."

Patricia rubbed her face. "Already short-staffed," she said.

"The secretary, Cheryle or whoever, she talked my ear off about what a good woman you are, how dedicated you are even when on your deathbed. She was very admiring." Valeria smoothed back Patricia's hair. "And she said to stay the hell away if you're sick."

The presence inside her soothed at Valeria's voice and touch, sat coiled and purring like a cat below her rib cage.

"I have paperwork here. Needs to go back."

"They're fine without you, Pati. You're in no condition to go to work."

"Then let me take a shower."

"Fine, but I'm staying in the bathroom. You don't get to be alone for a second until I'm sure everything's all right."

Patricia felt a chill, fragments of conversations over the years coming back to her. A disoriented ghost could kill its host accidentally, Valeria had said once. It could come back malicious, or simply angry to have been brought back at all. Even the kindest ghost could panic and cause its host damage in the early hours.

"What did you do?" Patricia asked, her disorientation shifting to anger.

"Exactly what I planned to do," Valeria snapped. "Until you broke the ritual."

"You were screaming! There were men with guns."

"You can't just step into a ritual like that and—"

"You told me—"

"You don't know what you're messing with! You could have killed yourself —"

"Me? I did what you told me. There were men with guns, Valeria! Guns, shooting at us."

Valeria's jaw clenched. "You didn't have to come."

"And, what? Let you run out on us again?" A wave of dizziness washed over Patricia, as though the fight was agitating the alien presence inside her. She gripped the edge of the counter to keep from falling.

"Pati?" Valeria grabbed her arm, helped her stand. "You OK?" Marco surged at the touch. "I'm sorry, OK, Pati? I'm really sorry. I didn't mean for this to happen."

Patricia watched the emotions play over her sister's face in the mirror. She looked like she hadn't slept in days, grief and exhaustion making her seem much older than thirty-eight. "How do you get him out of me?"

"Lucho's on his way."

"Valeria..."

"We'll get you taken care of. Both of you. Now take a shower—you'll feel normal again."

Valeria sat on the toilet and thumbed through a magazine to give Patricia a semblance of privacy while she undressed, but Patricia still turned her back. It had been too many years since she'd been naked in front of someone.

"Did Adrian come home last night? I can't remember anything after..."

"He was home already, and he and Ava both got off to school on time this morning. He ate like six scrambled eggs, Pati. Jesus. I can't even imagine what you paid for groceries when Gabe was still living at home."

"They killed a box of cereal in seven minutes flat one morning. I timed them. Did they win last night?"

"Yeah, sixty-two to fifty-six."

"Good."

The water felt divine. Normally Patricia was wary of the energy bill, but this morning she lingered, letting the water flow over her. Deep within her chest, Marco began to quiver in the silence.

"Keep talking, Val. He likes it. It calms him down."

"Yeah? You can feel him?" Valeria's voice held anticipation, longing, hope. "Marco, can you hear me?"

The presence swirled, then settled once more. "He can hear you. But he, I don't know, he moves around when you talk to him directly. It's making me nauseous. But he's listening. Did Adrian tell you any more about the game?"

"Not really. He spent most of breakfast texting. Is he always that quiet in the morning?"

"He's never quiet when he can give you a play-by-play. Did Ava remember her science project?"

"She did. That girl goes overboard, doesn't she?"

Patricia laughed. "Every time."

She rinsed the last of the conditioner out of her hair, then reluctantly turned off the shower. She toweled off behind the curtain, then dressed discreetly in the bedroom, wary both of her sister's eyes and of the new strange male presence within her. "I'm watching you, Marco," she whispered when her sister was out of earshot. "Don't get any ideas."

Lucho would be here at ten, Valeria told her as she fixed cereal for them both. There was a note from Adrian stuck to the kitchen counter by a ring of milk. *Hey mom, try tomato juice + fried eggs people TELL ME it works, haha. Going to a movie w/ L on friday, home late tonight after practice DONT WORRY—A.*

"Tomato juice?"

Valeria read the note and laughed. "I told him we'd been out dancing."

"You told him *what*?"

"Relax. He's a grown kid, he can handle thinking his mom got a little drunk. You looked like you'd been hit by a truck full of tequila, so what, was I supposed to tell him you were out getting yourself possessed by ghosts?" Valeria sloshed a bowl of Wheetie-Ohs down in front of Patricia. "Who's L?"

"Lucy."

"Oh, yeah. Glad they're still together. She's a sharp kid."

"She's good for him, but she got into Texas State. Music scholarship. Adrian says they're going to make it work, but how many college freshmen do you know who can make it work with their high school boyfriends back home?" Patricia sighed. "You never want to see your kid go through his first heartbreak."

"First ever. Gabe still hasn't gotten himself a lady, has he?"

"Not that he'd tell me."

"He come home much?"

Patricia shook her head. "You'd think UW was on the other side of the country."

The cereal tasted like cardboard, and the coffee Valeria brewed up left an oily slick over the tongue. Patricia pushed the food away.

"You have to eat, it's important. If you don't start feeling like yourself right away, the ghost can get too strong. The important thing is that you stay stronger than the ghost, or he can take over."

"Wow, thanks. That sounds great."

"Don't, Pati. I already feel like shit. Just eat."

Patricia took another bite of the cardboard cereal, washed it from her mouth with a swig of water. "How long?"

"Lucho should be here in a couple of minutes."

"I meant for the ghost. He'll get it out of me?"

Valeria cracked her knuckles. "It's not so easy, Pati."

"What's not so easy about it?"

"I'm going to let Lucho explain. He knows this stuff way better than I do."

"Obviously."

It was a testament to how badly Valeria felt that she didn't respond, and Patricia was torn between feeling guilty and letting herself get even more angry. She settled on self-righteous indignation and slurped at her coffee, burning her tongue.

A knock on the door finally saved them from the awkward silence. Lucho, smelling of stale cigarettes and wearing his standard pair of frayed grey sweatpants and torn Nirvana T-shirt, his fingers stained black with... ink? A well-patched, neon-pink JanSport bag was slung over his shoulder, probably left over from when his daughters were in high school. It reeked of the same herbs Valeria had carried the night before.

Patricia had seen some of the more famous resurrectionists on television, but it was almost always the white hippie types, with their mystical tattoos and amulets for sale, who made the big cases and advertised their services at exorbitant rates. There was a Jamaican man who also got some press—he looked the part, with his "yah, mons" and his dreadlocks plaited with bones.

Lucho looked like if you saw him on the street you'd turn away, expecting him to ask for a handout. He had to be well-off, though, with his constant stream of government contracts. Valeria said he had a nice house in West Seattle, and was putting both his daughters through private colleges.

That was part of being a resurrectionist, Patricia guessed. The black

Jamaican who practiced his accent, the white hippies who made shows of their stones and tattoos, the Tibetan shamans who pretended not to speak English, and the leathery Mexican *curandero* who looked like he'd just walked in from the Sonora chewing on snakeskin.

It was all part of the show.

Lucho sat on a chair beside her and took her chin in his gnarled hand, looking deep into her eyes. "How you doing, Pati?" he asked finally, releasing her chin but continuing to examine her face with an intensity that reminded Patricia of a doctor encountering a particularly fascinating ailment.

"As well as could be expected."

"What I expect is to see you throwing up this cereal in a few minutes."

"I already did that."

"Ah. Good. Nena, *café*?"

Valeria set a mug on the table beside the old man. For his age, his hair was still a strong grey-black; his face was leathery and wrinkled, but mostly from the sun. This close, Patricia was starting to wonder just how old he actually was. His facial muscles still seemed firm. Another illusion for the job, perhaps?

"Marco, *cabrón*, you hear me in there?"

Patricia felt him stir. "He hears you."

"You can feel him already? Damn, these Ramos sisters are naturals."

"I'm not a natural."

Lucho ignored her and took a long drink of his coffee. "Has he tried to say anything?"

"Um." Patricia looked at her sister. "He's said your name a couple of times."

Valeria's face lit up. "Really?"

"Don't you start, Nena," Lucho said, sparing her a scowl. "Hey, Marco. You listen, OK? I don't want you to try to answer me right now, just listen. You're probably feeling pretty scared, and I don't blame you. But you're safe, we won't let anything happen to you. How this works is that I'll take you and Patricia through some exercises over the next few days, and pretty soon you'll be strong enough to speak. I'll tell you when that is, so don't worry about figuring it out. And don't worry about trying to tell us anything—there's plenty of time for that."

"Why did you both tell him not to try to speak?" Patricia asked.

Lucho sat back. "The ghosts, when they come back, they always have something they want to say. A few want to tell someone they loved them or something like that, but with most it's something really stupid, like 'The keys to the car are in my sock drawer,' or 'Tell Amanda to register for next semester.'" He took another sip of coffee. "The ones we bring back for the courts were mostly murdered, or they have some big-ass secret and they want to tell us what's wrong. They can overdrive a host's brain trying to talk."

That explained the rush of panicked obsession whenever Marco saw Valeria. "I think he was trying to tell you something at first, Val. He was pretty excited, and..." She touched her throat, trying to think of the words. "It was like my throat was working without me. Like he was trying to make me say something."

Lucho frowned. "Marco, *güey*. Don't try to control Pati, yeah? You need to calm down, and we'll get you out on your own. It's bad manners to try to control your host. You'll be fine, everything's fine, you're safe."

Marco fluttered in her breast, then settled with a sense of melancholy. "I don't think he meant to," Patricia said. "He feels contrite."

"'Contrite.'" Lucho sat back, laughing. "I like you, *profe*. Now. You good for a minute? I need to yell at Nena for being an idiot. You just sit tight, then I'll come back and teach you some tricks on how to control that *pendejo* boyfriend of your sister's."

Valeria cringed, but followed him meekly outside. Patricia almost felt bad for her.

Almost.

Chapter Four

Patricia pushed away the bowl of soggy cereal, nausea winning out over hunger for the time being. She could hear Lucho outside, caught a faint whiff of Valeria's cigarette wafting through the open kitchen window.

She scraped out her bowl, then began to wash the dishes—tidying her anxiety along with the kitchen. Counters wiped, coffee mugs washed, and all the clean dishes set to dry in the dishwasher.

Valeria always made fun of her for that, but it saved space, and it had been years since the dishwasher last ran. Maybe when Adrian graduated from high school she'd have a few extra dollars to fix it. Get him a good scholarship for basketball, and money might not be quite so tight. If he could just finish out this season as strongly as he started, colleges would come calling.

Patricia had a litany of repairs to the house she planned to tackle after Adrian graduated—starting with the bathroom door Valeria broke this morning. She had no doubt Valeria would promise to pay for it, but Patricia wasn't going to hold her breath. At the very least maybe Valeria would drive her to the RE Store—Patricia couldn't imagine trying to get a door on the bus.

"So they didn't see you, eh?" she heard Lucho say, his raspy voice sharp with anger. "What's it matter if they saw you, Nena? Who else they gonna think did it?"

"Lucho, quiet!"

Patricia turned off the faucet.

"This is my livelihood you're fucking with," he growled, softer now. "Or you even think about that?"

"That's not—"

"You fix this. You lose me my best client, we're through."

"You can't do this without me."

"Val."

The silence drew out, and Patricia busied herself with the dishes once more, afraid to be caught eavesdropping. She turned the faucet to a quiet trickle, and let a few forks clatter in the sink.

"You fix this," Lucho said. "Or you're in way worse trouble than being out of a job. *No voy contigo.* This is your road."

Inside her, Marco lurched. Patricia gripped the edge of the sink, bile rising in her throat. "Calm down," she whispered. "You're making me sick." Marco settled, slightly, the sensation of his presence only a faint pressure below her rib cage.

The door banged open, and Patricia opened the faucet to full blast.

"Pati! So sorry we left you so long." Lucho entered with a wide smile, a jovial *abuelito* greeting his favorite daughter. Valeria slunk in after, reeking of cigarettes. "I was just telling your sister—ay, sit down, *profe.*"

"I'm OK." Patricia straightened and wiped her hands on the dish towel. "He just moved and startled me, but we're fine now. Aren't we, Marco." She could feel him, as sullen as Ava when she knew she was in the wrong. "You're worse than Ava in a fit," she told him, and felt his... embarrassment?

"I'm fine. We're both... fine," she said.

Could you say that a ghost was fine?

:tell val:

"He just said: 'Tell Val.' He wants to say something," she said.

"Don't say anything," said Lucho. "Wait up, *güey.* We'll get to you."

"It seems important."

Lucho studied her a moment, and she saw a fleeting hint of concern on his face. "It always is. You can hear him?" Patricia nodded. "And you think you feel his emotions?"

"Sure—Marco, you with me?" He swirled, and Patricia's knees buckled. Lucho was at her side in a heartbeat, his strong arm around her waist.

"You're sitting now. Dishes can wait." He led her to a chair. "You can understand his words? Normally that takes a coupla days, even for a pro host and a relatively sane ghost."

"Sane ghost?"

Lucho pursed his lips, a noncommittal gesture. "They go... stale. If they're left dead too long."

"How long is too long?"

"You're fine, *profe*. Marco's gonna be a good ghost, aren't you *cabrón*?"

:take care:

"He says he'll be careful." Patricia closed her eyes, trying to concentrate on what else he was saying. She caught the half-formed image of a milk carton. A faint tapping disturbed her, and she opened her eyes to see the cabinet where she kept the cereal rattling. She laughed. "And he thinks I should eat something, I guess. What?"

Lucho met Valeria's gaze above Patricia's head, his expression deadly serious a moment. Then he smiled. "Marco's right," he said. "You eat up, and then get some rest. I gotta go, but I'll be back tonight. Val can walk you through some of the exercises I taught her when she was first learning to host."

"I don't want to learn to host," Patricia said.

Lucho shrugged. "Too late for that," he said. He took her hand in his, his leathery skin as soft as a well-worn paper bag and just as brown. His nails were clean, the tips of his fingers bent at odd angles. Patricia wondered if they hurt him. He didn't move as though he were arthritic.

"OK, *profe*. We gotta teach you some things so you can keep this sonovabitch in line. Marco, *escúchame*." He wrinkled his nose. "*¿Habla español?*" he asked Valeria.

"Nope."

"What kind of man you with, anyway?"

"Italian."

Lucho sucked at his teeth. "So, Marco Polo, listen up. It's gonna feel weird, someone having this type of control over you, but don't you worry. It's just for now, just cuz you're weak. But you're gonna get back to your full strength soon, you'll be with your *chica*, things'll be just fine. But you gotta cooperate, cuz if you don't, things'll go bad for Pati here. *Capisce*? And if things goes bad for Pati, things goes bad for you." This last part came out in his best Marlon Brando.

Patricia stiffened. "How might things go bad?"

"It's, uh... Don't worry, kiddo. We'll be fine, huh? It's like those Cialis commercials, 'May cause vomiting,' you know. You had kids, so think of it that way—it's like being pregnant, you got all these hormones and morning sickness and weird cravings, but it's all smashed into two weeks instead of nine months. Right, Nena?" He didn't look at Valeria for confirmation. "And now I go. You girls play nice today, and I'll be back tonight. I don't wanna hear about no fights. I get enough referee time when my own girls are home." He patted Patricia's cheek, then he was out the door, pink JanSport bag slung over his shoulder.

Patricia stared at her hands. Valeria slouched against the fridge. *If you can't say anything nice,* thought Patricia, wracking her brain for conversation.

Not that she had any shortage of things to ask: *What did Lucho mean, "You'll be in worse trouble than being out of a job?" Why the hell were men shooting at us last night? Where do you think you get off playing with life and death?*

She kept her mouth shut. She didn't want Valeria barging out the front door just yet.

Dealing with Valeria was always such delicate business. Like she was a wounded mountain lion that might take your hand off, or a grenade that might or might not be live, or a volcano that could erupt without notice. Had she been this volatile with Marco, too? *How on earth did you deal with her?*

As if in response, Patricia felt Marco stir, stretching toward Valeria with longing. Valeria looked up suddenly, blinking.

"Lucho wants me to teach you some tricks to keep Marco under control," she said. "It's pretty simple stuff. Are you tired? Or do you want to do this now?"

Patricia sighed. "Let's do this."

They spent the rest of the morning going over proper hosting techniques. After the arcane incantations of the night before, Patricia was surprised to find today's exercises achingly mundane. Valeria led her through some simple meditations, and then combed through Patricia's possessions for a talisman. To help ground her, she said.

Valeria brought an armload out to the coffee table: Patricia's favorite scarf; a drawing Ava had made her; their grandmother's opal ring, brought out without comment. Patricia's job was to concentrate on each, and tell Valeria when she felt the most "herself." Patricia felt like an idiot.

"This is my talisman," Valeria said, holding out her hand. On her wrist was a fraying black leather bracelet, the thongs knotted through a metal chain.

"You've had that since we were kids," Patricia said.

"That's why it works. It makes me feel like me." She stood. "None of these work. What happened to that Van Halen shirt you wore to death when we were in high school?"

"Seriously, Val?" Patricia leaned back against the couch, racking her brain for something that made her feel "like herself." She considered the paraphernalia of motherhood, of housework, of her job. But did those things make her feel like herself? Why couldn't she answer such a simple question? "My Bible?" she asked.

Valeria shook her head. "Nothing spiritual—there's too much openness to God and the world and all that. Too ungrounding."

"'Ungrounding' is a word?"

"You know what I mean. You want something that closes you off. That makes you feel like yourself."

"Val, I have no idea what you mean."

Valeria was prowling the small living room, examining the family vacation photos and knickknacks. The room had always seemed dark to Patricia, despite the bright curtains she hung and Gabe's colorful paintings on the walls. "What are you—"

"What's this rock?" Valeria cut her off. "Why is it here?"

Patricia craned her neck to see Valeria holding an agate from the kitchen windowsill. "It's just an agate, Val. From Cannon Beach, I think."

"Catch," Valeria said, flipping the rock to her.

It was nothing special, just a mottled brown agate flecked with amber. She'd found it on their last trip to the Oregon coast as a family before Gabe left for college.

They'd gone in spring, when the hotels were cheap and the ocean was frigid. Ava and Adrian had wanted to swim in the pool, and so Patricia left Gabe to watch them and spent a precious afternoon by herself. She'd hunted through tide pools and run barefoot in the sand. She'd let the surf break over her feet until her toes went numb, then stopped at a little beachfront restaurant to indulge in a glass of wine and a cup of clam chowder. She'd pocketed the oyster crackers to take back for Ava.

And she'd found this agate, directly across from Haystack Rock. Nothing special, nothing shiny, but it was like a gift from the ocean she'd spent the day frolicking with. She'd felt electric, thrumming with the energy of the crashing waves and the possibilities of the future. She'd felt like herself.

"That's perfect," Valeria said when Patricia told her the story. "Totally perfect."

Patricia turned the agate over in her hand, watching the little glimmers of amber catch the light.

"Val? What did Lucho mean about ghosts going stale?"

"Don't worry about it. He's talking about ghosts that have been dead for years, but never really left our realm. Like a murder victim's ghost that's been wandering untethered for years—you can't try to host them, because they can drive a host crazy."

"Untethered?"

"Like Marco's tethered to you right now. Ghosts have to be tethered to a host in order to stay stable in this realm, otherwise it's like they get ripped apart. They want to stay here, but they have nothing to hold on to. They start to break up."

"So Marco can't exist outside of me."

Valeria took a deep breath. "No."

"When it's time for him to go, we send him back?"

"Or transfer him to a new host."

"Have you done that before?" The way Valeria paused told Patricia everything she needed to know. "Val..."

"We'll figure this out. Don't worry."

"This is crazy." But Patricia said it without rancor, and Valeria simply looked tired, not angry. Patricia bit her lip. They'd made it this long without an argument. She decided to press her luck. "Who were those men last night? The ones with the guns."

Valeria straightened. "Just some guys Lucho and I work with on occasion," she said. One index finger scraped across the cuticle of her thumb.

"Do all your clients shoot at you?"

"No, these guys are—well, they're not nice guys. The resurrections we do for them aren't always legal."

Shocker. "So, what, they're into drugs? Murders?" Patricia kept her voice friendly. Wounded mountain lion, live grenade, erupting volcano. She tried to stay calm. What kind of guys with guns needed a resurrectionist on call?

"I don't know what they're into, just that sometimes they call us."

"And they want Marco." Marco swirled, agitated. "So, what, you're working for a band of wannabe Los Ciegos or something?" At the look on Valeria's face, Patricia felt cold. "Val. Tell me you're not working for Los Ciegos."

"I'm working for Lucho."

What kind of danger were they in? What kind of danger were her children in? "Val..."

"How do you even know who Los Ciegos are?"

"Because I have teenage sons," Patricia snapped. "Who have stupid teenage boy friends who do stupid teenage boy things like join gangs and get killed. But you—"

"It's not like that. They hired Lucho once, and we did a job, no questions asked."

Once? Patricia thought. *Sure.* "And they want Marco why?"

"He did some work for them, too. Just some cars. Nothing illegal, he wouldn't have gotten mixed up in that. But he learned something they want to know."

Patricia raised an eyebrow. "About their engines? You brought Marco back from the dead to tell them they need to replace their carburetor?" Tears welled up in Valeria's eyes, but Patricia was too angry to care. "What kind of danger have you put my family in?"

"Nothing, none," said Valeria. "We'll get it worked out, I've called them already. I just wanted to make sure Marco wouldn't be hurt. I just—I just needed him." The tears began to spill over, now, and Patricia's compassion broke through her anger. She reached out to touch her sister's thigh. She could feel Marco inside her, aching.

"You should be smarter than this, Valeria," Patricia said.

Valeria slapped her hand away. "Well, I'm not. We can't all be perfect, with our perfect little lives and perfect little kids."

"I'm not perfect, but at least I don't get involved with gangs!"

"You have no idea. You don't know what my life is, but you think you can just tell me—"

"Were you in trouble, Val? Because you've got a family who can help you if you need it. You can—"

"I'm not in a fucking gang, Pati. Calm the fuck down." Valeria pushed herself to her feet.

Patricia tried to follow, but a wave of nausea forced her back onto the couch. "You're getting shot at by gang members," she said.

"That's not the same thing."

"No one I know gets shot at by gang members."

"Maybe you should expand your social circle beyond your church friends!" Valeria was shouting now.

"I don't think I'm the one with the problem."

"No, you never do. And that's your problem."

"I'm not getting shot at!"

"Of course not, Miss High-and-Mighty Queen Bitch with the perfect life."

"Valeria!" But she was gone, slamming the front door behind her.

Marco swirled, desperate to follow, and Patricia could feel waves of energy emanating off his presence. The door rattled on its hinges, and a dining chair flung itself toward it, slamming against the wall in a sickening, splintering crash.

Patricia gripped the agate as hard as she could, her fingernails digging into the palm of her hand. "Don't you start," she muttered. "Don't you dare, Marco." And in response she felt a roiling stew of exhausted sadness, regret, and apology. She collapsed on the couch, clutching the agate, uncertain which emotions were hers and which came from the alien presence drifting within her.

Chapter Five

PATRICIA TRIED TO keep busy at first, but she felt terrible, sluggish, like she was wading through molasses. Like she was hungover. She took a look at the broken chair—the leg was shattered. She grabbed the duct tape.

A broken chair, a broken door.

Patricia ran a tight ship—she had to with three kids and a receptionist's salary. She'd lived a good life, she worked hard to provide for her kids and keep a roof over their heads, to give them furniture to sit on and doors to close, and Valeria came in and destroyed it all. Every time.

She was no stranger to life's curveballs. She'd seen how hard her parents worked after they left Nicaragua—her proud mother bagging groceries when her philosopher father couldn't get a position at a U.S. university.

Patricia had worked hard, too. Worked herself through college, finished her degree even after marrying Joe and becoming pregnant with Gabe, and she'd gone back to work again as soon as Adrian was old enough for preschool. She'd scrimped to save enough money not only for her children's education, but to go back to school herself, to start the master's degree she needed to work in the field she'd gotten her BA in.

You could plan as much as you wanted to in life, but in the end you had to work with the curveballs. One month into her new master's program, she and Joe both got surprises. She had an Ava-bean growing in her belly. Joe had cancer growing in his.

She'd quit her program and gone to work for a friend who needed a receptionist at his clinic. Joe had held on until the week before Ava's third birthday.

Patricia finally lay down on the couch, her anxious sense of industry defeated by her body's insistence on rest. Her eyes wouldn't focus enough to read, so she flipped on the TV and scanned randomly through channels, finally dozing off to the horrors of daytime television, and waking only to hunger and the rattling of her kitchen cabinets.

"Yes, thank you," she said to Marco. "I'll eat something. You're not going to fix it for me, too?"

:wish go eat:

"I know." She pushed herself to her feet. "No one ever told me ghosts could be so bossy." She scoured her cabinets for something that didn't require much preparation, finally settling on a can of chicken noodle soup.

Lucho knocked on the door as she was finishing the soup. "Where's Valeria?" he said, glancing at the broken chair.

"I pissed her off. She stormed out."

"She break the chair?"

"Marco did."

"Wha— Marco?"

Patricia shrugged. "I guess. I didn't know ghosts could throw things around so much."

"Oh, yeah." Lucho rubbed the back of his neck, staring at the chair. "Don't worry about it. But Marco, *güey*, you stop that, you got it? And Pati, you listen to me, too. I don't know what the problem is with you two, but you need each other right now. I'll talk to Valeria. She shouldn't have left you alone. You feeling OK?"

"Kind of tired." She touched the back of the chair, wary now. "He shouldn't be able to move things, should he?"

"Some ghosts are a bit more physical than others."

"I've never heard that."

Lucho patted her cheek with a leathery hand. "You know the courts always sequester the hosts. They don't tell people everything that goes on. So you don't worry yourself about it, OK, *profe*? I still need to run a coupla errands, but you call me the second something seems weird. I'll be here in a heartbeat."

"What would seem weird?"

He shrugged. "Oh, feelings, like that aren't your own. You know, sadness or you wanting to go somewhere you wouldn't normally go. Anger toward your kids for no reason."

Patricia's jaw clenched. "My kids?"

"It can be hard for ghosts to recognize people. Hardly ever a problem, though. Don't worry about anything. I'll get Valeria back here with you before the kids come home. What's your number?" She told him, and he punched it into his iPhone. "OK, I'm calling you, so you got mine now. You call me you need anything at all. Even if you just have a question."

"Wait," she said, and he paused in the doorway. "I do have a question. This morning you said you needed to do some research. Why? I thought you'd done a lot of these."

Lucho flashed her a grin. "Nothing to worry, *profe*. It's just been a while since I trained a new host. I want to make sure no details have gone rattling off in this old brain." His expression turned serious. "And Marco, you don't know how strong you are, güey. Don't break anything else, you hear me?"

"Sorry, Lucho," Patricia said without thinking. "I didn't mean it."

Lucho paused, his hand on the doorknob, a steely look in his eye. "I'll get Valeria right here," was all he said. "You two just sit tight."

But Valeria never came. Patricia texted her twice, called Lucho, and got nothing but silence on either end.

Ava breezed through the door in time for dinner, chirping with excitement about how well her Mars rover project had gone over. "Ms. Stucke wants me to put it in the elementary-school fair at the Museum of Flight—here, she gave me a poster for it. See?"

Ava carefully unfolded the flyer on the dining room table, smoothing it flat.

"Sweetheart, that's fantastic!" Patricia reached out to tuck her daughter's hair behind her ear, and felt a stirring within. She remembered Lucho's worry about her kids, and snatched her hand back.

Marco was distraught at Ava's presence, she could feel that clearly. He radiated emotion, and after a moment of fear, Patricia recognized it as a variant of the overpowering sadness that she sometimes felt herself. That jealous, crushing love mixed with a despair that this tender moment would someday cease, that Ava would someday grow up. That longing to enfold her in the most fierce of hugs forever and never let her go.

Marco slumped within her. She could feel his despair. :tell tío marco misses: Tears sprang to Patricia's eyes. "How?" she asked, saying it out loud before she realized. How on earth could she tell Ava that she was getting messages from her dead uncle?

"What, Mom?"

"How did your teacher like the story you wrote?"

While Ava told her, Patricia pulled herself together enough to make dinner. Fish sticks in the microwave and cut-up vegetables with ranch was about all she could manage, and she promised herself she'd do something a bit more gourmet when this was all over. Ava picked out the bits of cauliflower, crunching into them with relish as she talked.

Patricia's phone rang while she was clearing her plate. Patricia snatched it up, hoping for Valeria or Lucho. She didn't recognize the number. "Hello?"

"Hi, Patricia? This is Toby Ng. Adrian's coach?"

"Oh, hey, Toby."

"Is Adrian there? I'd like to talk to him."

Patricia glanced at the stove clock: 5:48 p.m. "It normally takes him longer to get home from practice."

"He wasn't at practice today. One of the other kids said he wasn't feeling good, so he went home."

"What?"

"That's what I need to talk to him about. I made an exception for him to play yesterday, but I told him that if he missed any more practices I'd have to bench him for the next game."

Bench? "What?"

There was a pause, then Toby sighed. "He's not at home, is he, Pati?"

"No." Patricia glanced at Ava, who quickly looked back at her food. "How many has he missed?"

"This makes five in the last three weeks. Pati, I've been worried about Adrian. This is probably none of my business, but is everything all right with you guys?"

"We had a death in the family," she said. But that was two weeks ago, not three. "His uncle."

"Your sister's, ah..."

"My sister's boyfriend."

"I'm so sorry to hear that." On the other end of the line, Toby Ng cleared his throat. "I'm really sorry, Pati. How are you doing?"

"Things have been... tough around here."

"Would you maybe have some time to come by and chat this week? In the, in my office?"

"I can come in tomorrow," she said. She might as well. There was no way she was going to work tomorrow if she still felt like this.

"Oh, great. I've got a free period at one thirty."

"That sounds fine."

"And Pati, I'm so sorry to hear about... I know Adrian was really fond of his uncle."

Marco pulsed briefly in her chest. "Thanks," was all Patricia could manage to say. She breathed deep, unsure how much of the ache inside was hers, and how much was Marco's. "Thanks for calling, Toby. I'll see you tomorrow."

She hung up the phone, and Ava ducked her head as though suddenly very interested in her dinner.

"Ava? Your brother has been missing practices." Ava shrugged one shoulder. "Did you know this?"

"No."

"Ava."

Ava broke up a fish stick with her fork, smashing the tines into the meat. "Yes," she said finally. The fork clattered as she dropped it on her plate, scattering shards of fish stick onto the table. "But I only knew once, and he said you knew and not to say anything."

"Why would he have told you not to say anything if I knew?"

Ava glared, ignoring the question. "He said it was all right."

"Where was he going?"

A shrug.

"Is there anything else I should know?"

A shake of the head.

Patricia sighed, and finished cleaning up dinner. She dialed Adrian's cell, but got no answer. She called three more times, letting it go to voice mail each time, then collapsed on the couch beside Ava. Her phone buzzed, and she glanced at the screen.

Adrian. A text. *Home late.*

She tried calling Valeria again after Ava went to bed. Four, five, six rings, and she dropped the phone to her lap, listening to the faraway trill. Maybe it was ringing somewhere in an alley, and some passerby would hear it and find her sister's unconscious body and take her to the hospital and save her life.

This wasn't the first time Patricia had had this conversation with herself.

She tried to quell the anxiety rising within her, and was keenly aware that not all of it was hers. "Marco? How are you doing?"

:worry:

"Me, too. This is all so unreal."

The phone call disconnected, and Patricia dialed once more and let it ring —for good measure. In case the Good Samaritan was still searching that dark alley for Valeria's body.

"What does Valeria normally do when she's hosting?" She felt a mental shrug from Marco. "Right, so she'd be sequestered for all the court cases, but what about the ones she and Lucho do on the side?" The illegal ones. Like this one.

:take her:

"Take her what? Or like they would take her somewhere?" He seemed to agree with her. "Where?"

:gone plane maybe:

"On a plane?"

:come back tan:

"Tan? Marco, that girl could go get groceries at midnight and come back tanned." Patricia, on the other hand, had gotten their father's fair skin and susceptibility to sunburn. "So you've never seen her while she's hosting." He swirled in agreement. "You're no help, Marco. I figured when you die at least you get to be mystic and wise."

:nope:

A key turned quietly in the front door. Patricia glanced at her cell phone. Ten thirty.

"Where have you been?" she asked as Adrian pushed open the door.

He yelped. "Shit, Mom."

"Adrian Peter Waites."

"Sorry. You scared me."

Her phone buzzed in her hand, and she glanced at it. A text from Valeria. She dropped the phone onto the couch.

"And you scared me. Where have you been?" She searched her son's face. He was the spitting image of Joe: sharp cheekbones and a quirky, puckish smile, but with Patricia's brown eyes and thick, dark hair.

"Practice went late," Adrian said. "Then I drove a couple of the guys home. I left you a note."

"Coach Ng called, Adrian. You weren't at practice. He says he's benching you next game."

Adrian shrugged. "OK," he said after a minute.

"Just OK?" Patricia stood, drawing herself up to match Adrian's height as much as possible. He'd gotten his lanky form from his father, too. "You're lying to me, you're lying to Coach Ng, you're jeopardizing your chances at a scholarship, and you say 'OK'?"

"It's not a big deal."

"Then where were you?"

"I was out."

"Out where?"

He shouldered past, and she caught his arm, yanking him back so hard he stumbled.

Patricia let go, heart pounding at her sudden strength. "Adrian—"

"Just out, Mom," he said, rubbing his arm. "Leave it alone." The door to his room slammed behind him.

Adrenaline, Patricia thought, staring at her hand. It made you stronger sometimes, right? Well, she was definitely running on pure adrenaline by this point.

Patricia rubbed her eyes, exhausted. Her track record was two for two today—she'd chased out Valeria, she'd alienated Adrian, and all because she dared to care what they were doing with their lives.

Heaven forbid family should care.

She thumbed her phone on to read Valeria's message. *Something came up. Be by tomorrow.*

Patricia dropped the phone back on the couch. Damned if she was going to wait by it for anyone else tonight.

She paused in front of Adrian's door and whispered his name. It was silent inside, but she doubted he was asleep. "Adrian?" she said again, louder this time. "I'm sorry." There was no answer.

Patricia sighed, then locked herself in her own bedroom. As an afterthought, she pushed her dresser in front of the door. Marco felt... offended. "I'm sorry, Marco," she said. "I just don't know what could happen."

:won't hurt:

"I don't know that, Marco."

:good mom:

Patricia collapsed into bed, tears pricking at her eyes. "I don't know about that, either," she whispered.

$\mathcal{C}$

The night was long.

During the day, numbed by the whine of the television and her worry for the kids, she had mostly felt alone; now, Patricia could sense him lying still at the edge of her mind.

It was as though she'd come home to find a stranger's child—one who couldn't speak her language, and was too young to communicate. Marco felt a little feral, a little scared, able to make his needs known only though half gestures that she had to guess at.

She couldn't wait for this to be over, for him to be gone—but what exactly did that mean? If he couldn't transfer to a new host, it meant she was his last chance to be on earth before returning...

To heaven, she supposed. Had to suppose.

She felt a pang of grief at the thought of losing him once more—but then, he was dead. He had died. They'd buried him. They'd mourned.

He was dead.

She could feel him at the edge of her mind, but he was still now, very still. She could sense the effort he made to be quiet and let her rest, as though he was aware of his intrusion and trying to make himself as small as possible.

Patricia was too tired to try to reassure him, and then, embarrassed, she wondered how many of her thoughts he could read. All of them? Could he understand what she was thinking about him right now?

And as exhausted as she was, she roused herself mentally like a good hostess and went to greet her guest.

"Marco?" she whispered. His presence uncoiled. "Where are you?" Her toes tingled, her fingertips, her scalp. :... you:

Was that an echo, or an answer? "Are you all right?" In response she felt a deep sadness. "I'm sorry, Marco. About everything."

:sleep:

"Yes. OK." And they did.

Chapter Six

PATRICIA CALLED IN sick again the next morning, promising that it was just a twenty-four-hour bug, and that she'd be fine the next day. With a strange delight at the unexpected day off, she pulled out the waffle iron. Ava was thrilled, but Patricia had planned it mostly as a lure for Adrian. He was prone to slipping out without breakfast if he didn't feel like talking.

A knock on the door pulled her away from the waffle iron before he appeared. She opened it to find a white man about her age, wearing a dress shirt and slacks under a green softshell rain jacket. The morning's faint mist was beading on his shoulders.

"Hello?" Patricia held the door firmly in her hand. The chain beside the door rattled—a message from Marco, maybe, meant to comfort? Or warn?

The man glanced past her into the house, a quick, professional glance that took in everything and filed it carefully away. "Ms. Ramos-Waites?"

"Yes?"

"Sorry to disturb you at breakfast. I'm Dave Bayer—I'm a detective with the Seattle Police Department." He drew a badge out of his jacket pocket, held it out so she could examine it. "I have a couple of questions. About Marco Caruso. Can I come in a minute?"

Ice flushed through her blood, and her heart began to race. *Stop it*, she thought, though she wasn't sure if the fear was hers, or Marco's. "My kids..."

"I'll just need a minute of your time, ma'am. We've opened an investigation on the accident, and I just want to ask you a few questions. It's routine."

Relief followed so quickly on the heels of fear that she stood for a moment in silence, blinking at him. She could feel Marco tugging at her. :*invest?*: "What do you mean you're opening an investigation? It was a car accident."

Bayer took a deep breath. "We have reason to believe the car may have been tampered with."

A surge from Marco, and Patricia caught herself, dizzy, against the door frame.

"Are you all right, ma'am? You look white as a ghost."

"It's been a terrible few weeks."

"I understand. I apologize for catching you off guard like this—but I do only need a moment of your time."

"Of course, please, come in." Bayer's gaze swept her home again as he entered, and Patricia imagined how he saw it: clean but faded upholstery, the dining chair with its newly duct-taped leg, the cracked kitchen window. "Let me get you some coffee," she said, unplugging the waffle maker. "How do you take it? Ava, go get ready for school."

"With milk, if you have it," said Bayer. "Hi, Ava. I'm Detective Bayer." Ava looked him up and down, and Patricia could see the same calculation in her daughter's eyes as in the detective's.

"Can I see your badge?" Ava asked.

"Ava!"

Bayer smiled. "It's fine, ma'am." He handed Ava his badge, and she examined it thoroughly, turning it over in her hands. Finally she handed it back and gave him an arch nod of approval. "That's cool," she said.

"Ava. Get ready for school." Patricia cleared away Ava's plate to set a coffee mug on the table for Bayer, then sat down with one herself. "Now. How can I help you?"

"I've tried to get ahold of your sister, Valeria, but she's tough to find."

You can say that again. "She's been grieving," Patricia said. "But I can have her give you a call when I see her."

Bayer nodded. "I'll leave you my card. Ms. Ramos-Waites, to your knowledge, was Marco Caruso involved in anything?"

"Involved?"

"With anything illegal."

Marco swirled inside her, agitated. She looked away, fighting nausea. "He's a good man—he was a good man, I suppose. Everyone loved him."

"Did he have any enemies?"

"A man like Marco? I can't imagine why anyone would hate him. He was the sweetest man, he loved my sister, and my parents loved him. He was great with the kids. Why are you asking?"

"We're just investigating the accident, is all."

A door opened in the hallway, and both she and Bayer looked up to see Adrian stalk into the room, his jacket and shoes already on. "Adrian, this is Detective Bayer. Detective, this is my son Adrian. Honey, eat some breakfast. We'll talk when I'm done here."

"Hey," he said absently to Bayer. "I'm late for school, Mom," he said to Patricia, grabbing a banana and leaning to kiss her obediently. The front door clicked shut behind him. Bayer watched him go, and Patricia wondered what information he filed away: young Latino male, red jacket, five foot nine, hair close cut and spiked, athletic, poor neighborhood, single-parent family.

"Why are you investigating the accident?" she asked, uncomfortable, trying to draw the detective's attention away from her son.

"This is all still preliminary, but we found evidence that his car had been tampered with," said Bayer.

Marco surged with fury. "I was murdered?" And at the detective's expression, Patricia wrested back control. "You think he was murdered?" she said.

Bayer shook his head. "No one's saying that right now. There's just a problem with the car that seems strange for someone who was a mechanic."

"He loved that car," she said. "He worked on it constantly."

"That's what I understand." Bayer finished his coffee and set the mug down. He handed Patricia a card. "Please do tell your sister I'd like to talk to her, and feel free to call me if you think of anything. I'm sure you'd all just like to wrap this up so you can move on."

You have no idea, thought Patricia. *No idea at all.*

Marco didn't like her being in public. Patricia could feel that by the way he paced like a caged tiger. His presence surrounded her like the day's fine mist, and she was paranoid that everyone on the bus could feel it, too.

It wasn't very far to Highline High School, but the bus was hitting every stop, and Patricia realized with a sinking feeling that she was going to be late for her meeting with Toby Ng. Marco stirred within her, as if sensing her discomfort. A cool finger brushed her cheek. *:fine:* "Thank you," she whispered.

She was beginning to understand what Lucho had said about a ghost gaining power. As the morning wore on, she'd begun to have thoughts that were decidedly not hers—vague impressions about places, memories she shouldn't have. She'd feel an odd déjà vu while walking through her own home, and, once, an uncomfortable thought with regard to her sister crossed her mind. "I don't need to know any of that," she'd snapped at Marco, and he'd recoiled, embarrassed.

Adrian's high school was a stately building of red bricks and clean lines, set back from the street by a sodden expanse of lawn. Patricia signed in at the office, let the security guard shine his flashlight into her purse, and then was escorted down the hallway. Toby's office was close to the locker rooms, and the faint scent of pine disinfectant and sweat wafted out into the hallway. The door was open.

Her phone buzzed. Valeria: *Where are you.*

Highline HS. Meeting.

Pick you up right now.

Seriously? Patricia sighed. *Be done at 2:30.*

She knocked on the door frame, and Toby Ng waved her in. He was shorter than most of the kids he coached, but he was slender and well-built, and Adrian boasted he had better ball-handling skills than the entire varsity team combined. He'd coached Gabe, too—although to a lesser degree of success, given her eldest son's middling interest in athletics.

Today Toby wore a tweed sports coat over grey sweats and a purple Highline Pirates T-shirt. He pushed aside paperwork and stood to greet her with a warm handshake.

"I'm sorry I'm so late," Patricia said. "The bus..."

"I know how that goes, no worries." He waved her into a chair, then gestured at his outfit ruefully. "Sorry about the sweats—I've got practice after this."

"And you always wear a sports coat to practice?"

Toby laughed, scratching at his temple. "It's, ah, just for receiving visitors." During the heat of a basketball game his expression was always one of pure business; on the rare occasions he smiled, it lit up his entire face. Today that smile was all for her.

Inside her, Marco squirmed, combative. *Simmer down, boy,* she thought.

"I'm glad you called me last night," she said. "How long has Adrian been missing practices?"

Toby's smile faded. "About three weeks. I know kids are kids, and Adrian's not the first of my starters to test the limits. They usually come bouncing back, but Adrian seems a bit... preoccupied. I'm so sorry to hear about his uncle."

"Thanks. I know this has been hard on Adrian." She took a deep breath. "But you said it's been three weeks. So he was missing practices since before Marco's accident. Is something going on with Lucy, maybe? You know boys, he wouldn't tell his mother anything like that."

"Pati, I gotta say I'm a bit worried about some of the kids Adrian's been hanging out with lately." Toby held up his hands. "Nothing terrible, but you know. Some of the kids sneak beers and smoke pot. Stuff like that."

"Adrian?" No. *What do you know about this?* she thought, and felt Marco give her a mental shrug. "Have you talked to him about it?"

"I wanted to talk to you first. Has anything seemed off with him lately?"

"I can barely remember the last few weeks. With work, and Marco..." And Marco again.

Adrian was always gone—at practice, or at a friend's house, or with Lucy. Or with the church group that he and Lucy both belonged to—but they weren't those sorts of kids, were they?

Oh, Lord. Was she raising one of those boys she read about in the newspaper and clucked her tongue at, thinking, Where was his mother?

Toby must have seen it in her face. He leaned across the desk and took her hand, only for a second, but his fingers were warm and strong. Comforting. "I'm sorry, Pati. I didn't want to upset you. I shouldn't have said anything like that, not without any proof."

"It's fine, it's just—" Marco lurched, swirling wildly. *Stop it,* she thought, but he didn't seem to hear her. She felt a pressure like a hand on her arm, pulling her toward the door. *:valvalval:* She held firm, and he tugged at her, nearly toppling her from the chair. Nausea threatened to overwhelm her again. "Excuse me," she said to Toby. "I haven't felt well today. The ladies' room?"

He pointed her out the hallway, and she barely made it into one of the stalls before being sick. "You're worse than being pregnant," she snapped.

:val trouble:

"'Val trouble' is the story of my life," she said. She wiped her mouth. She hoped the wan cast to her skin was just the bathroom's fluorescent lighting, but she was beyond caring now. Toby was wearing sweatpants, after all.

Patricia made her way back to the office, but at the doorway, Marco surged within her, angry. His presence was like a wall, barring her way. "This is not the time, young man," Patricia whispered in her best mom voice. She clutched the agate in her pocket; it was warm and solid. Grounding. She felt the wall waver. "Acting up isn't helping either of us."

Marco slumped in her chest, throbbing sullenly. The wall disappeared. The agate pulsed.

:val trouble:

"I know," whispered Patricia. "We'll be right there."

Toby glanced past her as she stepped back in, as though looking to see who she'd been talking to. "I'm sorry," she said. "I really haven't been feeling well today."

"Do you want—I've got some Emergen-C in my drawer, I think. Do you want some water?"

"I'll be fine, thanks."

Toby nodded, but he didn't look convinced. She must look worse than she thought. "Do you need a ride?"

"My sister's picking me up, thanks."

"OK, well..." He reached out to shake her hand, and she held it maybe a fraction of a second too long. "I'll talk to Adrian, Pati. He's a good kid." He smiled. "And, hey?"

"Yes?"

"I—it'll be all right, don't worry, OK? Adrian's gonna be fine."

But with Marco's panic rising by the second, not being worried was the farthest thing from Patricia's mind.

Marco pulled her through the school parking lot as though drawn by a magnet —straight toward Valeria, who waited by her ancient silver Subaru wagon, smoking furiously.

"Val? Is everything OK?"

Valeria took one last drag, then flicked the cigarette into a puddle. "I'm fine. Let's go." She moved piles of old mail off the passenger seat and threw fast-food wrappers into the back.

"Where are we going in such a rush?"

"Nowhere," Valeria snapped. "I'm just making sure you're OK." Her hand shook as she tried to get her keys into the ignition, and Marco surged, then checked himself, circling inside Patricia like a dog before settling, pulsing with frustrated concern toward Valeria. :hurt?:

"Marco wants to know if you're hurt," Patricia said, and Valeria looked up in surprise.

"You really can understand him? Normally it takes at least a week before the ghost can communicate with its host."

Patricia shrugged. "He can still only give me a few words, but he's more coherent than he was last night. He's very concerned about you. He was restless in Toby's office. He even got physical." She settled back against the seat, closing her eyes. "He tugged me almost out of a chair, and then barred the door so I couldn't go back in."

"Shit, Pati. You serious?"

Patricia opened her eyes to find Valeria staring at her. "Yeah. What is it?"

"We need to see Lucho. I mean, I saw him rattle that cupboard, but that's the most physical I've seen a tethered ghost get. He shouldn't be able to manifest at all."

Patricia felt a chill. "He broke a chair last night."

"What?"

"Lucho said sometimes ghosts can do that. We just don't hear about them because the hosts are sequestered."

Valeria jammed the shifter into reverse. "He would know more about that, I guess." But she didn't sound convinced. She turned her head to check behind them, and Patricia caught a glimpse of an angry row of red half-moon marks marring the back of her neck.

"What happened to your neck?" Patricia asked, and Valeria's hand flew to cover the marks.

"Nothing," she said too quickly.

"Valeria Ramos Marquez, why are you lying to me? Those are fingernail marks. Was someone choking you?"

"It's nothing, OK? I ran into an old boyfriend when you were inside, he works as a security guard here now. He was pissed, that's all."

Marco seethed, and Patricia felt his presence as a hand on her wrist, fingers gripping hard. "Let me go," she whispered, and he did.

Valeria glanced at her. "What was that?"

"Marco's upset."

"I'm fine, Marco. Stay cool, all right?"

But as they drove from the school, Valeria's attention scarcely left her rearview mirror. "Red light," Patricia said, and Valeria slammed on the brakes barely in time. Patricia craned around in her seat to see what had captured Valeria's attention. "Val, are you in trouble?"

"I'm fine, OK? Just stay out of my business."

"You made this my business, too." Marco swirled inside her, anxious. "Stop it, Marco," she snapped, irritable. "You're giving me a headache. Green light."

"I see it." The silver Subaru lurched forward. Valeria was silent a moment, focused on weaving through the sparse northbound traffic on First Avenue. Patricia kept an eye on the side-view mirror. She didn't have much of a view, but she had enough to see the huge red pickup truck keeping up with their lane changes.

"How are you doing with this?" Valeria said after a moment.

"Don't worry, I won't throw up in your car."

"That's not what I'm worried about. Hosting is dangerous, Pati. You shouldn't have gotten involved."

"You're the one who asked me to come out with you."

"Stop it, Pati. I'm not trying to pick a fight. I'm trying to apologize."

"For getting me possessed?"

"You got your own damn self possessed."

"You looked like you were *dying*, Val. I thought I was doing the right thing."

"That's what I'm trying to say, dammit. That you didn't know what you were doing, and I shouldn't have gotten you involved."

"So if I hadn't been so ignorant—"

"God*dammit,* Pati." Valeria slammed her palms against the steering wheel. "I'm sorry, OK? You've got your world, I've got mine, and now I've dragged you way over your head into some shit no one should be involved in in the first place."

Inside Patricia's chest, Marco swirled uncomfortably.

"Something involving the guys in the red pickup?" They were still behind them, blinker on to follow Valeria's Subaru north on the 509. Patricia swiveled in her seat to try to see their faces. Two men, both Latino, dark-skinned. Tattoos blazed across the hands of the driver.

"Sit down, Pati, I'm trying to drive."

"Who did you—" Patricia felt her cell phone vibrate, an unfamiliar number. "Yes? This is Patricia."

"Hi, Pati? It's Toby Ng? Is this a bad time?"

She glanced at Valeria, who was glaring at her rearview mirror while she wove through highway traffic. "No, this is fine. Is everything all right?"

"Oh, of course. Listen, I feel ridiculous calling after you just left my office, but I really should have asked you before you went. It's just, could we talk some more some time?"

"About Adrian?"

Toby coughed on the other end of the line. "Not necessarily. About anything, really. I'd, ah, like to take you out to dinner."

"Oh!" Patricia sat back, startled.

In the left lane, the red pickup, a Ford F250, pulled even with Valeria's Subaru. Valeria ignored them, staring resolutely ahead, hands clenched on the steering wheel. Patricia looked past her, straight into the steady gaze of the passenger, a thin man with a buzz cut, coal-black eyes, and a crooked nose set in a handsome, chiseled face. He lifted his chin in greeting, and the diamond stud in his earlobe glittered. Behind his ear was a tattoo of a closed eye.

Los Ciegos.

Patricia remembered she was still holding the phone. "Ah, can I call you back?"

There was a long pause on the other end. "Right, sure," said Toby. "Any time is fine."

"OK, thanks."

Patricia hung up, staring as the F250 pulled ahead in a caustic haze of exhaust fumes.

"Who was that?"

The question came in chorus, each sister turning to the other.

"What?" said Patricia. "On the phone? No. You go first. Those guys are Los Ciegos, aren't they."

Valeria tapped a fresh cigarette out of the package, felt around in the ashtray for her lighter. "I've never seen them before in my life."

"That's bullshit."

"Language, Pati! OK. I think those guys are clients of Lucho's."

"They're Los Ciegos. I saw his tattoo: the blind eye."

"I just know that they're Lucho's clients. Who called you?"

Patricia glanced down at her phone. Had Toby Ng just called to ask her on a date? She realized abruptly that she'd blown the question off. He probably thought she'd been offended.

An acrid blast from Valeria's fresh cigarette brought her back. "Earth to Pati."

Patricia slipped her phone into her purse and shook her head. "Toby. You remember, Toby Ng?"

"What, Adrian's basketball coach? What did he want?"

"To, ah, to ask me out for dinner."

"What?" Valeria laughed, rolling down her window. "Nice work, Pati. He's cute."

"I suppose."

"So call him back and say yes."

Patricia turned to stare at her. "Val. I'm kind of possessed right now."

"Right." Valeria took a deep drag on her cigarette, then blew the smoke out the window. "We can fix that. Don't worry, babe. We'll fix all of this."

Chapter Seven

BUTTON-UP BLOUSE, DARK-BLUE skirt, warm tights, sensible flats: Patricia dressed for work. She wound her thick, dark hair into a bun at the nape of her neck, then leaned into the mirror, scrutinizing her face for signs of Marco's ghost.

Her eyes looked a little bloodshot, and there were maybe a few more crow's feet, but that wouldn't seem out of the ordinary; her coworkers thought she had been home sick. And she had been, hadn't she? In a matter of speaking.

Marco shifted—could he feel her thinking of him?—then settled into a feeling of fullness below her sternum. Patricia had realized with some horror last night that she'd started thinking of that place as "his spot." She thought she saw a flicker of something alien in her eyes and tore her gaze away from the mirror.

She stuffed her small makeup bag into her purse. She would finish up on the bus.

Ava was still in her room, coloring at her desk. "Ava-bean," Patricia said. "Grab your coat, sweetheart. We're leaving in a few minutes."

She glanced at the clock. Just enough time to pack a lunch.

Normally she loved the morning ritual of walking Ava to her friend's house, where Ava would wait for the school bus and Patricia would catch her grown-up Metro bus to work, but this morning Patricia was finding it hard to shake the feeling of dread. *Just get this week over with,* she told herself. They would figure out what to do with Marco soon enough.

Patricia was tiptoeing through the kitchen when the form on the couch stirred.

Valeria had refused to go home last night, and though she'd told Patricia it was to keep her safe, Patricia doubted that very much. If Valeria had wanted her to be safe so badly, she'd have stayed here the night before, too.

:sisters worry:

Patricia nearly dropped her yogurt cup. The quietly intruding voice in her head still startled her, even after two days of living with Marco's presence. *Sisters worry.* Was he chiding her? Patricia rolled her eyes at him, and felt a twinge of annoyance back.

:didn't know: Marco drew up a brief flash of memory, a chair sailing through the air to splinter against the front door.

No, Patricia granted. The other night Valeria hadn't known that Marco was manifesting, throwing chairs, moving objects—he'd nearly pulled Patricia physically out of her chair at Toby's office.

She and Valeria had had a long talk last night after the kids had gone to sleep. *Just the three of us*, Patricia thought wryly. *Just me, my sister, and a ghost.*

And maybe ignorance actually was bliss, because before last night, Patricia had had only her imaginary fears. Hearing her sister's take on what Marco should and shouldn't be able to do had only doubled what Patricia was worried about this morning.

Ghosts couldn't manifest like Marco had been doing, Valeria had said. She'd never seen it, never heard of it. Sure, if you got a particularly nasty ghost it could "go all *Exorcist* on you"—Valeria's terribly comforting words—but it wasn't likely.

"Not likely?"

Valeria had waved an impatient hand. "It's even less than your chance of being killed by a shark, which is like one in two hundred and fifty million."

"How do you even know that statistic?"

"I looked it up because Marco—" Valeria had stopped then, fiercely blinking away tears, her voice on the verge of breaking. And Patricia had caught just a glimpse of a memory that was not her own: *Steel-colored waves crashing on a beach, the sky bright through a veil of clouds. Westport, a cold wind*

gusting on a July afternoon. Valeria in her wet suit with curling strands of hair
plastered to the side of her face. She was grinning, and Patricia didn't want to go—

"He didn't want to go surfing with you."

Valeria's eyes had been glassy with unshed tears—but there was more than grief in her expression. There was worry.

Communicating lucid memories to a host within the first few days of a possession was apparently another thing Marco shouldn't be able to do.

So, yes. Maybe Valeria was worried about her. Or maybe—though Valeria wouldn't even come close to admitting it—she was worried about being at her own home alone with a bloodthirsty gang of drug smugglers after her.

"I'm right, aren't I?" Patricia whispered. Marco didn't respond.

"Pati?" Valeria's sleep-tousled head appeared over the back of the couch.

"*Buen día*, sunshine. We're just out the door. I need to walk Ava to her bus before mine comes. Adrian should be up any minute."

"I'll drive you."

"I really need to be on time, Val."

"I'll get you there on time." Valeria sat up, burrowing out of her cocoon of crocheted afghans and Ava's old Mulan sleeping bag. She kneaded her face in her hands. "What time is it, anyway?"

Patricia glanced at the microwave. "Seven oh four."

"And what time do you have to be there?"

"Eight thirty."

"No problem."

Patricia sighed. It would be nice to avoid the bus ride, and with a good amount of motherly coaxing, she might just get Valeria going in time. "What do you want for breakfast?" she asked.

"Coffee?"

Patricia glanced at the clock again, then plugged in the coffee maker. She could use some, too, after the last few days. She dropped two slices of bread into the toaster without asking. She hadn't seen Valeria consume anything but coffee and cigarettes for a few days.

"Ava-bean?" Patricia called. "Come out here. We're leaving in a couple of minutes." A moment later, Ava slunk to the dining table to spread out her papers and colored pencils. Valeria hauled herself over to join her, the Mulan sleeping bag draped over her lap. She raked her fingers through her tangled mane. "What're you working on, kiddo?"

Ava's shoulder twitched in a careless shrug. "It's a house. It's where we'll live when I grow up." She jabbed at the paper with her pencil. "See, here's Mom's room with all the plants. And there's a rain catcher on the roof with a hose that comes in to water them automatically so she doesn't have to." She jabbed again. "That's going to be my room, and behind this bookshelf is a secret passage that leads to the basement where my laboratory is."

Valeria leaned closer. "The basement is a maze?"

Ava nodded solemnly. "To keep intruders out of the laboratory."

"Good call. So where does Adrian live?"

"With Lucy." Ava started sketching in the corner of the paper. "They can live in the garden when they get married, and I'll even build them a basketball hoop so he can practice."

"How was the couch?" Patricia asked, rooting through the fridge for jam. Nearly gone. She marked it onto the list.

"Mmmf."

"Sounds lovely. And speaking of Adrian, you should get into the bathroom before he does. I've heard his alarm go off twice already."

Valeria threw back her head in a lion's yawn, then shook out her hair. Tiny specks of silver glittered on her cheek and forehead, and Patricia started to laugh. "Your face," she said, shaking her head. "You've got bits of foil stuck everywhere, from Ava's project." Valeria swiped at her forehead. "Val, it's everywhere. You should look in a mirror. I'll have the coffee ready to go when you're out. Now get."

She turned to Ava as Valeria shuffled down the hallway. "Ava-bean, I need you to vacuum the couch when you get home tonight, OK?" Ava nodded, humming softly as she constructed a garden cottage for her brother. Patricia returned to making coffee, relieved to have Valeria out of the room; the sight of her sleep-tousled state was provoking an uncomfortable reaction from Marco. She poured the coffee into a travel mug and, on a whim, doctored it with milk and two spoonfuls of sugar. It felt right, though she couldn't remember the last time she'd made coffee for her sister.

Patricia shivered. The line between her thoughts and Marco's was getting blurrier by the day.

Glitter-free and freshly caffeinated, they dropped Ava off at her friend's house, then stuck to the side roads on their way to First Hill. Traffic wasn't quite so bad yet. Patricia sipped at her coffee, trying to stay optimistic about her chances of getting to work on time.

"Adrian was quiet last night," Valeria said.

"He's been quiet a lot lately." Patricia leaned her head back against her seat, feeling suddenly very tired. "It's why I went to see Toby yesterday. He's been missing practices."

"Adrian? He lives to play basketball."

"I know. But Toby has to bench him next game because of his attendance." Patricia realized with a pang that she still hadn't called Toby back after the scare with the men in the red pickup yesterday. She'd do it on her lunch break. "He's worried about the kinds of kids Adrian's been hanging out with."

"What kind of kids, like stoners? Gangbangers? The chess club?"

"Ah, stoners, of the three. I'd guess. Toby said the kinds of kids who sometimes sneak beer between class, but he didn't think they were into anything harder than that."

Valeria raised an eyebrow. "He's a good kid. So maybe he and his friends sneak a beer every once in a while. I did in high school, and I turned out just fine."

Patricia turned to snap off a sarcastic comment, but Valeria was smiling. "Easy, Pati, I'm kidding. Besides, he's already gone down the path of dating a band geek. He may be lost to us already." She glanced at Patricia. "Maybe he's taken up the flute," she said sadly.

"If he was joining the band, it would probably be to play something much louder than the flute," Patricia said. "Adrian's never been quiet, not like this. And skipping practice?"

"Did you talk to him?"

"Yes."

"So what's he doing when he's skipping practice?"

"I don't know. He won't say."

"Hanging out with Lucy?"

"I have no idea."

"I'll tell you what, I'll talk to him. I'll sneak him a six-pack and we'll talk like bros." Patricia shot her a glare. "I'm kidding, Pati."

"Are you? I hear you gave him Marco's flask." Patricia sighed. "A flask, Val?"

"It's a family heirloom." But Valeria was looking straight ahead now, all laughter gone from her face.

Was this a moment to stir the coals, or back away from the volcano?

Patricia bit her lip and decided to stir. "I know what the flask meant to you," she said. "It's why I decided to help you that night."

Valeria glanced over. "What?"

"Sometimes..." Patricia chose her words carefully, probing each for incendiary properties before she said it. "Sometimes before you go, you give me things. And then you disappear. I was afraid that when you gave Adrian that flask and Ava your necklace, that you were planning something really crazy. Crazier than doing a resurrection solo." She paused, aware she was on shaky ground. "I was afraid you were going to run away again."

Valeria's knuckles were white on the steering wheel. "Run away?"

Inside Patricia, Marco fidgeted, a brief flutter in her chest. *:run?:* An echo, or a question? She ignored him. "It's just what I thought," she said to Valeria. "I was afraid you would."

"I wouldn't run away from you again," Valeria said. "You're the only family I have."

That's never stopped you from running in the past. But Patricia kept that thought to herself. No need to throw gasoline on the fire. "You know I'm here for you," she said instead. "I'm here for you, for whatever you need."

"I know." Valeria paused, and Patricia could see her thoughts conflicted in her expression. For the first time she wondered if Valeria might be choosing her own words as carefully. Did she imagine Patricia as a volcano, too? Or did Valeria have her own metaphor for her older sister's moods? Patricia caught a glimpse of white: a blizzard, maybe. A glacier. *What was that?* she thought crossly, but Marco went silent again.

Valeria sighed. "Thanks, Pati. For coming that night. I mean... I'm sorry how it happened. But I want you to know that I appreciated you coming."

"I love you." Patricia reached tentatively to pat Valeria's thigh, but withdrew her hand when Marco shifted inside her.

Tears glistened in Valeria's eyes. Patricia looked away.

They were almost to the office, Valeria's Subaru growling up the steep incline of Madison. She swore when she had to stop at a light, wrenching up the emergency brake and stomping on the clutch. Patricia grabbed the door handle reflexively.

"I turn at the next light, right?"

"Yeah." The light turned green, and Valeria eased the Subaru into gear with minimal lurching. "Will you call that detective back today?" Patricia asked.

"Sure." Valeria nosed into the loading zone in front of the clinic and hit her blinkers. "Will you call that cute basketball coach back today?"

Patricia felt her cheeks go red. "Planning on it."

"Good." Valeria was smiling. "Call me when you get off work. I'm going to go see Lucho, and we should be able to figure this whole thing out. Tell Toby you can make plans for the weekend."

"Really?" Patricia was too wary to feel optimistic, but she felt a surge of hope nonetheless—welling not just from her own self, but from Marco, too. He wasn't enjoying this any more than she was.

"I'm sure. Patricia?"

"Yes?" Patricia turned back, one hand on the door handle. Valeria caught her in an awkward hug of seat belts and purse straps and strained spines. "We'll figure this out," she whispered, her breath hot on Patricia's ear. "I promise."

Chapter Eight

MARCO RECOILED THE moment she walked through the office door. *:hate hospitals:*

"Good thing this isn't a hospital," Patricia muttered under her breath. The clinic's waiting room was sparsely populated this morning, which was always a good sign. "Good morning!" She waved a greeting to Marie, an older woman with pink-streaked hair and a workers' comp claim for her bad back. A little boy played with the toys in the corner—ones Ava had grown out of, actually—while his mother thumbed through an issue of *Mother Earth News*.

Patricia's desk was a disheveled pile of paperwork and sticky notes, the usual results of Cheryle's pinch-hitting administration. The voice mail button on the phone blinked furiously. Patricia breathed a quick sigh. This was why she was never sick. This above all else.

"Pati, how are you!" Cheryle greeted her with little pat on the shoulder in lieu of her usual hug, and Patricia caught a whiff of hand sanitizer. "I was worried about you—you're never sick! How are you feeling?"

"Better." Did she look better?

:look beautiful:

Stay out of this, Patricia thought furiously. Please, God, if Marco could only keep quiet today.

"Well, I brought you some zinc, you know it does wonders for me when I'm feeling under the weather. And hangovers, too, though I actually think those sports drinks, like runners use? With electrolytes? Those are the best for hangovers." Cheryle smiled and tucked back a strand of the sharp blond bob that knifed past her chin. She was quite pretty when she smiled, when some of her true beauty sneaked past the defenses of the foundation she caked on to hide her first signs of aging.

"Can I make you some tea? I brought some of my mom's blend, it's amazing when you're sick. It's all stuff she grows on Vashon." Cheryle laughed. "But not all the stuff she grows, don't worry. I'm not trying to get you fired—oh, God, can you imagine what this place would be like if I was running it? You're not allergic to nettles? Good. I'll make you some tea." With another shoulder pat, she disappeared into the back.

Patricia sank into her chair and attempted to make sense of Cheryle's Post-it system, smiling as she did. Despite her questionable organizational skills, Cheryle was definitely the right person to have in your corner.

A day in the life of a medical receptionist was difficult enough without a ghost rattling around inside her head. The phone rang constantly for the first few hours. Two patients back-to-back didn't believe there were no appointments available today, though only one asked to speak to Patricia's manager. "Your turn, 'manager,'" she called to Cheryle, putting him on hold. The next was a woman wanting a script without seeing a doctor. It took Patricia nearly fifteen minutes to get the woman off the phone.

:asshole moron:

"Shh." Patricia glanced at Cheryle, but of course she'd heard nothing. Marco had been trying to stay out of her way all morning, but she could feel him starting to get restless. *She's just sick and scared,* she told Marco; these were the same words she told herself whenever she dealt with frustrating patients. *I'm just the closest punching bag. It comes with the job.*

Cheryle plied her with a constant supply of natural remedies: a ginger tea which Patricia gladly drank, home-brewed kombucha which she sipped with reservations (*:the hell is that?:*), and a noxious mix of cayenne, honey, and apple cider vinegar which Patricia refused to touch.

:don't like hot?:

Val got all those taste buds. "I'm really feeling better," Patricia said out loud, pushing the last drink away. And it was true, wasn't it? She and Marco were developing a friendly rapport as he learned to navigate the confines of her body and mind without wracking her with nausea. If that wasn't the definition of "better," Patricia didn't know what was.

She polished off the last of her sandwich, then grabbed her purse. "I'm going to take lunch if you'll be fine without me for an hour."

Cheryle nodded as she punched the button to answer a call. "Dr. Hsao's office," she said. She cradled the phone on her shoulder and mimed holding something. "Umbrella," she mouthed. Patricia nodded and patted her purse.

Taking a walk on her lunch break was one of her little pleasures. Sometimes she went to the Frye Art Museum—she appreciated the free admission—or sometimes to St. James just to sit and think in the cathedral. The cathedral was so grand, so different from the small, plain, Disciples of Christ church she was used to. She felt small there, as though the building transformed her from a person with a world of problems to an insignificant, tiny thing. Although Patricia hadn't been raised Catholic, and generally subscribed to a more personal version of Christianity, she could see what it felt like to sit in awe. Here, God wasn't a feeling you felt or pretended to feel when you closed your eyes with others during a worship song. God was a presence.

God was so close in the cathedral—so close, yet so untouchable.

Like Marco, she supposed, probing, as she walked, for the small flutters that signaled his presence.

Patricia went to St. James at least once a week, never speaking to anyone else, always seeking the clarification that came from being crushed into insignificance by the enormity of God.

Quiet meditation would have been welcome today, what with all the questions that had arisen in the last forty-eight hours. Whether or not God intended for ghosts of the departed to return to aid the living—and that depended on who you asked—Patricia believed in a loving God who did things for a reason. If Marco was here, it was for a reason, and maybe with a quiet hour's meditation, God would grant her clarity in dealing with his purgatoried spirit.

But Patricia's questions were hardly all philosophical. Why could Marco manifest the way he'd been doing? Why could he communicate with her so clearly? Why was Lucho pretending everything was all right, when clearly there were problems? Who were the men in the red pickup?

Why were both Lucho and Valeria trying so hard to keep her from worrying?

Patricia needed to know what she should be worrying about.

What Patricia needed was information. She snapped open her umbrella and headed down the short, steep blocks to the Seattle Public Library.

This was a different sort of cathedral, one dedicated to public learning, to architecture. On her first visits, Patricia had found the library unsettling—the jutting planes of the windows were too disorienting, the unexpected colors and abstract seating absurdly futuristic, the concrete interior too cold.

The support beams tilted at disturbing angles, and the knowledge that it was engineered to withstand earthquakes was visually undermined by the fact that it looked already retrofitted post disaster. It reminded Patricia of photos in her parents' album of her parents standing in front of what was left of their home in Managua. Patricia was swaddled in her father's arms; an earthquake had destroyed the city the year she was born.

Patricia stepped onto the neon-yellow elevator, rising up into the stacks.

:the hell?:

Marco pulled her attention toward the babbling heads embedded in the far wall, their weirdly distorted images projected onto egg shapes.

Haven't you been here before?

:course not:

It's public art.

She could feel Marco rolling his eyes—how strange was that sensation?— and with the eye roll she remembered clearly his lanky, exaggerated, Italian– New Jerseyan shrug, and that accent he pulled out when he was trying to charm. Tears pricked her eyes, and he pulsed, a wash of anger, regret, and frustration pouring over her. *:is fine:*

God. How did you mourn someone who couldn't leave?

Patricia took the elevator all the way to the top of the library, aiming to walk the spiraling stacks downward to the right floor. Here, the vast expanse of glass was more humanely scaled; the reading room noisy with clicking fingers on laptop keyboards and warm with the must of wet canvas and steaming wool.

Patricia descended slowly, tracing the generous path of human knowledge from top to bottom until she reached the seventh level. Occult Studies. She hadn't dared look up any titles on the work computers, and she was too nervous to look up anything on the library computers while logged in under her own account. That could be traced, couldn't it? She could always check the catalog on a public computer later if she didn't find what she was looking for on the shelves.

The titles here seemed amateur. *Beyond the Veil. Ghosts and You. Of Heart and Spirit: A Practitioner's Path.* There were *True Ghost!* horror stories, ghost-hunting guides, and illustrated guides to séances that seemed more suitable for teenage vampire fans than truly informational.

Dared she approach the help desk? It could be that anything with actual information would be kept in a special collection. These all looked—

"Can I help you?"

Patricia whirled, heart pounding in her chest.

A woman wearing a librarian's tag stood at the head of the aisle. She was a little older than Patricia, but not much. Her brown hair, streaked with grey, braided, and rolled into a bun, reminded Patricia of wool yarn left natural and coarse. Faint wrinkles feathered out from her eyes.

She looked so normal, so mundane. Patricia forced herself to relax. Toby hadn't noticed anything strange about her, and neither had Cheryle. Surely people not possessed by ghosts became curious about the occult from time to time.

"I'm just trying to learn more about..." She paused, not certain how to ask. "I have a few questions." The librarian smiled warmly. Patricia took a deep breath. Easiest to lie when the truths were half, right? "My... niece has been wanting to host ghosts for the courts, and I wanted to know what she's getting herself into." Patricia cleared her throat. "Do you have any books on, ah..."

The librarian smiled. "On hosting?"

"Yes. On what it does to you—on what it would do to her. What she'd experience."

"Of course. Most of our collection can't be checked out, but I do have one or two which may interest you. Come with me?"

Patricia fought down a flutter of panic. This was not an arrest. The librarian—Sophie, her name tag said—was simply leading her to the help desk.

Sophie disappeared into the back.

:act too nervous:

You're not helping, Patricia thought crossly.

Sophie returned a moment later with a small clothbound book. The worn spine was fraying, though someone had tacked down the stray threads with yellowing book tape. It was a normal sort of cover, with no lurid ghost paintings or pseudo-Wiccan symbols. The title said, simply, *Crossing Over: An Introduction.*

"Do you want me to check it out for you here?"

"Oh, yes. Thank you."

"If it doesn't answer all your questions, feel free to come back and ask for me. We have some others in the collection that dig a bit deeper." Sophie smiled, handing the book back across the counter. "And good luck to your niece."

Patricia still had a few minutes to spare, so she found a spot in her reading nook on level nine, near the biographies. There, a series of sleek black tables looked over the manicured courthouse lawn, though since the rain had started back up in earnest, the view was blurred and watery.

She felt Marco's interest perk up as she opened the book. "Can you read this?" she whispered. "Can you read through my eyes?"

:if try:

A bit unsettling, perhaps, but Patricia pushed the feeling away. Maybe another set of eyes would help her make sense of this whole thing.

"Our world is not so different from the one inhabited by the spirits," began *Crossing Over.* The introduction was breathless, ethereal, dancing delicately around distasteful words like *death* and *ghost.* Patricia flipped to the author bio. Jasmynne Barrineau was a white woman with flowing hair and round cheeks, vamping for her photo in a medieval-looking gown.

Barrineau worked her way through a dizzying number of metaphors to describe the relationship of the ghostly plane with that of the living. Air pockets in rising bread, a sheet of ice melting back into the surface of a lake, oil and vinegar shaken as a salad dressing. The point, if Patricia understood it, was that there were constantly shifting points of intersection between the two planes.

According to Barrineau, most ghosts were called from the plane of the living to the spiritual plane either by the angels or by the ghost's deceased relatives, depending on your beliefs. That's what it meant to "follow the light," Barrineau said. "Once a spirit is beyond our plane, however, we have no way of knowing what has happened to them."

Insert your favorite afterlife here, Patricia thought. Most souls left the purgatory of this plane relatively quickly, though some stayed for reasons unknown. Barrineau used the vague motive of "unfinished business" as a catchall, and speculated that some spirits may balk at what they fear waits for them in the afterlife. These spirits may haunt the place where they lived, or appear to their loved ones. A marginally skilled medium could communicate with these lingering spirits, said Barrineau, but spirits that had crossed from our plane into the next required the deft skills of a resurrectionist.

Patricia glanced at her watch, then slipped the book into her purse. *Does that mean you crossed over? she thought to Marco. What was it like?*

He was a long time in responding, and for a moment Patricia wondered if he'd heard her. She opened her umbrella and began to hike her way back up to the office.

:don't know: Marco said at last. *:can't remember:*

Patricia remembered at the door to the office that she'd meant to call Toby, and checked her watch again. She waved at Cheryle through the window, miming a phone to her ear. Cheryle gave her a thumbs-up.

Her phone rang in her hand as she started to dial. "Oh, hello?" she answered, startled.

"Ms. Ramos-Waites? This is Detective Bayer. Is this a bad time?"

"Ah... no? Has Valeria not called you back?"

She heard papers shuffling on the other end of the line. "I haven't heard from your sister yet, no. Ma'am, I'm sorry to interrupt your day, but I just had one quick question. Do you have any idea if Mr. Caruso had connections with any local gangs?"

"Gangs?"

Marco?

She felt him react. *:course not:* But she could feel his anger, directed not at the detective's statement, but at himself. At... Valeria? She would ask him later.

"Specifically one called Los Ciegos. They're active mainly in South Seattle, so you may have heard of them."

"Yes, I think so." She cleared her throat. "Did they, did they mess with his car?" She couldn't bring herself to say the words: *Did they kill him?* She forced herself to smile at an entering patient, an older woman who came in regularly. "Nice to see you Mrs. Leyma," she said. "I'll catch up with you inside."

"I can't say, ma'am. I'd still like to talk with you and your sister in person, but I want you to know beforehand that Mr. Caruso may have gotten himself mixed up in something very serious. I need you to call me if you see anything suspicious."

"Is my—are my children in danger?"

"No, no. We have no reason to think that you or your family are in danger at this point, but we want to cover all our bases."

"I'll make sure Valeria calls you, and I'll bring her—we'll come in as soon as possible."

"Thank you."

Dammit, Valeria. She glanced through the window. Cheryle didn't seem overwhelmed, so she composed a quick text. *Detective wants to see us. Says important, maybe dangerous. Today after work?*

She took a deep breath, then began to pull open the door.

:toby:

"Oh, thank you," Patricia whispered. She dialed the number, praying he wouldn't answer. She didn't want to have a conversation with him, not right now.

She breathed a sigh of relief when the call went to voice mail. "Hi, Toby, it's Patricia. Sorry to be so abrupt on the phone yesterday, I was with my sister at the time and"—*Let's not mention Los Ciegos,* she thought, with the men's menacing faces etched in her memory—"something came up," she said instead. "I'd love to have dinner sometime. Maybe near the end of next week? This week is... this week is a mess. I hope you have a good day."

She sighed, and went back into the office, where Mrs. Leyma and all the other patients with normal, solvable medical problems were waiting for her attention. She put on a smile and slid behind the desk.

Chapter Nine

PATRICIA STILL HADN'T heard back from Valeria by the time she shut the office doors, so Detective Bayer would just have to wait another day. She could feel Marco's unease gnawing at the back of her mind, but she ignored it. She was hardly surprised that Valeria had disappeared at the mention of law enforcement.

Grateful to find a seat on the 60—the bus was usually so crowded at this time of day—Patricia settled in and cracked open the library book. She glanced at her seatmate, then shielded the book with her purse.

Jasmynne Barrineau had never claimed she would teach the reader to resurrect ghosts, but still Patricia was disappointed to flip through the table of contents and find no mention of hosting. She flipped to a promising-looking chapter about séances, and found herself drawn into a surprisingly interesting discussion of the herbs, anointing oils, and incenses that could attract or repel ghosts. *So no peppermint gum*, she thought, and Marco shrugged.

:never liked:

She was reading about banishing herbs when the hair on the back of her neck began to prick. Marco was agitated by the topic, she thought, or—the book snapped shut in her hands. Her seatmate glanced over at her, then went back to his phone.

Patricia looked up.

A quartet of elderly Asian women in rain bonnets were gathered around a cell phone, voices raised in annoyance at what they saw there. A man in scrubs and a faded fleece was having a spirited debate about *Twin Peaks* with a homeless woman whose tower of plastic bags threatened to spill into the aisle at every turn. A man was paying his fare, his dark features obscured by the collar of his puffy jacket. Impractical in the rain, Patricia thought, and yet these younger Latino men insisted on the fashion—

Her blood ran cold.

It was the man from the red F250 yesterday. Crooked Nose. Boarding the bus, paying like anyone else, reaching for the handrails as the bus stuttered away from the stop. Patricia ducked her head as he came toward her, but he walked past.

Had he seen her?

Patricia slipped the book into her purse, her cold, sweaty fingers fumbling with the latch.

Was it coincidence? Or did he know where she worked? He must, or else why would he be on the bus? If he had been watching her—

Patricia took a deep breath. She was being crazy, wasn't she? How on earth would he know? And why on earth would he ride the bus if he could drive? She shook her head; she was paranoid. It wasn't him, of course. Or it was, but he wasn't here for her. *Get a grip, Pati.* She glanced behind her.

Crooked Nose met her gaze and smiled.

Patricia whipped back around, heart racing. She should talk to the bus driver— No. Call the police? He hadn't done anything... yet. She could try to run, maybe, or ignore him, hope that he got off before she did. Or she could ride the bus forever until the passengers slowly dwindled and only she was left with the driver and a Los Ciegos thug. *Dear Lord, a sign please?*

:thirty-six:

"What?" In her surprise, Patricia had spoken out loud.

Patricia's seatmate looked over at her, and scooted toward the window.

She felt a ghostly finger on her chin, soft as a lover's, tilting her face to the right. The 36 bus was waiting at the corner of Twelfth and Jackson, crossing paths with the route of the 60. Patricia tensed. Could she make it? If she had the element of surprise, perhaps.

The red Stop Requested light was lit, a little mercy. Patricia wouldn't have to betray her move by pulling the cord.

As soon as the bus's doors opened, Patricia scrambled for the exit, pushing her way past the young man in scrubs, scattering the homeless woman's plastic bags, knocking into one of the Asian grandmothers with her purse—the women shouted after her in their language—elbowing past a silver-studded punk teen who was digging for his fare, and splashing out onto the puddled street.

She didn't look back, but :coming, run!: screamed Marco inside her head, and she dashed across Jackson against the crosswalk sign, against the blaring of horns, shoulders tensed against the report of a gun and the tearing bullet that would surely follow. She waved wildly at the driver of the 36, who reopened the doors just long enough to let Patricia inside before lurching away from the curb.

Patricia caught herself against the handrail, then dug through her purse for her ORCA bus fare card. "You trying to get yourself killed?" asked the bus driver, shaking her head. "I shouldna let you on, not like that."

"Thank you," Patricia gasped. "Thank you, thank you. I had to get away."

The bus driver spared her a glance, then laid into her horn as a car cut her off. Patricia clung to the handrail like a rag doll. "You in trouble? You got a boyfriend or something coming after you?"

A few other passengers on the crowded bus were looking her way, and Patricia felt her face flush. "No," she said quickly. "I'm fine."

"Honey." The bus driver clucked her tongue. "You need help, you just wait till I get done with this line, we'll call someone together."

Patricia glanced out the window, but she could see nothing but blurred neon through the rain-streaked, breath-fogged glass. "I'm fine, really."

The bus driver slammed to a stop at a red light and gave Patricia a hard look, with pursed magenta lips and a raised, sharply manicured eyebrow. "Mmm-hmm."

By the time she got off downtown, Patricia had finally accepted from the driver a business card with the number of a domestic violence hotline. She made her way to the Third and Pike stop that she normally avoided. Tonight she felt safer in the mass of people waiting there. The crowd was its usual odd mix of homeless folk trying to get out of the rain, scab-lipped drifter kids looking to score, and office workers staring intently at their phones in an attempt to ignore the seedy chaos and drug deals going on around them. She quickly assessed the best spot to wait: near a pair of women in casually professional dress, as far as possible from the small knot of teenagers with pants around their knees who were screaming insults at each other.

She craned her neck, heart racing, expecting at any moment to see that buzz cut and crooked nose again.

Nothing.

She dialed Valeria's number, listened as it rang into infinity. "Dammit, Val," she muttered.

Marco swirled, agitated, sending a rush of fear through her. Patricia looked up. Crooked Nose?

Nothing.

What is it?

:answer val:

Yes. It would be fantastic if Valeria would answer her phone, just once. Just one time out of the literally hundreds of times Patricia had tried to call her with important news in their lives. Patricia's fear ebbed in the face of a much more familiar emotion: fury with her sister.

Patricia started to tuck her phone back in her purse, but her hand stopped. She struggled a moment before recognizing Marco's presence, like a hand on her wrist. The two nice-looking women in professional dress paused in their conversation a moment, then moved a step away, as though Patricia were yet another sideshow at the Third and Pike bus stop, a disheveled Latina in sensible flats, mumbling to herself and twitching.

Marco was trying to move her thumb. *:answer val:* he said again, insistent.

"Stop it," she hissed. The women moved farther away.

She plunged her free hand into her jacket pocket to clutch at the agate waiting there. It leapt at her—*leapt?* Patricia thought—as though it had been waiting, and sat warm and pulsing in her hand as though alive. Patricia gripped it tight, remembering that day the ocean spoke to her as Patricia, not as "Mom" or "receptionist," but as Patricia, a woman who loved nature documentaries and biographies from the eighteen hundreds, travel and the feel of a cat's fur, and her children, and pancakes with peanut butter and strawberry jam on them, and the color green, and—

Patricia stumbled against the wall as Marco's physical presence disappeared.

The two women moved farther away still.

Patricia slipped her phone into her purse, with no resistance from Marco. Now he was only a sullen pressure tucked into his spo— into that place below her sternum.

Don't do that, she thought. *Please, Marco. Don't do that.*

He didn't answer.

Patricia leaned against the wall behind her, rubbing her thumb over the agate's smooth surface as though she could memorize the shape of it, the tiny divots and imperfections. She breathed deep, trying to think of nothing but her own breath.

A flash of headlights: the 120.

She boarded.

Chapter Ten

PATRICIA HARDLY FELT the rain as she walked the last few blocks from the bus stop to her house; every car headlight and crunch of tire in gravel made her heart leap in her throat, but none were the red F250.

None were hunting her.

The lights were on inside, though the porch light was not, and she could hear the whine of the television through the door.

Ava was sitting on the couch, a bowl of cereal in her lap. On the screen, a SWAT team was taking up position around a suburban house.

"Honey!" Patricia dropped her purse and coat in a heap on the dining table, then switched the television off. "You can watch your videos when I'm not around, but I don't want you watching TV. These shows are terrible for you."

"But Mom, they're about to catch the killer!" Ava said, throwing her hands theatrically into the air. She pouted a minute. "I think it's the ex-girlfriend, because she knows how to make soap."

"Ava-bean, please." Patricia sighed. *Mother-of-the-year award*, she thought. Her daughter was eating cereal for dinner and being raised by the television, learning all about life from crime dramas. "Don't you have homework?"

"I'm doing it." And she was, her math book open beside her, her notepad covered with chains of long division.

"Then why don't you finish, and we'll watch something after. Together. Something age-appropriate." Patricia turned to stare at the kitchen, trying to remember what sorts of food might be hidden in those cabinets. "And"—oh, she shouldn't ask—"what do you mean it's the girlfriend because she knows how to make soap?"

"Mommmm." Ava arched herself over the back of the couch to give Patricia an upside-down look. "Because you need fat to make soap."

"Ava-bean, you really, really can't watch those shows." *Dear Lord, why couldn't you have afflicted me with Disney princesses?*

Marco expanded with pride. :smart girl:

Yes. Very smart. Patricia felt a twinge of annoyance. Marco hadn't spoken to her the entire trip home, either embarrassed or angered by the way she'd used the agate to control him at the bus stop. Was he done hiding, come out to chide her about how to raise her own daughter?

She sighed. She needed to figure out another solution for Ava, and fast. Last year, Gabe had almost always been able to cover if Patricia couldn't make it home quickly from work, and when he left for college, she had thought she could make things work without him. It was rare that she was this late home, but it had been twice this week that Ava made herself "dinner" and filled her head with murder mystery shows on the television.

Patricia should find an after-school program, maybe, something to keep Ava busy a little longer. The elementary school must have something— although now that Gabe was out of the house, maybe she could even afford a paid program. Hadn't Ava been talking about one her friend had joined last month?

Patricia opened up the fridge, surveyed the sad contents, then opted for cereal herself. She was hunting for a clean bowl when she heard the television click back on.

"Ava!"

Ava whirled, caught red-handed. "I have to know how it ends!"

"No. No, you absolutely do not. Ava Maryam Waites, when I say you can't watch a show, that means you can't watch it. Now hand me the remote." Patricia switched the television back off. "I asked you to finish your homework. You can do it at the table or in your room, but you've lost television privileges for the rest of the week."

Ava let out a bloodcurdling shriek that was half horror-movie ingenue, half Chewbacca, then snatched up her homework and slammed the door to her room.

Patricia collapsed on the couch with her cereal.

:jesus:

Patricia sighed. "You get used to it," she said. Lord have mercy, but these were going to be a rough next few years. She sat in silence, listening to Ava's pretend sobs from the other room and eating her cereal, then finally reached for her phone and started a new text. *Saw one of those guys today. On the bus. Tried to call you. Where are you?*

Her phone buzzed nearly ten minutes later. Valeria. *Are you OK? Which one?*

I'm not OK. The one with the broken nose. He was looking for me. Where are you?

With Lucho. Can't talk. You at home?

Y

He follow?

I don't know.

Stay there. Don't talk detective yet. I'll call you.

When?

But there was no answer. Patricia wished to God she were home alone so she could recreate Ava's shriek of frustration without her daughter overhearing.

She should never have said yes to this. What would have happened if she hadn't? Valeria would have just walked away once more, just disappeared, and taken her ghosts and gangbangers and horror with her. And good riddance.

Had anything good ever come of getting involved with Valeria's problems? Not once, Patricia thought. And this time was no different.

Except that it was most definitely the last time. "I've been a crutch to her," she muttered bitterly. "And you were a crutch to her, too."

Marco recoiled, angry. Maybe she'd hit a little too close to the truth there. "She's used us both, and now she won't even let you rest. She's got Los Ciegos after me—and they were after you, too, weren't they? Detective Bayer said he thought they were involved."

Marco's anger snuffed. Was Patricia getting close to something? "You know, don't you? What the detective is talking about? And Valeria probably knows, but neither of you cares to tell me." Patricia's jaw clenched, and she turned her fury inward. "Are you protecting her from something? Or is she protecting you?"

She could feel Marco cringe, feel the anguish of conflict within him.

"Do you think these guys won't murder my children?"

:love val:

"I love her, too, and that means I don't enable her, or turn a blind eye when she gets into trouble. And believe me, I've seen her through a lot of trouble. A lot more than you have. And you—"

The latch turned on the front door, and Patricia whirled.

Adrian kicked the door open, and Patricia settled back against the couch with a racing heart. She heard the heavy whump as he dropped his gym bag, probably in the middle of the entryway as usual. She heard the skittering of his keys across the kitchen counter, and made a note of their location for when he asked tomorrow morning. "Hi, honey," she said, in what she hoped was a normal voice.

"Hey, Mom." Patricia heard the fridge door open.

"There's stuff for sandwiches. I could make you one if you wanted."

"That's cool." The fridge door shut; she heard the clanging of pots and pans.

Patricia levered herself to a seated position, then settled back against the arm of the couch so she could see him. "How was practice?" He'd gone, or at least made an effort to make it look like he had. He had that glow of exertion reddening his cheeks, his hair damp from the shower.

"Good." Pans clattered in the drawer as he pulled one out, and he instinctively glanced over his shoulder at Ava's closed door. He closed the drawer more carefully.

Patricia closed her eyes and listened to the sound of the faucet, the crinkle of plastic, Adrian's unself-conscious hum as he waited for the water to boil.

Adrian had more than a touch of Valeria's skittishness toward confrontation. Gabe was straightforward—quick to fess up, but equally quick with a logical justification or philosophical argument for his actions. Uncomplicated Ava was showing hints of preteen moodiness, but could still be confronted directly. Adrian... Adrian had far too much of Valeria in him, which was why this mess with the bad kids at school worried her more than if it had been Gabe.

When something went wrong, Adrian became a martyr, withdrawing into himself rather than letting someone else help him. She'd mused on it a hundred times before. Was it a fear of admitting his mistakes? A feeling that he alone could deal with it?

Patricia opened her eyes at the snap of the range unit being turned off, the telltale *tik-tik-tik* as the metal coils began to cool. Adrian was doctoring his Top Ramen with gouts of Tapatío and a packet of red pepper flakes left over from some pizza delivery. He looked up at her, tilted his head.

"You OK, Mom?"

"What?"

"You feeling OK?"

"Oh." Patricia forced herself to sit more upright. "I'm just tired."

Adrian brought his steaming bowl to sit beside her on the couch, and Patricia reached to clear the cereal bowls so he'd have room. "Breakfast for dinner, huh?" he said, and a hint of a smile quirked at his lips.

"The dinner of champions."

"Is Ava asleep?"

Patricia shook her head. "She's sulking in her room because I wouldn't let her watch NCIS or whatever it was."

Adrian screwed up his face. Joe's expression. "I don't know why she likes that stuff. That show's tough."

"You've got me." Patricia let him take a few bites. "I met with Coach Ng yesterday."

He didn't flinch. "I know."

"Did he tell you?"

"He talked to me before practice." Adrian slurped at his soup, blowing on the red-flecked, spring-loaded noodles to cool them. He didn't look at Patricia.

"He said he's got to bench me next game, but if I don't miss any more I'll be back starting like I should be."

"That's good." Patricia took a deep breath. "Honey, Marco's..." It felt rude to say "death" with Marco right there, so she stumbled a moment. Then, "Marco's been hard on us all," she said finally, awkwardly. Which probably sounded ruder. *No offense*, she thought. Marco gave a little huff of irritation.

Adrian chewed his mouthful of noodles a long time. "Tía Valeria looks really rough," he said finally.

"She's had a hard time. It's hard when..." But Adrian didn't need to be told that. He'd been ten years old when Joe had died. "How are you?"

Adrian shrugged.

"You can tell me anything," Patricia said, then added, without thinking, her father's family creed from years ago: "We don't keep secrets in this family." The words came out before she could stop them, and she instantly felt guilty. Marco curled inside her. Accusing? Nervous? She couldn't tell.

"You're going to a movie with Lucy after practice tomorrow, right?" she asked, to change the subject. Adrian nodded. "What are you seeing?"

"We don't know yet."

"Anything you can take your sister to?"

"Mom!"

Patricia smiled. "I'm joking. Maybe she and I will have our own movie date. Why don't you invite Lucy over for dinner after church on Sunday? I can make *tres leches*."

"She might be busy," he said, too quickly. Then, "I'll ask."

"It would be nice to see her."

"OK." Adrian finished off his bowl, slurped down the rest of the salty broth. "I'm tired. I'm going to bed." Patricia heard the clatter of the bowl in the sink. "You should probably, too."

Patricia smiled. "Yes, son."

⌣

Patricia did go to bed, but she didn't go to sleep. She opened the library book,

Crossing Over, and scanned it for something that would help.

As Patricia read the table of contents, she kept a portion of her attention on Marco's responses. Their last conversation had unsettled her—he knew something more than he'd let on, of that she was certain. She wondered if there was a section on compelling ghosts to speak.

There wasn't, but one chapter had the vaguely promising title "Guests on Our Plane." A pun? Did the ethereal Jasmynne Barrineau have a sarcastic streak?

In the chapter, Barrineau described the different stages that ghosts—"our spirit friends," she called them—went through when trying to cling to the plane of the living. At first they might remain interactive and coherent, retaining a grip on the person they'd been before their death—especially if tethered to a host or another object. Those that weren't tethered somehow in the plane of the living could begin to lose their grip on both worlds and develop fragmented consciousness.

Tethered?

She felt Marco perk up, as well, and she flipped back to the index—but there was no index. Patricia let out a sigh, then scanned the table of contents again for a chapter titled, oh, she didn't know. "How to Tether Your Unwanted Guest," maybe, or "Regaining Your Mental Privacy Without Destroying Your Familial Bonds."

Nothing.

There was a chapter on Emmaline Cook and Sarah Prichard, however. Out of curiosity, Patricia turned to it; she'd heard the names, of course—everyone had—but she realized she'd never actually read about the case. It had been one of the first studied by science, in the late eighteen hundreds, and one of the first that had paved the way for resurrected ghosts to give court-permissible evidence.

Emmaline's best friend, Sarah, had been killed in an accident, but because of the suspicious circumstances of her death, Sarah's stepfather had been accused of murder. Emmaline had become possessed by Sarah—the exact mechanism was unclear—and the communication between the two had been extraordinary.

The court was convinced to accept Sarah's testimony through the means of Emmaline, and Sarah's stepfather was cleared of murder.

Patricia found herself engrossed in the girls' story. When the phone rang, she let out a yelp and dropped the book. "Pull it together, Pati," she whispered. She fumbled for her phone, which buzzed against her nightstand.

She reached over to check the number. It had a 206 area code, but she didn't recognize the number. She stared at it. Valeria in trouble? When else had she gotten strange phone calls in the middle of the night?

Patricia licked her lips and answered. "Hello?"

"Yeah, hey, Pati? Good, you're awake." It was a man's voice, scratchy and soft like comfortable old wool.

"Lucho?"

"You were awake, right? Sorry it's kinda late."

"That's OK. I was awake." She slipped a bookmark into Crossing Over and set it aside. "What's going on? Is Valeria with you?"

"Yeah, Nena was here. She just left. I think we got something figured out for you two."

"For me and Val?" *Hardly likely.*

"Marco. You and Marco Polo."

Oh.

"He still treating you all right in there?"

Patricia took a deep breath. "He's fine. I think we're both a little antsy to get this over with."

"Oh, yeah, I bet. So we're gonna get this over with. Tomorrow," Lucho said. "You come over after work."

Patricia's heart skipped a beat. Marco expanded like a sigh. "Tomorrow?"

"Tomorrow. You been doing so good, *profe*. We'll get you taken care of." On the other end of the line, she could hear sirens flare and die in the distance. "You have any questions for me?"

"I..." Did she have questions. Patricia licked her lips. "I've been reading up on ghosts," she said finally. "I think there might be a way to tether Marco outside of me? Or, I read that at least." She paused, waiting for him to laugh. Instead, the silence stretched on. "Is that true?"

"Yeah," Lucho said slowly, after a moment. "You can. I won't, though."

"You can't?"

"No, I can—I mean, no. No. I won't. So, *profe*, first off it's illegal. And, sure, Marco Polo, it probably sounds good until you know you'll just be trapped inside a pot eating chicken blood and telling fortunes for the rest of eternity." She heard Lucho take a sip of something. "Anyway, it's not right—well, I don't think it's right. There are religions that do it, like Palo, they build these little altars, *prendas*, and they fix them all up with graveyard dirt and sticks and somebody's bones, then they call that person's ghost into it."

"And the ghost... stays?"

"They get its permission first, I guess. And then you gotta feed it. Animal sacrifice and all that." Marco squirmed in his spo— in that place below her sternum.

"So, it's an evil cult?" Patricia asked.

"Oh, no, no." She could hear static as he shifted. "Just not my, ah—I'm a good Catholic, you know? You gotta let the dead go to their judgment, not leave them purgatoried here in our plane forever. But I got some friends from Colombia who are *paleros*, they're the nicest people, you know?"

"The nicest people who sacrifice chickens to feed ghosts."

"Hey, hey. I used to kill chickens all the time growing up. Difference is I just drained the blood into the sink, but my *palero* buddies give it to Grandma to drink. Besides, when's the last time you ate a Chicken McNugget? I guarantee that chicken got a worse death. I just think it's weird is all. And we don't see eye to eye on where the party's at in the afterlife."

Lucho cleared his throat. "Why are we talking about this, anyway? Oh, right. Can you tether a ghost outside a host. Yeah. You can."

"You just didn't want to tell me about it because it's illegal."

"I didn't think to tell you because we aren't going to do it."

Right. Making that decision for her.

"What else aren't you telling me?" Patricia asked.

On the other end of the line, Lucho sighed deeply. "A lot, actually, *profe*. There's a lot I'm not telling you, and you know why? Because there's a lot to know. I've been doing this probably since before you were born, and here's the thing, let me tell you. Sometimes I go to my wife and I say, 'Hey, Lindsay, why won't you let me drink Diet Coke?' And then she starts telling me about artificial sweeteners and chemical bonding and carbon molecules and electrons and my eyes glaze over and I wish I hadn't asked. Because I don't know a tenth about science as her freshmen Intro to Chem students. Do I want Lindsay to tell me everything? Hell no. I just trust her and don't drink the Diet Coke."

The line went silent for a moment, then Lucho took a deep breath. "I know you don't know me that well, and I know you got problems with your sister, but you really gotta trust me, Pati. I promise I'll start making your eyes glaze over with gobs and gobs of arcane facts if you want them."

Patricia stared at the ceiling, trying to think of how to ask her next question.

"You still there?"

"Yes," she said.

"You pissed?"

"No."

"You trust me?"

"I think so. Lucho... I have one more question."

"Go for it."

"Is Marco acting different from a normal ghost."

"Yes," Lucho said without hesitation. "He shouldn't be nearly as powerful as he is. You want me to make your eyes glaze over?"

"No. But am I in danger?"

"Not if you keep up the training Nena taught you. You got a talisman, right?"

"Right."

"Good, Pati, that's great. You just hold tight and we'll get you taken care of tomorrow night. Then we can do all the research papers you want, and you read all the books you want. But for now you trust me, *entiendes*?"

"I trust you."

"Good night, then, and Marco Polo, *güey*, you be a gentleman. I'll see you both tomorrow."

The other end went silent, but Patricia lay cradling her phone in her hand for another hour, unable to sleep.

Chapter Eleven

PATRICIA WAITED IN the rain, beads of water dripping from the edge of her umbrella and splashing onto the cuffs of her pants; she could feel the damp there seeping through her socks, a slow, top-down, icy creep into her shoes.

Adrian was out with Lucy tonight, and she'd arranged for Ava to stay with a friend, so she supposed that there really wasn't any hurry—other than the fact that she was cold and damp, and Valeria had said she'd be here twenty minutes ago.

She'd spent today's lunch break reading Crossing Over, but had found no more references to tethering ghosts outside of a host. That would make sense, if what Lucho said was true and it was illegal to do so.

But if Lucho wouldn't tether Marco outside of her, what was he planning to do tonight?

Marco had been a nervous coil of energy all day, his anxiety interfering with her ability to work no matter how hard he tried to fade into the background. She couldn't blame him. For Patricia, whatever happened tonight meant she'd go back to normal, to having only a single set of memories and emotions and thoughts rattling around in her brain.

For Marco, there was no longer any such thing as normal. Whatever happened tonight would be yet another new border to cross. Yet another new way of existing.

Or not existing.

Patricia glanced at her watch. Valeria was now twenty-five minutes late.

You coming? she texted.

2 min. Traffic.

Patricia sighed. Of course there was traffic; there was always traffic. Which is why you planned ahead when you made appointments.

As annoyed as Patricia was to be kept waiting, she hated even more to be late herself. Detective Bayer was expecting them at the police station ten minutes ago, and Lucho after that—well, but maybe Lucho was used to Valeria's constant tardiness.

Patricia stamped her feet to stay warm. At this rate she should have just taken the bus down to the police station and had Valeria meet her there. At least then she would have been sitting, and relatively dry.

:drive you crazy:

Yes. She could drive you crazy. Patricia tried to ignore the undercurrent of longing that came from Marco's version of that sentiment.

She scanned the rows of headlights inching down Ninth Avenue. Or maybe she should have taken the bus to somewhere easier for Valeria to get to in rush hour.

Or maybe something was wrong.

Or maybe—

Patricia stopped herself. She was driving herself batty speculating on what might or might not be happening.

Valeria had always said she'd worry herself into a psych ward if she didn't stop herself, but Patricia had always brushed it off. As if Valeria knew the first thing about—

Well, it hadn't just been Valeria who'd told her that. Joe had said it, too. "You're scared of your dinosaur eggs before they've even hatched," he'd always told her. "Wait to see what happens. It may not be as bad as you think it'll be."

Patricia blinked against the burning in her eyes. She'd been letting her imagination run wild with worry lately. First she'd let fear of what Valeria might do trap her in this situation in the first place. If she'd just sat her sister down to talk, if she'd just taken time to understand what was going on before rushing headlong into a cemetery...

Then she'd let her imagination run wild with visions of Adrian's problems, imagining hoodlums, drugs, and juvenile hall, and finally prison, when most likely it was nothing more than a fight with Lucy.

Finally, she'd let Lucho's cagey responses send her into a frenzy of amateur ghost-hunting research, filling her head with crazy theories when she should really just trust Lucho. He was the expert, after all. And despite his reluctance to share all of his information with her—which, to be fair, Patricia could understand—she didn't have any reason not to trust him. And if she was honest with herself, most of her frustration with Lucho stemmed from her irritation with Valeria.

Not that there was nothing to worry about, of course. She hadn't imagined her sister's involvement with Los Ciegos—the conversation with Bayer yesterday had confirmed it. And Crooked Nose had come after her on the bus. She wasn't making that up.

Patricia steeled herself. Her sister might be in way over her head, but tonight at least they could get past the speculation. Tonight they would talk things through with Bayer, they would work things out with Lucho, and Patricia wasn't going to let herself get lost in speculative worries: not her son's supposed decline into juvenile delinquency, not how Toby would run screaming from her life if he knew she was hosting a ghost, and not whether they would be arrested for arriving so late to a meeting with a detective.

A tap of the horn jolted her from her thoughts. Patricia squinted against the glare of the headlights: Valeria's silver Subaru sat at the bus stop, wipers slapping against the rain and smearing reflected streetlight over the windshield like mercury.

A second horn blared, from the bus that was about to pull up behind Valeria. Patricia hurried toward the Subaru, shaking out her umbrella as she went. She didn't notice the passenger window rolling down as she reached for the handle, until the bus sounded its horn again and she looked up.

She jerked her hand back with a stifled scream.

Dark eyes met hers, set in a handsome face with a crooked nose. Gold glittered in his earlobe. The closed-eye tattoo branded his neck.

"Patricia." The man shifted so she could see the pistol in his hand, its barrel pointed casually toward the driver's seat. Toward Valeria. "Get in."

"I'm so sorry, Pati," Valeria whispered. "Please get in."

Behind them, the bus driver laid on his horn once more.

Patricia slipped into the back of the Subaru.

Valeria peeled away from the curb.

"Get behind your sister," said Crooked Nose. "So I can see you." His voice was soft, his accent strong but not impossible to understand. Central American, maybe.

Patricia gingerly cleared a space on the other side of the back seat, then slid over. Marco was coiled inside her like a jaguar. Not the panic she had felt from him yesterday on the bus, but rather a cold fury. *Let me deal with this*, she thought, terrified at what would happen if he got in the way. She thought she felt assent. Hoped she felt assent.

"Val, are you OK?"

Valeria was pale, her knuckles bone white as she clutched the steering wheel. She didn't look injured, but from this angle, in these lights, it was impossible to tell.

"Pati," said Valeria, "meet Javier Mejía. Javi, this is my sister."

Javi? Patricia wasn't the only one to react to the nickname. Marco shifted. Between his coiled tension and Valeria's jerky driving, Patricia's stomach was beginning to turn. She fought down a wave of nausea and buckled her seat belt.

Javier adjusted the rearview mirror to see her. "Nice to meet you," he said.

Can't say the same, thought Patricia, though she kept her tongue. "What is this?" she asked instead.

"It's just a little kidnapping. Just I gotta talk to the two of you, and your sister isn't being talkative."

"What are you going to do with us?"

"That depends on you. You don't do anything stupid, we can have a conversation, OK?"

"Javi." Valeria's voice sounded hoarse. "She doesn't know anything about Marco. She doesn't know about any of this."

"Yeah, I bet she doesn't." Javier tilted his head. "Patricia, *te juro*, I'm not gonna hurt either of you so long as you're honest with me."

Patricia swallowed, trying to work moisture into her dry mouth enough to speak. "I don't know anything about this," she whispered. "You have to believe me."

The sickly wash of streetlights flickered over Javier's face—faster now as Valeria slipped out of the mess of traffic and onto Dearborn. His dark eyes glittered. "Course I don't believe you," he said. "You wanna play rough, that doesn't surprise me." He reached up to twine a strand of Valeria's hair in his tattooed fingers, grinning at Patricia in the rearview mirror. "I know your sister, always likes to do things the hard way."

Marco roared.

"Hands off her, asshole," Patricia heard herself shout as she surged forward against the seat belt, having forgotten about the restraint. She tried to land a punch, to gouge him with clawed fingers, but Javier was faster. He spun in the passenger seat, gun in hand. The barrel was aimed directly at her forehead.

"Back off, Marco," Javier said coolly. "Or neither of you gonna be in this world much longer."

"Stop it!" screamed Valeria.

"Keep driving, Val. Marco, *pendejo*. Back down."

Patricia could hear him speak, but it was from a distant place, the words burbling and distorted as though through water. Her presence was diminishing, fading, receding to that spot below her sternum, maybe, while Marco groped for the reins—his indecision, his seething anger, strained her muscles taut as he decided how to take this asshole down. *Because what the hell is there to lose, I already died once.*

Horror dawned on Patricia: she was no longer in charge.

She struggled to reach Marco with her thoughts, to force her words through his—*her!*—vocal cords. Through the depths she could hear Marco howling like a caged beast, could feel the seat belt scoring her torso, could feel —

She could feel her fingers moving when she willed them to, just ever so slightly. Her right hand twitched and grasped on command. Marco's full attention was held by the pistol's barrel and the need to destroy the man behind it. Patricia thrust her hand into her coat pocket, clawed her fingers around the agate.

Marco flinched, then threw her body back against the seat.

:notakingback:

She focused all her thoughts on the agate, on the glowing sense of her own being spreading outward from her chest. It was a power struggle beyond any other she'd known, a tug-of-war with oblivion, an arm-wrestling match with herself—against herself?—and for a moment she wasn't certain she would win. *C'mon, Marco. I'm Patricia. I'm in charge. This is my body. I'm Patricia, remember? I'm Patricia. I'm—*

:fucknbastard:

Patricia ignored him, concentrating on the stone. The icy waves of the Pacific Ocean had washed over *her* frozen feet. She had found this agate, while *her* children played in the pool. Haystack Rock was *her* memory. The sand on *her*—

And she was alone.

Patricia took a deep, shuddering breath, probing her mind for traces of Marco. She smelled roasting coffee, baking bread, diesel fuel, and she forced herself to open her eyes. Javier's pistol was still pointed between her eyes, glinting neon from the Tully's factory sign. Valeria's Subaru was still flowing steady with the traffic along Airport Way.

Patricia was still alive, and Marco was still dead.

Javier gave her a long, searching look, then eased on the safety and tucked the gun into a bag at his feet. He fished a crumpled fast-food napkin out of the glove compartment, passed it back to Patricia. "For your nose," he said.

Patricia touched it to her nose. It came away black with blood. Her head felt like it was about to split open.

"Fuck you, Javi," said Valeria.

"Me? This is your fault. You don't answer my calls, you don't wanna talk about where Marco is, I gotta figure this out on my own."

"You could have killed her."

"How was I supposed to know that? I never seen a ghost do that." He glanced back at Patricia. "Ghosts can't do that."

Valeria's jaw clenched.

Javier leaned back against the door, one eye on Valeria, the other on Patricia, though now he seemed less interested in threatening the two sisters than in keeping an eye out for his own safety.

"You're a sick bitch, Valeria Ramos," he said. "Putting a ghost in your sister, vos. That's twisted."

"It wasn't the plan."

"Maybe that's why you're not supposed to make the plans."

"When Chente—"

"Shut up and drive."

"When you take—"

"Just drive."

"No!" Valeria slammed on the brakes, skidding to a halt in a bus lane. A semi screamed past them, its horn blasting a fading yowl. "Promise me you won't let them hurt her. This isn't her fault." Tears spilled down Valeria's cheeks. "She really doesn't know anything, Javier."

They sat in silence a moment, the windshield wipers slapping furiously against the sheets of water thrown up by the wheels of passing semitrucks.

Finally Javier sighed. "Val. I'm not taking you to Chente. Now drive."

Chapter Twelve

VALERIA NOSED THE silver Subaru into her driveway and killed the engine. No one made a move to get out.

Patricia sat silent, one hand clutching the door handle, the other fisted around the agate in her pocket; Javier's profile cut a sharp silhouette against Valeria's flickering porch light.

"Please," Valeria said at last, her voice so soft Patricia almost didn't hear her over the patter of rain on the Subaru's roof. "Leave my sister out of this. I'll talk to Chente. I'll tell him whatever he wants to know. But please leave my sister out of this."

"You'd give up Marco?" Javier asked. Marco pulsed; Patricia clutched the agate even tighter. When Valeria didn't answer, Javier swore under his breath. "He's dead, Val," he said, opening the passenger door. "No offense, Marco. Anyway, if I was gonna take you to Chente, you think we'd be stopping by here to grab your nightie and toothbrush? Get outta the car, Val. Come on, Patricia."

While Valeria stabbed her shaking keys at the dead bolt, Patricia stood shivering in the rain, unwilling to share the stoop with Javier. He wasn't much taller than her, but he carried himself in that wiry way of fighters and swaggering boys that said he wouldn't hesitate to draw blood. That, and the tattoos which painted his skin in rainbow hues of bruises. And the broken nose.

And the gun, of course, which was tucked safely away, though Patricia thought she could still sense it like a red-hot presence, waiting to strike. Javier held the door open for her. She edged past him.

Patricia had been to Valeria's place once since Marco's death, so she was expecting what she found. But Marco's flutter of dismay was so strong she had to catch herself in the door frame.

Valeria had purged after his death, donating garbage bags full of clothes to the Goodwill, giving to friends anything with too much sentiment to donate. Nothing remained of the warmth he had spread through Valeria's one-room junker, not a thing of his on the cracked walls or the empty bookshelves. Two olive-green folding chairs and a ratty couch covered with a floral sheet were the only pieces of furniture. What few belongings Valeria had kept were strewn about, cluttering up surfaces and drifting into corners, Marco's neat influence no longer there to stem their tide.

His absence was palpable.

Patricia could almost hear Marco's laugh coming from the kitchen, where he would cook dinner while the sisters talked with the news flickering on the TV. Marco was just about to walk out of the kitchen and give her a hug—she could feel it. Thank her for stopping by, ask if she was hungry.

Inside her, the very real ghost Marco stirred. Patricia gripped the agate.

Valeria was watching her, gauging Marco's reaction to his old home, maybe. He shrank away from her gaze, hurt and... accusing?

"You got anything to drink?" Javier asked, shattering the moment. Valeria broke away from watching Patricia to open the fridge: a few lone takeout boxes and a case of Modelo Especial. She pulled one out for each of them. Patricia took a sip of hers, then set it on a stack of unopened bills on the coffee table.

Javier settled onto one of the folding chairs, elbows on knees, head tilted. "What's in your pocket?" he asked, then he raised his hands. "Don't plan anything, OK? I'm not fucking with you two. We're just going to talk."

Patricia glanced at Valeria, then withdrew her hand. The agate lay on her palm, nestled alongside a line of fingernail marks.

"Pretty rock," said Javier.

"It's her talisman," said Valeria. "It helps her keep control when Marco..."

"When Marco gets all crazy and takes over her body?" Javier took a long draw of his beer. "What's wrong with him, Val?"

"Nothing's wrong."

"Something's wrong. I never seen a ghost do that." He leaned forward to get a better look at Patricia's face. She felt like she was in a museum. "Or is it because she's new? Did that happen to you when you first started?" Valeria didn't respond, but it was clear in her expression that the answer was no. "Shit, Val."

Javier settled back against his chair, gnawing his lower lip. Tiny metal shrieks came from Valeria's hands as she worried the tab off her beer can. Patricia cleared her throat. "So, how do you two know each other?" she asked. It was the most awkward of cocktail-party beginnings, but it was all she had right now.

Javier lifted his chin to Valeria.

"Lucho and I do resurrections for them sometimes." Valeria coughed. "For Los Ciegos."

"And who do you resurrect?"

"Immigrants, mostly. They want to see their families one last time."

"That sounds noble."

Javier cut in. "It's like the reverse coyote package. You paid to get across the border, and once you're here, you've got the insurance that if you die up north, you'll get a chance to say good-bye in spirit."

"So you're smuggling ghosts. Is that—is it actually illegal to cross borders with ghosts?"

"You need a special visa," said Valeria. "Normally. But we don't—ah, we don't bother. And no one's really watching out for it. It's not a big deal."

It was absurd, really, the thought of applying for a visa to travel with a ghost. Patricia actually laughed, a frayed and nervous chuckle at the cartoony, shimmering passport she imagined you would use.

So Valeria was crossing borders, to someplace warm, presumably; *comes back tan*, she thought, remembering her conversation with Marco. *And you never asked her?*

:her business:

Family gets in each other's business, she answered him. "So," she said out loud. "You're flying to... Mexico?"

Valeria snapped the tab off her can with an unsatisfying *tink*. "Nicaragua," she said uncomfortably. "It works out better for a cover story."

"You're going home and you're not telling Mom?" This made Patricia angrier than the ghosts, than the guns. Than Javier.

Valeria at least had the decency to look ashamed. "She'd tell the tías and make me visit. Or she'd make me bring her back cheese. And, Pati, I wasn't there to hunt down Mom's favorite old childhood friend and give her a hug. I was there to do *illegal things*."

"Smuggling ghosts? And what else? Are you a drug mule, too? Or just whoring your body out for ghosts?"

Javier slammed his palm on the coffee table, which shuddered from the blow. "*Basta ya*," he growled. "Valeria. Lucho wasn't part of this, right? Lucho wouldn't cross Los Ciegos like that."

"He wasn't a part. I called him when..." Valeria gestured wordlessly at Patricia. "I told him I'd make it right. He wasn't a part of this at all."

Javier's nostrils flared. "That won't stop Chente from getting rid of him if he's in a bad mood."

"I'll talk to him."

"Good, because I can't or he knows I talked to you. And you shoulda done that in the first place. You got cojones, vos, but you shoulda either talked to Chente or gotten out of town right away." Javier took a long draw of his Modelo, then regarded Patricia with a thoughtful expression. "I think you're telling the truth that your sister doesn't know a goddamn thing about this, huh?"

Patricia looked from Valeria to Javier. "What do you mean?"

Valeria paled. "He means the smuggling, the ghosts I was—"

"Shut up, Valeria!" Patricia snapped. Marco roiled inside her, and she clenched the agate again, focusing on the sensation of being "herself."

"What do you mean?" she asked Javier again.

Javier glanced at Valeria.

But pieces were starting to fall into place in Patricia's mind. She could sense Marco, trying to keep it to himself, but she focused on the agate, compelling him to tell her what no one else would. *Sharp tang of oil in the garage, and sickly sweet radiator fluid, it's puddling on the floor, this POS is more of a wreck than he thought, but it's a favor he'll do for Val's friend. It's not the radiator that he's working on now, it's the damn window that won't go down, and even though no one told him to check it out, he does good work, he'll find out why...*

Patricia's eyes went wide. "Who—"

"Marco found something he shouldn't have," Valeria said, too quickly. Patricia stared at her, feeling sick. "I know Marco can't talk to you yet," Valeria said with a quick glance at Javier, "but once he does, you'll learn about it anyway."

"And this... something Marco found?"

"Is highly illegal."

"More illegal than your normal above-board ghost smuggling?" Patricia shoved her hands back in her pockets to stop their trembling. *Screws clattering into their magnetic tray, jimmying the molded plastic liner off the inside of the door, the scent getting stronger, and maybe he's smelled it this whole time, covered up by the sweetness of the leaking radiator, this more earthy reek...*

"Yes," said Valeria. "But I didn't know—"

"She didn't know, Marco," said Javier.

A parcel, it's the length of his forearm and twice as thick, it's what's jamming up the window mechanism, and it smells like death, what the hell...

"Didn't know what?" Patricia asked, because even though she could see in her memory the sad, pale contents of the parcel laid open on the driver's seat, she still couldn't comprehend what it meant. Her voice seemed like an echo far away. Marco quivered.

"Val, you tell her later," Javier said. "I don't wanna hear about it, I don't wanna talk about it, I don't wanna be a part of any of this." He crossed himself.

Patricia took a deep breath. "So Marco found something, and now they, and you"—Patricia glanced at Javier—"want to make sure this dead man takes his secret to the grave."

"They do," said Javier quietly. "I don't."

"Why not?"

Javier picked up his beer can, found it empty. Set it back on the coffee table. "You know, this year Marisol stopped asking what I do," he said finally.

"Like she went through a phase in preschool where she wanted to tell everybody what her daddy did, so she started asking my girl and me. I don't want to lie to her, but I don't want to tell her the truth, you know. And I think she figured that out, because she stopped asking and just started telling the other kids I'm a carpenter." He smiled sadly. "My little girl started lying for me."

Valeria got up to grab him another beer.

"It started out with a bit of weed," he said after he'd opened it and taken a drink. "You can make some good money selling weed. You can make better selling cocaine, and who cares how some rich kids mess up their lives. But now it's heroin, it's crack, it's guns, its protection, it's ghosts, it's little girls, and now it's even—" Javier sat back in disgust. "And if I'd wanted to join the *maras* I woulda stayed in LA and joined the fucking *maras*. So here's what I got. I got something Chente needs right now, tucked inside her skull." He jabbed a finger at Patricia. "Maybe we get to the cops and tell them what Chente's messing with, once Marco's ready to talk. You and me, Val. Maybe we go to the cops and get out of this mess."

Valeria's eyes went wide. "You'd do that? What about your kids?"

"They're ready. They'll come with me if we gotta run. And my girl, too. She hates the rain anyway." Javier leaned forward, knuckles white, hands clutched against his knees. "Listen, Val. Chente doesn't know you got Marco outta the dirt—he only thinks you made it so no one else could. Me and you two and Lucho are the only ones who know he's here. So I go back to Chente, I tell him you're scared outta your mind and won't make trouble, and then we wait until Marco can testify and we go to the cops. We got, what, you think another four or five days until he starts talking?" Valeria gave Patricia a hard look. Javier missed it. "She ever hosted before?"

"No."

"Damn." Javier sighed. "So like two weeks, then. You—"

Patricia shrieked as her phone buzzed in her pocket. She pulled it out, then glanced up to see Javier with the gun in his hand, Valeria reaching for a knife on the counter. She raised her hands to show the phone. "I'm sorry, it rang, and I..."

Javier swore loudly in Spanish and shoved the gun back into his bag.

"I'll just, I'll just answer it then," Patricia said lamely. She saw the number and her heart sank. Detective Bayer. She'd completely forgotten about their appointment.

She pushed her way into Valeria's bedroom before answering.

"Patricia? Is everything all right?"

Patricia pushed the door shut. Valeria's bed was a wreck of tumbled blankets and dirty clothes; Patricia pushed aside a pair of jeans and sat gingerly on the edge. "Things are—I'm sorry, Detective Bayer. My sister had car troubles, she..." Patricia tumbled on, unable to stop herself. "She's been a wreck, and it was impossible to get her anywhere on time even in the best of times, you can't even imagine what my parents had to do to get her to the dentist."

Bayer cleared his throat when she'd finished. "Where are you now?"

"We're at her house. I was helping her with her car..."

:stop acting nervous, detective fine:

Patricia took a deep breath.

:you're a trip:

"We're at her house," she said finally. "In South Park."

"Have you eaten? I can meet you down there. My commute goes through there anyway."

"Oh?" Patricia glanced at the closed bedroom door. "Oh. Yes. Let's."

"How does Loretta's sound? In half an hour?"

"Perfect." Patricia swallowed. "I'll make sure we're there."

She hung up and stared at the phone a moment. She would do her best to make sure they were there, at least.

Javier and Valeria stopped talking as soon as she walked back into the living room. "Who was that?" Javier asked.

Patricia ran through a quick list of possibilities, and decided to settle on the truth. "Detective Bayer," she said. "Wondering why we'd missed our appointment."

"Did you tell him you'd been kidnapped by a *cholito* with a gun?" Valeria asked.

Javier shot her a theatrical smirk. "You the one didn't return my civilized phone calls." He gave Patricia a more serious look. "Who's the detective?"

"Bayer. He's working on Marco's... accident."

"And he doesn't think it was an accident."

"No."

Javier stood, gathering beer cans off the coffee table. "You should go. You talk to him, you figure out what he knows, you give him just a little hint of what you know. We'll talk tomorrow."

"I told him we'd meet him in half an hour. At Loretta's."

"We're supposed to go to Lucho's."

"We can go after."

"No. We—"

"Don't you care?" Patricia threw up her hands. "Marco was murdered, and all this guy wants is to talk to you about it. Does that not matter to you at all?"

"I—" Valeria cut herself off, then sank back into the couch cushions like a discarded doll. She stared at the glittering beer tab in her hands. Marco surged toward her, his presence an unreadable tangle of emotion and fear. "Fuck you, Pati," she whispered.

Braced for a fight, Patricia felt instead as though the wall she'd been leaning against had suddenly disappeared, the floor dropped out from beneath her feet; her stomach lurched like a carnival ride at the sight of her sister weaponless and wordless.

"She cares," said Javier softly. "She cares a lot." His hand brushed Valeria's shoulder as he walked by. "You guys talk to the detective, then call me tomorrow. You good, Val?"

"I'm good," Valeria said, her breath so soft Patricia could barely hear her.

Javier shut the door behind him, leaving the two sisters alone once more with a ghost.

Chapter Thirteen

PATRICIA PULLED BACK the living room curtain to watch Javier's F250 pull away from the curb. "Do you think we can trust him?" she asked finally.

Valeria still hadn't moved from the couch. "I trust him," she said after a moment. "He hasn't always been on my side, but he's not a backstabber. And he's a terrible actor." She scrubbed her hands over her face as though she could rub away the events of the last weeks.

Patricia let the curtain drop and sank down beside her sister. "Did you..." She sighed. "Did you and him have a thing?" she asked delicately. She sounded like a schoolgirl.

Marco pulsed, aching in his spot below her sternum.

"Are you asking?" Valeria said. "Or is he?"

"I'm asking." Patricia took a deep breath. "But he's awfully curious."

"Well, no, Pati. We didn't 'have a thing.' I have—" Valeria stumbled over the words, dropped her head against the back of the couch. "Marco, Javi's got a girlfriend of a lot of years, and they've got like the cutest kids you've ever seen. And Marco, you know I wouldn't. You know me."

:*know?*: Marco didn't feel reassured.

Valeria searched Patricia's face, her expression anxious. "What did he say? Is he OK?"

"He knows," Patricia said. It was almost what he'd said, anyway. "He'll be OK." *Except that he's dead.* Lord. And except that she understood what he'd really meant. Did either of them really know Valeria anymore?

Valeria's eyes were brimming with tears. "Good. Marco, I never wanted to hurt you with any of this. Any of this mess."

"And what is this mess? That even Javier was too scared to talk about?" Patricia shuddered. "Whose bones were they?"

"What?"

"The bones. In the car." Valeria just looked at her, puzzled. "Val, I saw what he found in the car."

"What do you mean, 'saw'?"

"Like a memory. I get them sometimes." Patricia paused, suddenly scared. "I actually get them a lot, especially when I'm around you. I try not to listen in, but it's weird—I can't not, really. Marco's using my brain to play them back. Isn't that how it works when you're hosting?"

Valeria shook her head slowly. "Only with very strong ghosts, and only after we've gotten to know each other for a long time. Then I meditate and, well, it's complicated, but it's like I step back and let them take over—just while I'm under oath. Then Lucho brings me back. I don't—I don't have conversations with them. Or see their memories, really. Not like you have with Marco." Her voice held a tinge of jealousy. "What did he find in the car?"

Didn't Valeria know?

"Bones, I told you," Patricia said. "In the door of the car. The window wouldn't roll down, so he decided to try to fix it, and he found bones wrapped in cloth stuck inside the car door."

"Human?"

Patricia shrugged. "I think so."

"Like a full skeleton?"

"In a car door, Val? No, just..." Patricia thought back to the memory, drawing on her long-ago anatomy classes and Marco's fuzzy assessment. "A femur, humerus, I think the radius and ulna, and three ribs. Seven bones. Small ones. A kid, I think." Patricia shivered.

"Why didn't he tell me?"

"He didn't know what to say. He thought maybe your friends had just bought the car, or..." Patricia sighed. "It belonged to Los Ciegos, didn't it?" Valeria looked uncomfortable. "Val..."

"They needed some work done, and I thought it would help everyone out. Marco would get some work, Chente would appreciate me for hooking him up with an awesome mechanic, and everything would be good." She took a deep breath. "Marco, I'm sorry. I should have told you... I should have told you a lot of things. But I didn't think..."

Patricia reached to take her sister's hand. It was dry, warm. Trembling. "It's OK, Val. You couldn't have known. He never said anything—not even to you—and he put them back exactly as he found them. So how would anyone have known he'd seen them?"

Valeria was silent a long while. "I have no idea," she said finally. "Chente only told me Marco had found something he shouldn't have, but he never told me what."

"Oh." Patricia's phone buzzed. Bayer. *Here early. Got a table.* Patricia glanced at her watch. "We should go. Bayer's waiting."

Loretta's Northwesterner wasn't far from Valeria's house, but with the rain, they decided to drive. "What do you do with the bones?" Patricia asked as they waited for the Subaru to warm back up.

"Me? Nothing. I mean, Lucho and I, we just work with the ghosts. You don't have to dig anybody up to do that." Valeria shrugged and put the car in reverse. "It's illegal, anyway."

"Like tethering a ghost outside a host would be?"

Valeria gave her a sharp look, face strobed with passing streetlights. "Exactly. Where did you hear that?"

"Lucho. He called me the other night, after the—after Javier scared me on the bus. You remember?" Patricia couldn't resist the barb. Valeria looked guilty. Good. "I asked him about getting Marco out of me and tethering him, and Lucho said no. He felt it was immoral."

"I guess it is."

Patricia raised an eyebrow at her sister's noncommittal wording. "Would you do it if Marco agreed?"

"I don't know how."

"But if you knew how?"

"In a heartbeat. If it meant..."

Inside her, Marco melted. Tears pricked at Patricia's eyes. She looked away.

They found one of the rare spots on the street out front of Loretta's; the pouring rain must have kept the crowd down, even on a Friday night. Patricia had only been here once before, but she felt Marco relax into the rockabilly rhythms and greasy combination of fries and faint cigarette smoke. Ancient bar signs cast their watery neon glow over the scene, painting their colors over the enormous rusty saw that perched above the liquor bottles.

Bayer was already in the booth closest to the door; he stood as soon as he saw them. "Ms. Ramos-Waites, I appreciate you meeting me tonight," he said, shaking Patricia's hand before turning to Valeria with a nod. "I'm Detective Dave Bayer, with the Seattle Police Department. We met several months ago at the courthouse."

"Yeah." Valeria took his offered hand, then dropped it like a hot coal. "I remember."

"I appreciate you coming out in the rain," Bayer said. "And I'm sorry for your loss, Ms. Ramos. I know this is a hard time. I have something I need to ask you about, and I don't think it can wait." Bayer glanced at the bar. "Did you —"

"I'll get a pitcher," said Valeria. "You drink Oly?"

"That sounds great."

"Good. Pati, burger?" Valeria cocked her finger like a pistol at Bayer's chest. "Burger?"

"Oh, sure. Can I—"

"I got it. Pati, give me a hand."

She dragged Patricia toward the ordering station at the bar. Patricia grabbed a damp menu off the bar mat. "What else do they have?" she asked, but Valeria just plucked the menu away.

"You want a burger. Trust me." She placed their order, then turned so her back was to Bayer. "Don't look at him. Talk to me. You said he was asking about Marco's accident."

"What? Val—"

"Don't look at him. Tell me what he said."

Patricia forced herself not to glance past Valeria at Bayer, who was checking his phone. "That's what he said, that it might not have been an accident. They were investigating it."

"Is that all he said? Think, Pati. Did he seem suspicious about"—she waved her hand vaguely—"at all?"

"About me?" Patricia whispered.

"You look so fucking guilty, stop it. You have to pull yourself together."

The bartender sloshed a full pitcher and a shot of whiskey onto the bar mat, then bent to grab a trio of chilled pint glasses. Valeria handed over cash and downed the whiskey.

"What's going on?"

"Bayer's the one who gets called in for the supernatural cases," Valeria said. "I'd forgotten his name, but I recognize him from the last case Lucho and I worked. SPD brings him in to work with the court resurrectionists, and to help investigate any other of the weird cases."

"Maybe he works on regular cases, too? There can't be that many supernatural crimes here."

Valeria set the shot glass back onto the bar mat and counted out the tip. "Or maybe he suspects. We'll just talk to him. We'll be cool. Patricia, you have got to stop looking like you're going to faint."

"I—"

"Listen, just let me talk to him, OK? We'll be fine."

Bayer was watching them as they sat down. "Let me," he said, taking the pitcher from Valeria and pouring three perfect pints without spilling a drop. "I'm just going to start right in, Ms. Ramos. Can I call you Valeria? Thanks. The department was investigating Marco Caruso's accident, just a standard procedure, but no one could find anything that had malfunctioned. They decided to rule it driver error, but when they sent the car on to be demoed, somebody pulled out the headliner and found something odd there." He reached into his briefcase and pulled out an iPad. "You understand that under the headliner is not the usual place we'd look for a vehicle malfunction."

He tapped at the iPad's screen for a moment, then handed it to Valeria. He watched her reaction closely. "Is this something you've come across in your... work?"

Valeria shook her head. "I'm not sure; it looks familiar, though."

Patricia leaned over to see the image through the glare of neon reflecting off the screen. It was faint, a chalky black outline against the metal of the roof. Squiggles, arrows, circles. "What is it?" she asked, reaching over to enlarge it. Something tugged at her.

"I have no idea," said Valeria. "Have you talked with my boss?"

"With Mr. Carrera? No. Not yet."

Valeria spoke again, but Patricia tuned out the words. Her fingers traced the symbol of their own accord. It was lovely, she thought, so intricate—

:pati hey: Marco's voice barked across her mind. She sat back, startled.

"Do you recognize the symbol?" asked Bayer.

Patricia shook her head, partly in answer, partly to clear it. "No," she said. "It just looked interesting is all."

Bayer frowned, then tucked away the iPad back to clear space as the bartender brought out the burgers. They were wrapped in paper and nestled into a plastic basket like at a fast-food restaurant. The bartender slapped a basket of hand-cut fries in the center of the table. Patricia raised an eyebrow at the presentation, but Marco was practically salivating at the memory of this burger. It couldn't be that bad.

Bayer unwrapped his and took a bite. "We're still investigating it—I just hoped you'd have some insight. I saw your testimony on that case several months ago, and I was impressed with your mastery as a host."

"Thank you," Valeria said. "But I don't know much about anything else. My experience is pretty limited to what I've learned from Lucho."

"And Mr. Carrera has an impressive record as a court resurrectionist. I understand he's the first on the list."

"He's good at what he does."

Valeria took a bite, but she was watching Bayer warily. "Where did you move to Seattle from?" she asked. "I thought the SPD had a different occult specialist. That woman. Georgina, or whatever her name was."

"She retired. I moved up here from Salt Lake."

Patricia braced herself and took a bite of her burger, relaxing now that the banter had become more neutral. It was delicious. She stared at it, surprised.

"See, it's good, right?" Valeria shook her head at Bayer. "She never believes me."

"This is a great spot," said Bayer. He took a sip of his beer. "How long have you worked with Mr. Carrera?"

Patricia hadn't realized how hungry she was. She polished off the burger, then started working on the fries, dragging them through the ketchup pooled in her basket. The ketchup streaked and swirled. A dab here, a dash there, and —

:patipatipati:

"The diagram isn't the only odd thing about Mr. Caruso's death," Bayer said. Patricia looked up. "It seems his grave was disturbed."

Patricia choked on a fry. Valeria thumped her on the back. "Jesus, Pati. Drink this." She handed her a pint of Olympia. "I'm sure it's not that bad. It's OK." She turned to Bayer. "Right? I'm sorry, Patricia's never been around this occult stuff. What do you mean, 'disturbed'? Not dug up?"

"No, the body is still there. But the gravestone was broken, and the earth was disturbed. Shovelfuls taken, but not dug down to the coffin."

Valeria frowned.

Marco shivered.

Patricia finally got her coughing under control, a strange mix of emotions tugging at her. Relief floated to the top. The detective wasn't looking for them, then—they hadn't dug into the earth, and they certainly hadn't broken Marco's headstone. But beneath the relief, unease blossomed.

"We, ah, scanned the area for ritual residue, and it's clear that a ritual was performed there, though we've been having trouble deciphering exactly what it was. We're not certain, but we think someone might be trying to bind Mr. Caruso in his grave."

"That's not my area of expertise." Valeria's jaw set. "Really, you should talk to Lucho."

"We will. We just haven't had need to. Yet."

Neither Valeria nor Bayer were eating anymore. Patricia crossed another fry through her ketchup as the words started to sink in. Yet.

"So you're not looking for an expert. You're looking for a suspect."

"I'm simply asking questions at this point. Was everything all right at home with you and Mr. Caruso? Any troubles?" Inside her, Marco was squirming. Patricia slid her fingers around the agate. *Be calm, Marco. You can't show yourself here.*

"Like did I catch him cheating and go all witchy on him?"

"Ms. Ramos..."

"You think I used some sort of voodoo to kill my boyfriend, and now I'm fucking with his grave."

Marco lurched forward, protective. Not now not now not now. "That's ridiculous," said Patricia. "Of course he's not suggesting that." *Marco!*

:bastard I'm trying:

"I'm not suggesting anything at this point," said Bayer. "I'm merely trying to figure out what this diagram is. But you have to understand it doesn't look good if this is actually an occult case, since you're Mr. Caruso's only known contact with a background in the occult. If you're innocent, then it's in your best interest to help me out here."

"But I don't have to talk to you without a lawyer. C'mon, Pati." Valeria started to stand, but Bayer held up his hands.

"I would appreciate your help, with or without a lawyer present," he said. "As far as we can tell, the damage done to Marco's grave is meant to bind him to our plane. I want to know why."

"What happens to ghosts?" asked Patricia. "If they're bound, I mean."

"That depends," said Valeria. "On what the person who's binding them is trying to do."

"At the very best, ghosts that are bound to our plane go mad," said Bayer. Marco fluttered nervously.

"So if someone did this ritual to Marco's grave, then he can't ever go back to where he belongs?"

Bayer shook his head. "No. Not until we know what's holding him here. And why."

"What if he wasn't in his grave when the ritual was performed?" Patricia asked.

Valeria shot her a furious look.

Bayer raised an eyebrow. "Then I'd guess whoever has been binding ghosts will be doing everything in their power to hunt him down." He stood, zipping up his coat. "Thank you for the beer, Ms. Ramos, I do appreciate you taking the time to meet me." Valeria glared at him. He smiled at Patricia. "You have my number if there's anything you'd like to talk about."

A blast of icy air washed over them as Bayer pushed through the front door. Patricia pulled up the collar of her coat, then reached for the last fry.

"That bastard," said Valeria. "If he..." She trailed off, watching as Patricia put the finishing touch on her ketchup drawing. "Pati? What did you do?"

There, scrawled across the basket's paper liner, was the symbol Bayer had shown them. Etched in ketchup as dark as blood.

"Pati? Hey, Patricia, answer me. Pati?"

Valeria's voice echoed from far away, and Marco writhed, clawing desperately for a hiding place.

For the briefest of moments, he wasn't alone.

Ahhhh, Patricia heard someone sigh, just before she blacked out. *There you are.*

Chapter Fourteen

PATRICIA WOKE UP alone. Her mind was blissfully empty, hushed like snow, and for a brief, beautiful moment, she was free.

She breathed deep and full, eyes closed. Felt the weight of unfamiliar blankets on her chest, the whipped-cream-thick pile of a duvet rustling. She stretched out her toes, her thoughts brushing up against a blank space in her mind where once...

"Marco?" she whispered.

Silence.

Blissful, terrifying silence.

Patricia snapped her eyes open and saw nothing but a dim blur of pastels. She clawed feebly at the duvet, suddenly smothered by its downy weight.

"Let me help." A woman leaned over her. Short blond hair and cold hands, and even without her glasses on, Patricia was sure she didn't recognize her. Patricia stretched to reach her nightstand, feeling for those familiar angles of hinged metal and lenses and... nothing. "Sit tight," the blond woman said. "I'll be back in a minute." She disappeared from Patricia's field of view; Patricia heard a door open, footsteps in a hallway. "Luis! She's awake."

The woman had left a pile of papers on the chair beside Patricia's bed, with a red pen lying across the top. In the dim light of the lamp—was it teddy bear shaped?—Patricia could make out bloody arrows and crosses and swirls scribbled across the papers. Her heart flipped end over end. She clawed once more at the nightstand, felt fingertips brush wire and glass.

She put her glasses on.

The room resolved into some teenage girl's paradise, complete with sheer pink curtains and piles of stuffed animals, a soccer ball behind glass scribbled with signatures, a Seattle Reign jersey tacked to the wall. Patricia's gaze fell to the papers the blond woman had left behind, but they were only tests being graded. Chemistry, she thought, those Cs and Hs with lines connecting them, circles around them. Answers crossed out. Annoyed question marks and stern scrawls crowded the margins: "Show your work" and "We covered this last week."

Where was she? *Marco?*

There was no answer.

The bright red marks on the chemistry tests triggered memories: the drift of fryer grease and cigarette smoke, the sweet-salty tang of fries in ketchup, a flash in her mind like a searchlight passing over, and a voice—

"Marco?" she whispered. She tried again, voice pitched high with fear. "Marco?"

"Pati, it's OK." Lucho appeared in the doorway.

"No. *Nonono*." Patricia flailed against the duvet, pressing her hand above her sternum—Marco's spot. It felt empty, her heart only a vacant fluttering organ, the pit of her stomach dropping out beneath. Her voice echoed inside her mind like a door closing in a long hallway, the sounds battered and thrown back by barren walls. "Marco!"

The fluffy down duvet settled back around her no matter what she tried, suffocating her with mounds of pale-blue frosting *almond flavored, for some reason her mother, Maryam, had always tinged the almond-frosted cakes blue*—

:maramos bes godam baker:

Lucho was there beside her, pulling back the duvet, his arm behind her shoulders.

"What did you say?" she demanded, gasping for breath.

"I said you're gonna be OK."

"No. About my mother?"

Lucho's bushy white brows knit together in a frown. "Pati, I don't know you well enough to make cracks about your mother."

:said mama ramos best goddamn baker:

"Marco?"

"Pati?" Lucho's arm tightened around her. "What's wrong?"

:still here sorry: Marco's voice came faint through her panic, cutting in and out like the car radio in a long tunnel.

Patricia collapsed back on the pillows, tears of relief pricking at her eyes. She remembered now what had happened at Loretta's. Marco's terror at the searchlight-hunting sensation she'd felt, that quiet, sighing voice she'd heard right before blacking out, that sing-song refrain. Ah, there you are.

She thought she'd lost him all over again. It was that same shock she'd felt sitting with her phone in the break room listening to Valeria's faraway voice breaking with the news. Except this time it would have been her fault. This second chance to say good-bye snatched out of her hands to disappear forever. Plucked away by... what? By that thing she'd... called? That voice...

"Patricia!" Lucho's rough fingers patted lightly against her cheek, jostling her back into the present. Patricia opened her eyes. "Pati. What's wrong."

"It's OK. He's still here. I thought..."

A pressure at the foot of the bed: Valeria perched there, her hand seeking out Patricia's, her grip verging on painful. This was all wrong. "Where are we?"

"You're at my house," said Lucho. "Nena brought you here."

Patricia's gaze rested on the Hunger Games poster taped beside the door. "Your room?" she said weakly.

Lucho allowed her a tense, humoring smile. "Nope. Me and Lindsay, we got our room full of Hanson posters. This is Jenna's."

"What happened?"

Valeria squeezed her hand. "We were at Loretta's, and that detective had just left. I was talking to you, but you didn't seem to be listening. You'd gone all pale and you were staring at the table—I realized you'd been sketching out that symbol Bayer showed us. Do you remember that?"

Patricia had a vague impression of bloody swirls and arrows on the paper liner, of the taste of salt, and she blinked her eyes shut hard, afraid of what would happen if she saw the shape of the diagram again even in her mind's eye. "I remember," she said finally.

"Why were you drawing it?"

"I didn't mean to. I didn't realize I was, not until it was all done." She turned to Lucho. "What was it?"

"I'd need to see it first to know," he said, and cold fear spiked through her chest. Lucho patted her shoulder. "No worries, *profe*, you won't have to draw it. Valeria called that detective to see if he'd send it over."

"Why would Pati react, and not me?" asked Valeria. "Or was it aimed at her? An attack spell or something?"

Patricia rubbed the bridge of her nose, suddenly tired. "Is that a thing?"

"I'd have to see it," Lucho said again. "Until then, *no sé nada*."

"It was aimed at Marco," Patricia said. "Whatever it was."

Valeria's grip on Patricia's hand tightened to crushing. Patricia tugged her hand free.

"Right before I blacked out, I heard a voice in my head—not Marco. It said something like, 'Well, there you are.'"

Marco shivered below her sternum, burrowing deeper as though to hide. *Who was it?* Patricia asked him.

:don't know I'm so sorry:

It's OK. We'll figure this out.

Valeria paled. Lucho sucked at his teeth.

"What was it?" Patricia asked.

The creaking of the bedroom door kept them from answering. The blond woman—Lindsay, Patricia realized—slipped through. "Looks like you're feeling better. Can I get you anything else right now?" Patricia shook her head, and Lindsay smiled. "Well, good night, kids. I'm going to bed, I've got a meeting in the morning. Val, remind Luis to show your sister where the extra towels and toothbrushes are. And Luis, I just started a kettle for tea, don't forget it." She scooped up her stack of papers, then kissed Lucho on the top of the head. "Seriously, don't forget it. If you burn the house down I'm going to be pissed."

"Good night, Linz," Lucho called after her.

"'Night, Lindsay," Valeria echoed.

Patricia took a deep breath, gauging her strength. She was feeling stronger, she decided, and she didn't need to be lying here with everyone gathered around like she was about to die. She pushed herself to sit up. Lucho leaned forward to help arrange pillows behind her back.

"Do you know what that voice was?" Patricia asked him. His answer was clear from the look on his face. "But you believe me, right?"

"*Claro*. Of course."

"Then what could it be? Another ghost, one that wasn't tethered? Or, like, someone telepathic?" Her head spun, both from sitting up and from the whirl of questions inside it. She squeezed her eyes shut briefly. "Is telepathy even a thing?"

Lucho shrugged. "I never heard of it."

"It felt like someone had turned a search beam on me. I could feel it all the way down inside my body, and Marco"—Marco shuddered again—"he was trying to get away from it. Like he was trying to hide."

"Does he know anything?"

"He said he doesn't know. He's been very apologetic. I'm trying to tell him it's not his fault." She frowned at Lucho. "It isn't, right?"

A faint whistle began to sound from the hallway, an alarm, Patricia thought with a jolt of panic. "Luis!" came Lindsay's voice, shouting from down the hall. "Kettle!"

Patricia took a deep, shuddering breath against her spiking heart rate. *Kettle, Pati.*

Lucho patted her hand and stood. "I'm gonna make tea, apparently," he said. "I'll be right back, don't you worry. Oh, hey," he said from the doorway. "You guys like what kind? Green, or with flowers in it, or what?"

"Um, something herbal?" said Patricia.

"Coffee," said Valeria.

He shut the door, and the room echoed with silence.

Valeria was still perched on the end of the bed, a throw pillow in her lap that was printed with a teddy bear holding a heart and the words I love you in scrolled fuchsia letters. Her gaze drifted toward Patricia but shied short, some magnet impulse spinning it back to her lap.

"There's so much pink," Patricia said finally, looking around the room.

"This would be Ava's nightmare." The corner of Valeria's mouth quirked up. "I'm feeling better, Val. I don't want to lie here anymore like I'm dying."

Valeria looked more ragged than Patricia had ever seen her. Her ponytail hung limp and fraying, and the makeup she'd been wearing earlier that evening had worn off, leaving the faintest of dark smudges below eyes shining with tears. "Pati, I'm so sorry."

"I'm fine," Patricia said again, automatically.

"If I'd known, if I'd had any idea what would happen, I'd never have—"

"It's OK, Val."

"No, it's really not. It's—"

"Val." Valeria looked up at her, one spilled tear shimmering in the last of her eyeliner. "Come here."

And in a heartbeat Valeria was lying beside her, the two of them tangled in sheets and pillows and each other's arms. The weight of her was so solid, the deep sweet musk of her hair hollowing Patricia out, leaving her aching for breath. Valeria's bony elbow dug into her ribs. Patricia pulled her even tighter.

The feel of Valeria's breath on her neck sparked something slow-moving and precious and deep—none of the trail of sparks left by a shimmering and quicksilver romance, none of that. It was simply as though each breath rekindled an ache so deep and secret that Patricia hadn't even known to try to heal it.

Valeria's breath was coming ragged, her face pressed hard into Patricia's shoulder. Patricia smoothed back her stray hair, kissed the top of her head. "We're going to be OK," she said, but Valeria didn't answer.

The moment stretched into tingling fingertips and cramping muscles, and Valeria's sobs finally stilled. Her breath smoothed back into a normal rhythm. Beneath Patricia's hands, Valeria's rigid muscles unknotted, and she melted into the whipped-cream duvet and pastel throw pillows. Patricia's shoulder was damp. She stroked Valeria's arm, realizing that this whole time Marco had been holding himself back—he was balled up in his spot, quivering with the need to hold Valeria, yet stepping out to leave this moment to the sisters. *Thank you*, she thought.

Something buzzed against Patricia's thigh. Valeria yelped, the tension instantly back in her muscles, the wariness in her eyes. She wriggled to grab her phone, then sat up. Its blue-white glow cast a ghastly light on her face. "I just got the email from Bayer," she said.

The nape of Patricia's neck pricked. From somewhere not so far away, she felt the flicker of a search beam nearing. "With the drawing?"

Valeria nodded. "Don't worry. You're not going anywhere near this thing. Let's go show Lucho."

She shoved the phone back into her pocket, but before Patricia could extract herself from the bed, Valeria pulled her into a sitting hug. "I'm so glad you're OK," she whispered.

Patricia stroked her back. "I'm fine, Val."

Valeria's shoulders rose and fell in a sigh. "We'll figure this out," she said.

Chapter Fifteen

LUCHO WAS WAITING in the kitchen with steaming mugs for each of them, wreathed with the scent of oranges and cloves. "We all get Market Spice," he said. "It's the only one I could find." Wearing a neatly patched wool sweater and baggy jeans, he looked completely out of place in his bright, modern kitchen. Patricia wondered if his jars of mysterious herbs and resurrection ingredients were tucked away behind the frosted glass cabinets. Probably not. Lindsay didn't seem the type to allow that.

She slid onto a stool at the breakfast bar, cupping her hands around the hot mug. Lucho leaned against the sink, his fingers curled around Valeria's phone as he studied the diagram. Valeria took up a spot protectively close to Patricia.

"All right, Pati," said Lucho. "Nena's told me everything she knows about tonight, but I want to hear it from your perspective."

Patricia glanced at Valeria, trying to gauge how far back in the evening to start.

"Since we met Bayer," Valeria said, a hint of warning in her eyes: Lucho didn't need to know about the visit from Javier.

Patricia traced her way through that meeting, remembering her intrigue over the diagram and its graceful swirls, remembering leaning over for a closer look at Bayer's iPad. "It was just..." She thought back to what she'd felt, frowning. "It was fascinating. It seemed special, somehow."

"I saw you touch at it, which seemed weird to me," said Valeria. "You reached over, and you looked like, I don't know. Like you were in awe. But I thought you were just curious."

Marco squirmed. :*tried to say:*

"Oh," said Patricia. "I remember that, thank you. Marco tried to warn me about it. He kept calling my name, but I thought he was just trying to get my attention because I wasn't listening to the conversation."

Lucho scratched his neck. "Marco, *güey*, you seen this thing before?"

"He says no," said Patricia. "But he felt afraid of it for some reason. And I think he knew I was acting strangely." An affirmative surge from Marco. "He knew something was wrong with it, but didn't know what." Patricia frowned into her tea. "I don't remember drawing the symbol, though. I was just listening to you talk."

"You copied it exactly," Valeria said. "In ketchup. After Bayer left, you looked really out of it. That's when I saw what you'd been doing." She looked miserable. "I should have caught it earlier."

Patricia flashed her a weary smile. "Bayer was accusing you of murder. I forgive you for being distracted by that. Lucho? What is it?"

Lucho rubbed his chin; it was salted by a day's worth of whiskers. "It's a *firma*," he said quietly.

"A signature?"

"Yeah, but like a..." He pursed his lips, thinking. "Like a football play. You ever play football?"

Patricia raised her eyebrows. "Lucho?"

"But you seen movies, right? Where you got the underdog team who just lost real bad, but now the coach is getting them all excited for the big game, so you get like this training montage where they're jogging through a bunch of tires and smashing into padded things. And then there's always a scene in the locker room where the coach is going over plays, right?"

"Lucho," said Valeria, rolling her eyes. "Your point."

"My stories have always got a point, don't you worry your cynical little head, Nena." He grabbed a piece of junk mail off a pile and started sketching on the back. "The coach draws these diagrams. All the circles and arrows, they tell the football players—or the dead—where to go."

He whirled his drawing to face Patricia. Swirling arrows, circles, Xs. She flinched away. "You know how to draw these *firmas*?"

"No worries, *profe*." He jabbed the paper with a crooked finger. "This is a fullback sweep."

Valeria tugged her phone out of his other hand and thumbed the screen back on. Patricia turned her head, not sure what would happen if she caught another glimpse. "Huh," Valeria said. "It does look like a football play." She switched the phone off. "I don't know that we needed to hear about the training montage, though."

Lucho waved a gnarled hand. "My stories are exactly as long as they need to be. You and Lindsay can start a support group called Women Bored to Tears by Lucho's Stories."

"But what do you mean it tells the dead where to go?" Patricia broke in. "I thought they were, well, dead. Or ghosts, like Marco, tethered to a person."

"That depends on what you believe," Lucho answered. "I believe in an afterlife that's not here. You get some ghosts stranded here or called back like our Marco Polo, and maybe sometimes the borders between our worlds shift a bit, but for the most part we live in two separate worlds." He seemed to be choosing his words carefully now. "But some people believe that the dead are all around us, and so you can consult them, or direct their energies. These *firmas* are one way to direct their energy."

"To do what?"

Lucho shrugged. "To protect someone, maybe. Or to make them unlucky."

Unlucky. Silence stretched after that word. Lucho stared at his fullback sweep, tapping a finger against the paper, gnawing on his cheek. Valeria was barely breathing. Patricia cleared her throat. "Unlucky, as in your brakes might go out while you're driving over a mountain pass?" Lucho didn't answer. "Did someone use magic to kill Marco?"

"That's ridiculous," snapped Valeria. "You can't do that. Lucho, this is crazy, right?"

But Lucho was staring at the counter, lost in thought. "I don't know anything about *firmas*," he said finally. "But I know someone who does. I'll call. Pati, can you stay here tonight?"

Patricia nodded. "I'll text Adrian, he's out with Lucy. And Ava's staying over with a friend tonight." And she was here, trapped in an insane conversation about the dead. "Lucho?" Patricia asked. "What do you mean that some people believe different things about the dead? I mean, this is real, right? I can feel Marco, we talk. How could people believe something different?"

Lucho shrugged. "Everything is as real as we think it is. Even weird stuff like this." He tapped a finger against the dark screen of Valeria's phone. "This is bad stuff."

"Do you think it has to do with the bones Marco found?" Patricia asked. At Lucho's puzzled expression, she described what Marco had seen: the seven child's bones wrapped up and stuffed inside the door of the car, smuggled from who knows where.

Lucho said nothing for a long while, sipping at his tea. "Was there a skull?" he asked eventually. Patricia shook her head, and he frowned. "Did he touch them?"

Patricia thought back. "Yeah. I think so. Valeria said you don't use bones at all in your work."

Lucho smiled grimly. "I don't," he said. "But the people I'm gonna call about the *firma*? They do." He pushed back his chair. "We're not gonna do anything else tonight, not until I get a chance to think things over and make a few calls. I had the idea to transfer Marco between the two of you, but until we know what's going on, I ain't gonna risk it. We've all had a scare tonight, so let's just take it easy, get some rest, and come back tomorrow fresh. Yeah? Good. Then, Pati, lemme grab you a toothbrush and we'll get you set up in Jenna's room." He squeezed Valeria's arm as he walked past. She looked up from her mug, her expression troubled. "I'll be right back if you wanna talk, Nena."

Valeria nodded, wished a halfhearted good night to Patricia, then returned her attention to the swirling depths of her Market Spice tea.

Patricia lingered a second, poised to say something to her sister, but not knowing what to say. "Good night," she whispered finally, and turned to follow Lucho down the hall.

Chapter Sixteen

PATRICIA AWOKE TO the smell of coffee and frying eggs, and to tiny claws kneading her breastbone. A rough tongue scraped her chin. She opened her eyes to meet the half-lidded gaze of an orange tabby.

The tabby licked her chin again and purred, the vibrations rumbling through Patricia's sternum and echoing through her chest. Marco fluttered in rhythm, radiating contentment.

"Nice kitty," murmured Patricia. She carefully extricated one hand from the blankets to stroke the cat's fur. The cat arched into her touch, digging its claws in deeper. Patricia yelped, Marco flinched, and the cat leapt from the bed to land near the doorway, where it eyed Patricia reproachfully. "Sorry," she whispered.

Patricia slipped on the fluffy robe draped near the bed and followed her nose to the kitchen. The breakfast bar was set with plates, and a steaming bowl of eggs took center stage. Lucho was rummaging through the fridge.

"I met your cat," Patricia said. "The orange one."

Lucho glanced over his shoulder. "She was probably saying hello to Marco," he said. He turned, orange juice in hand. "She like ghosts, *la loquita*. Most cats don't like ghosts."

Patricia slipped onto a stool. "Did you make all this?"

Lucho pursed his lips and tilted an eyebrow at her. "Please. Who do you think does the cooking here? Lindsay can barely manage to not burn toast. What you're looking at is the Lucho Scramble Surprise." He poured her a cup of coffee, dished the scramble onto her plate, then dug a pair of corn tortillas out of a towel and threw them on top. The eggs were filled with black beans, tomatoes, onions, flecks of green cilantro. Patricia breathed in the scent, stomach growling.

"Is Val up?"

"Not yet. We've got her in Kate's room. It's where she stays when she crashes here."

Patricia tore off a piece of her tortilla, mulling that over. "Does she stay here often?"

Lucho shrugged like he'd never thought about it. He turned back to the fridge. "A lot more since the accident. Here. You gotta try this hot sauce. Linz gets it at the farmers' market. Some kid on Whidbey Island makes it with ghost peppers. It'll wake you up real fast."

Patricia pretended to study the bottle, but her mind was far away. Valeria hadn't turned to her after Marco's death, she'd turned to her boss. She stayed with Lucho when she couldn't face being alone at her apartment. She talked to Lucho when she had problems.

A flickering tongue of jealousy flared reflexively inside her, but it found little fuel. Patricia hadn't been a model sister, had she? Let alone a friend. How had she reacted to all those late-night "Pati, I'm in trouble" phone calls? Certainly not with compassion. Obligation, expediency, selfless sacrifice, yes. Patience and love, no.

She didn't need to ask why Valeria had slept in Lucho's daughter's room rather than call Patricia.

"What do you think she needs from me right now?" she asked, and Lucho turned. His bushy eyebrows drew in.

"What do you mean?"

"Valeria. I don't, I know I haven't been there for her. And I—" Patricia didn't know how to say it. "I guess I just don't know where to start."

Lucho frowned. "Sisters don't gotta be best friends," he said finally. "You know I got a brother who lives in Arizona, and we haven't talked for probably ten years. I don't hate him, I don't think he hates me. But I don't need to call him up and see what he's up to, because we've never been friends. I know you and Nena love each other, but nobody's got a law that says you have to tattoo each other's names on your asses or be each other's bridesmaids or whatever. Family doesn't have to mean friends." He handed her a glass of orange juice. "You didn't try the hot sauce."

"I'm OK. And thanks, Lucho. I think."

He shrugged. "And anyway—" He looked up, smiled over Patricia's shoulder. "Good morning, sunshine."

Valeria looked better than she had in days—sleep-tousled and groggy, yes, but in a healthy, well-rested way that Patricia hadn't seen for... months, probably. Valeria paused in the hallway, uncertain. Patricia thought she could see it in her face: *What did I do now, what are they talking about me for.*

Did Valeria always assume Patricia thought the worst of her? Marco was silent, staying tucked out of the way. If he'd gotten an earful or two about Patricia, he wasn't about to share it now. And Patricia...

Patricia tugged out the stool next to her. "You want some coffee?" she said. "Lucho made a scramble. It's amazing."

Valeria perched on the stool like a bird.

Patricia poured her a cup of coffee. "How'd you sleep?" she asked. Her attempt at a cheerful smile only made Valeria look more wary.

"I was worried," Valeria said finally. "At first I had nightmares that thing was coming back after you. But eventually I got some real sleep, I think."

Coming after Marco? Patricia almost asked, but she bit her tongue.

"I'm glad you're OK," Valeria said. "I was really scared."

"I'm fine," said Patricia. She reached over to touch Valeria's hand. "I'll be just fine."

Lucho cleared his throat. "I made a call this morning to a couple of my friends that I think could help."

"Who?" Valeria was piling her plate with eggs, dousing them with the ghost pepper hot sauce without a glance at the label.

"You wanna be careful with that," said Lucho. He was eating now, too, leaning against the counter and scooping eggs straight from the serving bowl with pieces of tortilla.

Valeria lifted her chin defiantly and gave the bottle another dash.

"Isidro and Isabella."

"Oh." Valeria glanced at Patricia. "What did they say?"

"They wanna come over and see things for themselves."

"Do they think—"

"They don't think nothing until they see what's going on. You know Isabella. You couldn't get her to trust that it's raining unless she gets drenched herself."

Patricia glanced at the clock. She couldn't remember the last time she'd slept past nine in the morning. "This morning?" she asked. "I need to be home by noon to pick up Ava from her friend's house."

"No problemo," said Lucho. "You think you could come back this afternoon? You can bring Ava if you want. We got tons of the girls' toys around still to keep her busy."

Patricia nodded slowly. Adrian had an away game tonight, and it wasn't like she had anything more pressing to do this weekend than get rid of Marco's ghost. No offense. Marco shrugged. "That sounds fine," she said. "I'm free this weekend."

Valeria arched an eyebrow. "Not totally free, right? I thought you were setting up a date? With a certain handsome basketball coach?"

Patricia felt her cheeks go pink. "It's next weekend." She glanced at Lucho.

Lucho took another bite of eggs. "Maybe he's the type who liked *The Exorcist?* Invite him over."

"*What?*"

"You're too easy, *profe.*" Valeria's laugh turned to frantic coughing, and Lucho tossed her a handful of napkins. "Told you that ghost pepper stuff was hot," he said, pulling a milk bottle out of the fridge and pouring her a glass.

"It's not going to be that bad, is it?" Patricia said. Inside her, Marco was shifting anxiously. "Like *The Exorcist?*"

"Not that bad, no."

"Scout's honor?" asked Patricia.

The laughter left Lucho's smile. "I don't ever make promises when it comes to this stuff," he said quietly. "Even when it's just me, and no one else is going around chalking *firmas* or trying to resurrect ghosts into their own bodies." His eyes stayed locked with Patricia's, but the last was meant for Valeria. She looked down at her plate. "I can promise me and Val are gonna do our best to clear this mess up, though. For you and for Marco Polo."

"Thank you, Lucho."

He waved a hand. "Let's do this." Lucho shoved his last bite into his mouth.

Patricia stood to follow him. "Do what?"

Lucho led them down the hallway lined with family vacation photos. Lucho and Lindsay in hiking gear, posed in front of a waterfall. A family photo at Disneyland, complete with a pair of little girls practically bouncing out of the frame with excitement. The same two girls as teenagers, hugging in front of the Statue of Liberty.

The door to the basement was locked. "Keeps the cat out," Lucho said as he fished the key out of his pocket. "*Y las mujeres.*"

Patricia wasn't sure what to expect of Lucho's basement lair. She imagined dirt floors and spiderwebs, the scent of decay, pungent herbs bunched on the ceiling and rough workbenches covered by jars of preserved terrors.

Instead, she descended into a finished, carpeted room that was only a bit less neat than the spic-and-span upstairs. Where Patricia had expected a curandero shack, it was more a man cave, complete with overstuffed leather recliners and a huge TV. A signed Seahawks jersey was framed on the wall. The only nod to Lucho's job was the bookshelf stuffed with antique volumes and a desk covered with sheaves of papers. Some were scrawled with arcane symbols. Most looked like legal briefs. A child's drawing of a ghost was tacked up on the wall.

Patricia must have looked disappointed, because Lucho grinned. "Don't look so sad, *profe*. This isn't all of it."

He crossed to a door half-hidden by a weight bench. This one was double locked, and as Lucho turned the keys, Patricia caught the scent of must and herbs: a bitter aroma tinged with licorice and an undercurrent of soap. She sneezed.

The narrow open shelves above the workbench were lined with irregular sizes of Mason jars stuffed with herbs and powders. None were labeled. Bare bulbs dangled from the ceiling. Copper mixing bowls hung on nails below the shelves. Lucho waved Patricia onto a rickety wooden stool farthest from the door, then turned to his workbench.

A jar close to her looked like it contained a tumble of perfect stones in a hundred colors, and Patricia leaned closer, curious. Gourmet jelly beans?

"You want one?" Lucho said, and Patricia sat back, startled. "I gotta hide any candy in this house from Linz or she'll throw it out." He pulled a jar off the highest shelf, unscrewed the cap, sniffed at the contents, then shook some out into an oversized stone mortar. "Turns out it's bad for you."

"Are you going to transfer Marco right now?"

Lucho grabbed another jar, this one filled with what looked like black ash, and shook the contents, considering. "We can't just yet," he said. "First up, I want to get a second opinion from Isabella and Isidro, since things have gotten weird around here. Plus, after spending so much time in each other's heads, it can be tough for a host and a ghost to split up. I'm making you a tea that helps with that." He scooped out some of the ash. "Defines the edges a bit, but it takes some time to work."

Once all the ingredients were in, Lucho laid his hands on the mortar and bowed his head, his lips moving quietly. Valeria bowed her head, too. Patricia, feeling awkward, did the same.

Lucho finished up and smiled at her. "This was my grandma's *molcajete*," he said, patting the stone mortar like an old friend. "Whenever I work with it, I like to tell her I appreciate her letting me drag it all the way up to Seattle."

It was simple, though with no legs like the little *molcajetes* Patricia had seen in Jesusito's grocery in White Center. This was solid all the way through, carved from an entire piece of basalt. A large cat could have curled up comfortably inside.

Lucho worked the ingredients with a squat pestle, humming as he did so. Patricia thought she recognized the song as something her mother sang when she was a child, but she couldn't quite catch the lyrics.

The ingredients crushed into powder and the song sung, Lucho carefully swept the dust up into a paper pouch, using an artist's paintbrush to catch all the little eddies. He murmured something to Valeria, and she disappeared from the doorway. Patricia could hear her footsteps on the stairs.

"Nena's gonna make you some tea; it'll help get you ready for what we'll do tonight. Gets your energies and Marco's aligned better, so it's not quite a shock when we get him out of you."

"Will I feel anything?"

Lucho shrugged. "Probably not. Don't worry about it."

:famous last words:

Patricia agreed, but she kept her tongue. *We've trusted him this far, haven't we?* But one question was still bothering her. "Lucho? Why don't you use these *firmas*? I mean, if they work, then why wouldn't all resurrectionists use them?"

He frowned, and she was uncertain for a moment if he was angry, or simply trying to work out an answer. "They're not like, say, aspirin. It just works, right? I put a bunch in a bottle, and anyone can take one out and pop it in their mouth and their hangover goes away." He wiped a damp cloth around the inside of the molcajete, his brows knitting together. "No, that's not really right. They're not like massages, is what I mean to say."

:the hell?:

"What?"

"Stay with me, *profe*. You got a crick in your neck, you go to someone with special massage-therapy training, and he does a set of moves that get you sorted out. Anyone can learn to be a massage therapist, and use that set of moves, right? But a *firma* isn't like that. I could learn to draw one, but it wouldn't just work, because they're tied to a *prenda*."

"A *prenda*?"

"Remember, I was telling you about tethering a ghost to an object? A *prenda* is one of those tethers. Like a house, really."

"Which is illegal, right?"

Lucho sighed. "Yeah, but it's—ah, Pati, it's just... it's Palo. It's a different religion. And it's not like one you can just pick up and play with. You wanna work Palo, you gotta live Palo, and it's not something you can just take with a light heart.

"I got a legal business. I talk to the dead and figure out the truth of what happened to them. To do that, I have to manhandle them a bit, you know?

Bring 'em out and make 'em solid inside a host for a few weeks so we can chat. It's straightforward. I know who I'll be dealing with. Sure, there are hiccoughs in the road"—he shot her a meaningful glance—"but I'm dealing with something known. And I'm in control.

"Palo, you're giving the ghost too much control. You build it up with sacrifices, and you figure out a relationship. It uses you, you use it." He shrugged. "It's a mutual partnership, but one that's always a struggle. Like kids, maybe. When they're little, you just tell them what to do, but when they grow up they take more of the control for themselves. And it's rewarding, but it's way tougher than when you could just send them to their rooms." Lucho cleared his throat. "The last thing is, using a *firma*, it needs you to believe that we're surrounded by ghosts. That they don't go to a different plane after death, they just hang out here, milling around us like in Costco on Sundays."

"But if *firmas* work, wouldn't that be true?"

Lucho set his last ingredients away, shrugged. "The world is a weird place, *profe*. You gotta pick something and believe it, and I believe what I hear in mass."

Valeria walked in, then, and looked from one to the other quizzically. "Deep thoughts by Lucho?" she asked.

"Trying to talk about Palo," said Lucho, and Valeria shook her head.

"Good luck," she said. "You can ask Isabella and Isidro tonight if you want to get lectured." She handed Patricia a mug printed with a photo of Mount Rushmore. Patricia sniffed at it. It smelled like charred oranges with an undercurrent of pine-scented cleaning products.

She frowned at the glass. "What is this stuff?"

"Drink up," said Lucho. "It's gonna help us find the edges between you and Marco when it's time to pull you two apart."

The tea was bitter, with an ashen texture that made Patricia gag. It coated her tongue, seeped back into her throat. Though it had been barely warm when she drank it, she could feel heat spreading from her stomach.

She could sense Marco's reaction to it, as well, feel his displeasure at the texture. He shied away from the spreading heat, as though with every sip he was being corralled into a smaller place in her body. She finished the concoction, feeling strangely guilty. *I'm sorry, Marco.*

She realized suddenly that she wasn't quite ready to be rid of him. She could remember what life had been like without him sharing her body, but the arrangement had become familiar over the last week. Comfortable. A little less lonely, even.

:like you too: Marco's voice seemed distant, tinny, fading off on the last syllables. *:you'll be…:*

It's going to be fine, Patricia thought, but for the first time in days she didn't know if anyone else was listening.

Chapter Seventeen

PATRICIA TURNED HER key in the dead bolt, numbly registering each detail of her home in that scraped-raw way of someone who's been away for months, not just a single night. She couldn't remember her last night away.

She laid two days' worth of mail on the kitchen counter and looked around for signs of Adrian. His hurricane had been subtler than usual—or he'd decided to clean up after himself for once—but Patricia still saw the marks of his passage. A cereal bowl in the sink, an algebra textbook on the coffee table, his hoodie crumpled near the door to the bathroom.

Patricia picked it up. Tomorrow, maybe. Or Monday, when this was all over and she could breathe again, she'd make it a point to really talk with him. She'd step up her motherhood game.

Valeria would be back in an hour to drive them back to Lucho's. Just enough time for a good shower and to grab Ava from her friend's house. At least one child would get to see her mother today.

A dark shape flashed in the corner of her eye, and Patricia spun to face it. She blinked. Nothing.

"You had better not be a mouse," she said out loud, to hear her own voice in the silence if nothing else. "Did you see it?" she asked Marco, but though he stirred, he didn't respond. Patricia frowned, not sure which bothered her more, the fleeting shape or Marco's sluggishness. She took a deep breath.

It had been a mouse, she told herself. She made a mental note to pick up some traps.

She gratefully shed yesterday's office clothes and turned the shower up as hot as she could handle. Steam curled out from behind the shower curtain. Water—not quite scalding—beat down against the knotted muscles in her back.

Patricia was toweling off when she heard a knock at the door. Dammit, Valeria had been too fast. She wriggled into jeans and a tank top and dashed to answer the door in bare feet, mopping at her dripping hair with the towel.

She flicked back the curtain over the window and caught her breath. A single man standing respectfully off the front step, hands shoved in pockets, turned half away as if embarrassed for intruding. Crooked nose, glittering gold earring.

Javier Mejía.

Marco's presence tugged her back from the door, and she tripped backward, pulled off balance into the coat tree, which tipped in a clattering crash.

If Javier hadn't seen the curtain move, he'd certainly heard the crash; she saw it in the way he shifted, ready, though he didn't turn his head. Pretending she wasn't home was no longer an option.

He just wants to talk. He's looking for Val.

She took a deep breath and reached for the doorknob, but her hand felt as though she were pushing through wet sand, something abrasive and semisolid and achingly, achingly cold.

"Marco," she hissed. She tucked her free hand into her pocket, but the agate wasn't there. Her blood ran cold. She'd left it sitting on her dresser.

:warn:

"Don't you dare warn me." Was it always guns and power plays with these men? What happened to simply talking things out like civilized human beings? She summoned her most impressive mom voice. "Marco!"

The presence disappeared. She stumbled into the door, wrenched it open. "What do you want?" she snapped.

Javier took a startled step back. "Hi, ah, good morning," he said. "Is Valeria...?"

"No."

He met her gaze in silence, and Patricia tried to decipher what she saw. In his eyes, hesitation, uncertainty. He was young—she could see that now in the daylight—and looked almost harmless in a shirt buttoned up past most of his tattoos, the tattooed knuckles shoved deep in puffy vest pockets, his beanie pulled low against the slight rain.

Last night she'd thought he was closer to her age. It was his face that made him seem old, she realized. The crooked nose that must have been a decade or more old, bad enough to leave him marred for life, but nothing anyone had tried to fix. Last night, the thin scar under his left eye had seemed a crease of age, but it had no match. She'd be surprised if he was much more than thirty.

He cleared his throat. "OK," he said. "Thanks." He didn't move. Patricia's grip tightened on the door. She glanced at his red F250, parked in her driveway where Adrian's car usually sat. She had a vision of the nearly empty streets, the black patches of thick forest and steep ravines just blocks away, the shuttered industrial plants closed all weekend, where she wouldn't be found until the Monday morning shift, her body splashing down into the Duwamish, then drifting out and away into the Sound.

The F250 wavered like a mirage, ever so slightly, and Patricia blinked. What was—

:pati:

She glanced back at Javier, then braced her arm against the door as though she were strong enough to block him from forcing his way past her if he tried. "Hey," he said finally. "I'm sorry. About the gun and all that. And about... Marco. And to Marco, man, this is shit. I'm sorry."

Marco wound tighter within her chest, a coil testing the edges of its tolerance.

"It's OK," said Patricia automatically, then frowned. Javier's jaw tightened. "Why are you looking for Valeria?"

"She's not at home. She's not picking up the phone."

"She never answers for me, either," Patricia said. She'd meant it to lighten the tension, a joke, but the words came out raw and bitter. Patricia bit her cheek. *Be kind to her*, she reminded herself. "I can ask her to call you," she said. "But I need to go pick up my daughter."

Javier nodded, shoving his hands deeper into the pockets of his down vest. "I'm surprised she left you alone." Patricia tensed, but Javier raised his hands, empty. He took a half step back. "I didn't mean it like anything."

"Then what did you mean?"

"I meant with Marco and all. You shouldn't leave a host alone anyway, but like, I've never seen a ghost take somebody over like that. Looked like *Evil Dead II*."

Marco cringed inside her, embarrassed. How many more times was Patricia going to be compared to a horror movie this week? "How many ghosts have you seen?" she asked instead.

Javier shook his head. "I should go. Sorry for coming over." He turned to leave, shrugging his shoulders up against the rain.

"Wait." Marco swirled angrily. *Stop it.* "How many ghosts have you seen?"

Javier stopped with one foot still on the bottom step, as though deciding. "I helped out with maybe a dozen possessions," he said finally, turning back. "Make sure nothing goes wrong before they fly back to wherever so the ghosts can see their families one last time. Mostly Val, but there's another coupla hosts, too." He paused. "But I never seen a ghost. Not until last night."

Patricia felt a chill. "What do you mean?"

"Like the host, right, they talk to the ghost. But no one else does. One guy told me it's like having a toddler living in your head, and it's always right before nap time. Val always says it's like you're watching a really fuzzy movie of somebody's life."

"But eventually they get the two-way communication?" Patricia asked, curious in spite of herself. "So they can have conversations with the ghosts?"

"Yeah. Sometimes the host is just like, 'Hey, *vos*, your mom says she misses you,' but there are a couple who pretend to let the ghost take over, and speak in his voice." Javier shrugged. "It's just an act, though, always makes the families happy. What I hear, ghosts are just echoes, you know? Like you can tune the radio station to them, but that's all they are. They can come in stronger or weaker, but they can't take over. And they don't come out of the radio and move things around."

"Like what Marco did."

He shrugged, looking uncomfortable. "I'm sorry for, ah..."

Inside her, Marco stirred. She slipped her hand into her pocket before remembering the agate wasn't there. *Tranquilo*, she thought. "I'll be fine," she said.

Javier nodded, but he didn't look reassured. "Hey, let me give you my number," he said, pulling a scrap of paper from his pocket. "In case you have any trouble, or you need anything, or..." He shrugged. "Just for, you know."

Patricia wasn't sure she knew, but she took it anyway. His number was scrawled on the back of a receipt from Target: shampoo, eggs, laundry detergent, girls' socks.

"Thanks," she said. "And thank you for telling me what you know."

Javier shrugged. "Ghosts don't bother me. I understand what Lucho does. He calls the ghosts, the hosts care for them, they tell them what to do, they let them go. It's safe." A shadow crossed his face. "Ghosts shouldn't be bossing around the boss man. They had their chance in this life, and if they're back here, it should just be as our guests, not trying to take someone else's power." He looked up. "No offense, Marco."

Marco gave a whirl of irritation. Patricia frowned and shook her head, agreeing with Javier, although she wasn't sure what he was talking about. She'd preferred the world as she knew it, with defined edges—spiritual and personal. She couldn't wait for things to go back to normal. Marco twitched. *No offense, Marco.*

Javier nodded, a flash of gold catching Patricia from his ear. "Tell Val to call me," he said. "And, ah, *buena suerte*. I hope Lucho can help you out. He's good at what he does. *Adios*."

He turned and walked away, that swagger back in his step. Patricia cleared her throat. "*Vaya con Dios*," she replied—go with God—and Javier jerked to a stop. Her heart stopped, and she worried that she'd offended him. But when he turned, a tiny sad smile quirked at his lips.

"*Mamá* always said that," he said. "*Gracias*."

Patricia shut the door and turned the dead bolt, leaning against it until she could no longer hear the rumble of his truck.

Patricia knocked on the Kims' front door ten minutes before noon and was not surprised by the double look she got from Esther. Despite the shower and fresh clothes, she knew she looked a wreck.

Esther recovered gracefully, as always, dusting flour from her hands onto her apron before reaching to give Patricia a quick hug. Patricia's fingers tingled oddly at the touch, and she balled her fists to test them. The tips felt numb.

"Patricia! So good to see you." Esther looked as though she were about to ask how Patricia was, but decided against it. "Ava and Holly are just finishing tidying the kitchen, and the cookies should be out of the oven any second."

An electronic *beepbeepbeep* sounded from inside the house, cutting through the excited chatter of the girls. Esther waved Patricia inside, then lost herself in a bustle of fancy silicon baking sheets, black-braided girls, and small talk about elementary-school politics, while Patricia smiled and tried to nod at appropriate times.

Esther saw them off with a decorative paper plate full of peanut butter cookies, still warm in Patricia's hands. Patricia drummed her numb fingertips against the bottom of the plate while Ava chattered beside her.

"Ava-bean?" Patricia said once there was a break in the monologue. "I have something I need to do today. Do you mind if we go to one of my friends' houses? You can bring all your coloring books and things. It should just take part of the afternoon."

Ava shrugged. "Yeah, sure. Hey, Mom?" she asked, stopping suddenly with a serious look in her eye. "Is that detective going to find out who killed Tío Marco?"

"What?"

"When he came over to the house, he said he was investigating T?o Marco's death. Is he going to find out who killed him?"

"They're still trying to figure out if anything was wrong, sweetheart. They don't know what happened with his accident yet."

"He probably knows more than he's telling you," Ava said. She brightened. "Maybe you're a suspect. Do you think so?"

"Ava!"

"What?" Ava shrugged again, a slouching two-shouldered gesture that looked decidedly tween compared to her usual one-shouldered kid shrug. *Oh, Lord...*

"You have an alibi," Ava said. "You were at work when it happened, and we were at Adrian's booooring basketball game the night before." She tilted her head. "Also, you don't know anything about cars. I don't think."

"Not like that, I don't." Patricia sighed, resigned to the macabre game. "What's your alibi, Ava-bean? You told me you were in school, but can I believe you?"

Ava looked at Patricia sideways, eyes narrowed in thought. "All my teachers would have seen me, but then before Adrian's game, I went to Holly's house to work on my project. And the next day I could have snuck off from school."

"No, you couldn't have."

"Why not?"

"Because, Ava. No sneaking away from school." Patricia shifted her shoulder bag, feeling the ache of an unfamiliar bed and the stresses of the last night in a pinched nerve in her back. The numbness in her fingers was getting worse. "Besides, you don't have a motive."

"No," said Ava softly. "I loved Tío Marco."

Marco broke against Patricia's breastbone like a wave. *:love:*

Patricia fought back tears. "I know, honey. He loves you, too."

Chapter Eighteen

"YOUR FRIENDS WHO are coming. They're resurrectionists, too?"

Patricia was back at the breakfast bar, sipping a cup of coffee while Lucho's heavy knife snicked radishes into translucent, paper-thin slices. The hearty, earthy scents of soup stock and chiles coming from the slow cooker was making her stomach growl. It was about the only thing she felt, since Marco's presence had faded again over the last few hours. She could still feel him, but he was lying lethargic, only a light pressure cradled below her ribs.

Valeria had run to the grocery store for limes, and Patricia could hear Ava singing to herself from the den, having found paradise in the massive collection of Legos that Lucho's daughters had left behind.

Ava's voice sounded as though it were being played at the bottom of a well. Patricia shook her head, wondering if something was wrong with her ears.

"Nope," said Lucho. He popped a slice of radish into his mouth. "They work with the dead, but in a very different way. Remember, we talked on the phone about my Colombian friends, the *paleros*?"

Patricia helped herself to a radish off Lucho's cutting board. The feeling had come back into her fingers, but seemed to have disappeared from the tip of her tongue. She must be fatigued. "The ones who keep dead people in pots and sacrifice chickens?" she asked.

Lucho clicked his tongue at her. "You be nice when they come. They're doing us a favor."

"I'll be nice. It's just a bit odd."

"What have you seen so far this week that hasn't been odd, *profe*?"

Fair point. "What makes you think they know about what's going on?"

"The *firma*, for one. And I wonder about the bones Marco found in the car. It seems like something they might know about. If someone used the dead to harm Marco, they might be able to help us."

"I thought you said they weren't members of a crazy evil religion."

"Hey, hey, hey. No. You seen that movie Seven, right? You think that guy was really a Catholic? And anyway—" He frowned, then leaned in to stare at her eyes. "How are you feeling, *profe*? Maybe a little loopy?"

"I'm fine! I'm sorry, I didn't..." Patricia fumbled for an apology, but trailed off as the pieces began to click into place. "Wait, what do you mean, 'How am I feeling?'"

"Like, you seeing anything? Feeling anything weird?"

Oh, Lord. "Like my fingers being numb?" she asked. "Or if it sounds like voices are really far away? Or maybe objects are flickering in and out of my vision?"

"Yeah. Like that."

"The tea," Patricia said.

"It can make you a little loopy, you know? Nothing bad, just like you got a second-hand high."

"Lucho!"

"I probably shoulda told you. Sorry, *profe*. I didn't think about it." He swept the radishes into a decorative bowl and grabbed a handful of cilantro. "Anyway, glad to hear it's kicking in."

"It kicked in hours ago," Patricia said. "When I was convinced I was seeing mice run around my kitchen."

"Nah, that's just the feeling-stoned effects. The parts I need are still coming. That's why I had to give it to you so long ago."

"The 'feeling-stoned effects'?"

"Not actually stoned. Don't worry, *profe*, there's nothing in there your boss can find out about."

A key turned in the front door, and a pair of women's voices floated in. Valeria and Lindsay. Patricia could hear the scuff of Valeria's boots, the businesslike click of Lindsay's heels. Valeria was laughing.

"I got limes," she said when she entered the kitchen. She set a bag of them on the counter, and a case of Tecate alongside them. "And their best accompaniment."

"And I made cookies," Lindsay said. She was carrying a box of frosted sugar cookies from Safeway; she set them down on top of Valeria's Tecate.

Lucho leaned over for a kiss. "*Mi amor,*" he said. "Your best recipe."

She kissed him, then turned to Patricia. "We didn't get much of a chance to meet last night. I'm Lindsay. It looks like you're feeling better."

Patricia shook her hand. Smooth, cool, dry. Patricia tried to reconcile this vision of Mr. and Mrs. Carrera standing side by side in their gourmet kitchen. Lindsay was the same height as Lucho, at least in her heels, and looked like the type who'd spent plenty of effort on exercise and good living to keep herself aging so gracefully. Her ashy blond hair glimmered with silver, pulled back into a no-nonsense ponytail. "It's nice to meet you," Patricia said. "Thanks for your help last night."

Lindsay waved a manicured hand. "It's nothing. I've seen some strange things come out of Luis's job. But he probably knows what he's doing." She pulled a plate out of the cupboard and began arranging cookies. Valeria settled onto a stool beside Patricia, met her gaze with a warm smile.

"Luis told me you have a son at UW," Lindsay said. "Gabriel, right? What year is he?"

Patricia smiled back at Valeria. Sweet Lord, could things always feel this right between them? "He's a freshman," she said.

"Is he taking chemistry this quarter?"

"No, I don't think so. Not that he keeps his mother in the loop."

Lindsay threw her hands up in mock despair. "They leave the house and they're impossible, right? Well, tell him to look for Professor Carrera when it's time to take Intro to Chem. I'll make sure to include my famous 'call your mother to ask for her favorite cookie recipe' assignment."

Patricia laughed. "I will."

"Hey, Linz." Lucho snagged a cookie off the plate; she swatted at him and rearranged them. "Isidro and Isabella are gonna be here in about twenty minutes. You gonna stick around?"

"Heavens, no. I made plans with Christine for dinner. It breaks my brain to listen to them talk about the spiritual realm—give me science any day." She smiled at Patricia. "No offense. I understand you're hosting right now."

"It wasn't on my bucket list."

"Ugh, me neither. All right, kids. I'm off. Save the cookies until after your dinner, and save some of that pozole for me, Luis. Do you need anything from me before I leave?"

He lifted an eyebrow at Valeria. "Maybe," he said, following her back down the hallway to their bedroom. "Lemme check, *mi reina*."

Patricia nibbled on another radish slice.

:don't get them:

Patricia perked up. *Been napping?*

Marco uncoiled lazily; she could feel him stretching his... just stretching, she supposed. It wasn't like he had muscles to cramp up anymore.

:stupid tea:

Yes. Patricia sighed. *Oh, yes.*

Twenty minutes later, the doorbell rang.

"Isidro and Isabella," Lucho said, rubbing his hands clean on a towel and running his fingers through his wild hair. "Always on time. Nena!"

Patricia followed him and Valeria to the front door. In her imagination, she'd created a fantastical vision of what Lucho's *palero* friends would look like. She envisioned New Orleans, the voodoo parlors of movie fame: an ancient, dreadlocked witch with cataract-blind eyes and blackened teeth; a top-hatted black man with a gold-rimmed smile and diamond rings.

The couple at the door could have been ushers at Patricia's church.

Isabella came up to Patricia's shoulder, with the formidable linebacker density of a Latina grandmother. Her short, curly hair was dyed reddish brown, her lips were painted on and her eyebrows done up, but she wore a simple mocha-colored skirt and matching coat.

Isidro sported a full bushy head of white hair; his pale-blue polyester suit pants were impeccably pressed, and of the type Patricia was certain no one made anymore. Or maybe they did. She'd try to remember to ask him, since she was pretty sure her dad wore the same ones.

Lucho threw open the door, and threw himself into shaking Isidro's hand vigorously. "Chilo!" he bellowed, pulling the man to his chest. "*Y la princesa.*" He began to sing, something old and low that Patricia recognized faintly from her childhood, and Isabella began to dance, a slow, shuffling step, her boxy body agile on her polished leather heels, her hips sashaying with Lucho as she danced through the door, hands meeting his; he spun her once.

Isidro greeted Valeria with a kiss, then turned to Patricia. "Valeria's sister?" he asked. "It's good to meet you." Patricia leaned in awkwardly for a kiss, then clasped hands with Isabella, pressing her cheek into the old woman's powdered one. She came away smelling of a cloying blend of Isidro's cologne and Isabella's spicy floral perfume. She raised an eyebrow at Valeria, who smiled.

"Well, friends, dinner's ready whenever we are. Do you want to eat now, or later?"

"Now," said Patricia and Valeria at the same time.

Isidro pursed his lips. "*Ahorita ya,*" he said. "Now would be good. *Huelo pozole, no?*"

"Yes, you smell pozole." Lucho smiled.

Patricia went to ask Ava if she'd like to have dinner in the den so she could keep playing, and got a resounding yes, which relieved her. She had a suspicion conversation around the dinner table was going to be a bit beyond... Well, beyond.

Valeria took the older couple's coats, helped Lucho serve, then returned to sit at his right hand, in an odd gesture of acolyte to master. Patricia watched her, but said nothing, taking her place beside Valeria. She wondered if it was a nod to the other... not resurrectionists, Lucho had said. Practitioners?

Patricia was mulling over the correct word when she realized Isidro was watching her. Isabella and Lucho were bantering in Spanish while Valeria listened in with a smile. Isidro's short-sleeve shirt was pressed and bleached and worn almost translucent to reveal the lines of his undershirt through the fabric. "A toast to our silent friend," he said quietly, raising his Tecate. Pale cross scars marked the backs of his hands.

Patricia clinked her water glass with his can, and the hairs rose on the nape of her neck as she realized he wasn't talking about her. His gaze shifted past. Marco shivered.

Patricia turned to her soup as the conversation whirled from people she didn't know to esoteric spiritual topics she'd never heard of. Isabella jumped seamlessly from English to Spanish when she was explaining a more intricate point, her Colombian accent so thick, Patricia could barely follow along. She glanced at Valeria, who shrugged.

"Isabella's just pecking at me," Lucho said, translating without bothering to ask if they understood her. "About the ghosts. I tell her we can argue about all this later, but she wants me to tell you that the dead shouldn't be exalted like what we do. Singled out." He lifted his hands in surrender.

Isabella sighed, put upon. "The dead are like the ocean," she said. "They surround us. Like the sea, the tides. Our craft isn't spells and potions," she said with a meaningful look at Lucho. "We honor the dead with sacrifices, we sing to them, and we ask them for their help and guidance. We don't trap them like the poor man trapped here." Isabella reached out to clasp Patricia's hand.

Her fingers glittered with rings, the one nod to the dreadlocked witch of Patricia's imagination. Her hands clinked against her spoon, her water glass, her bowl, each ring studded with stones Patricia didn't recognize—not diamonds, nothing that looked precious. But all of them looked ancient. Like something you'd find in a pirate's treasure chest.

"How's the pozole?" asked Lucho, and Isabella shot him an annoyed look, pulling her hand away from Patricia's. As Isabella turned away, Patricia made out a small scar marked ever so faintly on the back of her neck: a tiny pale cross, faded as if after decades.

After Valeria cleared away dinner, they settled in the living room. It was decorated mainly with family photos and art, tapestries, and photographs the Carreras had picked up on trips together.

Isabella and Isidro examined the *firma*, while Patricia stayed carefully away. Lucho repeated the story she'd told him, glancing at Patricia for confirmation from time to time.

"It is a *firma* meant to do harm," Isidro said when Lucho had finished. "Only the one who wrote it can know for sure, but I recognize it at its base as a *firma* that is meant to bring bad luck to a rival. To put it in his car, his prized possession, it could mean someone was trying to attack him at his core."

Lucho looked puzzled. "I thought they had to be written up special each time," he said. "So if it was drawn for Marco, why would Patricia have responded to it like she did? None of the rest of us were affected."

"Patricia didn't respond," said Isidro. "Marco did."

Isabella frowned. "Why would you work Palo against a ghost? If a rival wanted to kill him, they might have worked against him then. But once he is dead? He's just another in the sea of dead." She peered over her glasses at her husband. "Who would work *brujería* against the dead?"

Isidro rubbed his chin. "You said that Marco found bones in a car before his death? He told you this?"

"I saw it." The Colombians exchanged a glance. "I mean, I saw Marco's memory of it."

Isabella wrinkled her nose as though she'd smelled something distasteful.

"There was no skull?" Isidro asked Patricia.

She shook her head.

"I would not make a *prenda* without a skull. A *nfumbe* needs a skull."

"I don't—" Patricia paused; Marco stirred sluggishly. :skull separate maybe didn't search: "Marco wonders if the skull might be separate," said Patricia. "He says he didn't search the car."

The Colombians stared at her, their expressions unreadable.

"That could be," Isidro said finally. "I would not transport a *nfumbe* in such a way, with the skull separated from its bones, but I have seen it done. Especially if the *nfumbe* was very hot and causing mischief during its journey. Separating the skull may cool it enough to keep its transporters safe."

"Hot?" asked Patricia.

"Active," said Lucho. "Awake. Also: stolen." Isabella glared at him. "Tell me those bones weren't stolen, *mi reina*," he said.

"From whom? They would not have been taken if the *nfumbe* was not asked to come and had not agreed." She jutted her chin at Patricia. "Did you ask this man if he wanted to be made captive like this?"

"Yes," Valeria said quietly. "I asked him."

"See?" Isabella turned back to the drawing of the *firma*. She said something in rapid Spanish to Isidro, her accent so thick that Patricia could only pick out a few words. *Light, path, change.*

"The bones were a child's," said Isidro, "which makes us believe that whoever is working with them used them to make a Lucero Mundo. It is a *prenda* that opens paths and smooths opportunities. The *firma* looks similar to one I would use with my Lucero."

His Lucero? A chill touched the back of Patricia's neck. Isidro and Isabella had a pot somewhere in their home with the bones of a child in it. Marco squirmed. :*they think I'm the freakshow?*:

"But Lucero is not predictable; like a little boy, he takes only suggestions, not orders. If someone has made a powerful Lucero and let it taste blood like this, it could grow beyond his control."

Isidro pulled a leather bag from his trouser pocket and shook it out over the glass-topped coffee table. Patricia had half expected to see bones, but instead they were pieces of a coconut shell, glossy and polished. Lucho leaned forward to watch, but said nothing.

"What—" Patricia fell silent at a sharp glance from Valeria. Now was watching time, apparently.

"We ask permission of the dead," Isabella said to Patricia. She began humming as Isidro fingered the coconut shells, a quiet tune that seemed to pull at Marco. His presence shimmered within Patricia, electric and pulsing with the rise and fall of Isabella's voice, quivering with the faint drumbeat of her fingertips against the couch's leather arm. Isidro's shells clattered against the coffee table. The old man frowned at the results.

Patricia felt Marco shift subtly in response to whatever question was asked there. Threads tugged at him through her, binding him close and present, inviting his attention. He felt flatter—or Patricia did, maybe, her own self stretched thinner across the bulk of his spirit. She—he?—leaned forward to see the shells.

Can you feel anyone else out there? Patricia asked him, and he shrugged.

:creepy thinking dead people everywhere: He curled inward. *:don't feel anyone though:*

But he was responding, no matter what else was happening, malleable in the *paleros'* hands and taut as a string.

Isidro frowned at the results of his cast shells and reached out to throw them again. Lucho sat back. "What's wrong?" he said.

"The spirits aren't..." Isabella pursed her lips, stopped. She began to sing again.

Isidro dropped the shells once again, but before they could fall—before she knew she was doing it—Patricia reached to catch two of the larger ones, placing them carefully on the table. One up, one down, nudged into the perfect position. Isabella snapped at her in Spanish, but Isidro held out a hand. "*Está bien,*" he murmured. "The dead are answering."

Isidro and Isabella seemed content with this latest throw of the shells, despite Patricia's—or rather, Marco's—interruption. "The dead say we can continue," said Isidro. "They invite us to."

Patricia caught a wave of skepticism from Marco. Lucho was sitting tight-lipped, his expression unreadable. His hands were knotted around one knee.

"You have become very sick with spirits," said Isidro to Patricia. "Someone is working Palo against the dead inside you." He frowned, and cast his shells again. "They worked against him in life, and now in death they continue their work. It is a strange thing to do. In life, they worked to make him unlucky, but in death it is a binding work."

"Binding?"

But Isidro didn't answer.

"What would this Lucero want with Marco?" Lucho asked.

"He could just be creating mischief," said Isabella. "But you said Marco's grave had been disturbed. Headstone broken, and earth taken, no?"

"I think so," said Valeria. She glanced at Patricia. "Yeah, Bayer said that earth had been taken, right?"

"Then someone may be using this Lucero to gain power. First we can speak to the dead to see what they say. Then, Lucho, you want to take Marco out of Patricia, no?"

Lucho nodded. "We'll transfer him to Val," he said.

Isabella frowned at Lucho. "It would be better to let him go, no?" She clucked her tongue. "*Vale.*"

Valeria stilled her fidgeting beside Patricia. She breathed out, her breath harsh with the cigarette she'd smoked just after dinner. Her hand slipped into Patricia's, cool and dry. "It's time," she said.

Chapter Nineteen

ISABELLA OFFERED TO stay upstairs with Ava during the ritual. "To keep distractions at bay," as she put it. Patricia thought she saw a touch of relief in her expression—it was clear how much she disapproved of Lucho's decision to transfer Marco instead of "releasing" him.

Ava took to the older woman immediately, and dove into explaining her Lego saga of a sea battle between pirates and the motley crew of astronauts and islanders who had stolen the pirate ship. Patricia kissed the top of her head. "We've got a little more adult business to take care of, and then we can go home," she said.

Isabella slipped off her polished leather heels and *oofed* her way onto the floor with Ava. "And why is this one in the jail?" she asked, flashing a smile at Patricia.

In the basement, the others had cleared away the couches and pulled back the rugs so that all that remained in the center of the room were a pair of straight-backed chairs set on bare concrete and a small folding card table. Valeria was helping Lucho set the table with an array of bottles and herbs while Isidro watched with respectful interest.

"Siddown, siddown, *profe*," Lucho said, waving Patricia in. "We've almost got everything ready here. No no, not that chair. This one."

Both chairs had been painted black and chalked with symbols that looked similar, but at closer inspection were more like two halves of a whole. Patricia sat in the one to Lucho's left, her bare arms crawling at the touch. The wood was strangely chilled, like the chairs had just been brought in from a cold garage. Marco flickered with energy once, suddenly, like a sharp sting in the pit of her stomach. She flinched. Lucho glanced over, nodded, and then went back to his preparations.

Patricia rubbed her arms. "Have you ever done this before?"

Lucho grinned at her. "I been practicing these arts since before you were born, kiddo. You ever ask a baker, 'I know you can make banana bread, but are you sure you can make chocolate chip cookies?' It's all about following the recipe and knowing when to stop mixing the dough."

"Sorry." Patricia glanced at Valeria, who looked deadly serious. "I didn't mean to offend you."

"No problem." Lucho unscrewed an unlabeled jar, sniffed at the contents. "If I were you, I'd be worried as hell."

"Not that you should be," Valeria cut in. She straightened, rubbing her palms down her jeans. "It'll be fine."

:had a nickel:

My thoughts exactly.

Valeria seemed to be talking as much to herself as to Patricia, the way she cracked her knuckles as she arrange the jars, the constant readjusting of her hair. Patricia wondered if she was nervous not only for the spell, but also for the sudden reunion with Marco.

As for Marco, Patricia could feel his restless anxiety, his anticipation, or... cold feet?

It's going to be fine, Marco.

:that's ten cents:

She smiled.

"Is something funny?" Valeria sat in the chair beside Patricia.

"He's ready," Patricia said. "We're both ready."

Lucho's magic was different than Valeria's. Patricia could tell, even as inexperienced as she was. Valeria had been stiff and self-conscious in the cemetery, where Lucho was easy and loose. She could see it in the careless, almost offhand way he picked from his ingredients. His analogy with baking seemed apt—he moved through his workshop like Patricia's mother moved through her kitchen: chatting and humming, tossing in a pinch of this, a dash of that, a frown, a dash more. He looked like it had been years since he'd consulted a cookbook.

"Chilo, plug that fan in the window?" Isidro opened a window to the cold night air, the box fan blowing air out as Lucho kindled a fire in the brass censer. "OK, now what this is going to feel like is static electricity—you know when you shuffle your feet and zap somebody with what you built up? Pati, you're gonna zap your sister. Bet you won't mind that." He grinned. "But, hey, it's gonna hurt you both. So just be aware."

He uncorked a vial of terrible-smelling liquid with his teeth, and daubed it onto both women's wrists. Patricia wrinkled her nose. Valeria's knee jostled nervously. "*Ptth.*" Lucho spat out the cork. "So what I'm doing is making you positive, Pati. Nena's gonna be negative, so it'll be easy for Marco to skip on over, right? He won't have a choice, just like that static electricity you build up don't have a choice but to jump on over to your friend. That tea that made you all stoned, that makes you the positive, right? Loosens Marco's grip on you and calms him down a bit."

He marked a pair of different symbols in black chalk on both women's hands, smudged their foreheads with the ground mix from his grandmother's *molcajete*, muttering in Spanish as he did. He stooped to chalk a circle around them on the concrete. With a little groan, he straightened.

Patricia could feel Marco inside her, gathering like the static charge Lucho had described. He was different than he had been in the past. Less responsive to her thoughts. *Marco? How are you doing?*

He surged, jittering as though trying to scent her out. :*val?*:

I don't know if you can hear me now, but good-bye, Marco. Patricia paused, not sure what to say in farewell to her unexpected houseguest. *And good luck out there,* she thought. *It was weird, but it was good.*

For a moment she heard nothing. She'd missed her timing, maybe, missed the opportunity to say good-bye. She felt a pang of grief, then took a deep breath. This was what she'd wanted more than anything for the past few days.

:*pati miss you bye kiddo*:

She straightened. Lucho glanced at her, but did not stop his incantation.

Bye, Marco.

The charge of him was almost unbearable, now. Her skin pricked with energy, the tiny needlepoints of static concentrating down her left arm, to the hand which held Valeria's. The heat coming off the places where their hands touched was nearly unbearable, and Patricia looked down, expecting to see smoke.

Valeria looked more still than she'd been all evening, a quiet calm masking her face and softening her features. The nervous energy was long gone. For a moment Patricia felt as though she'd gotten a glimpse of what her sister would look like in twenty years—at their mother's age—her features softened and gentled with time.

She looked lovely. Untroubled.

Before she realized what she was doing, Patricia lifted her sister's hand to her lips and kissed her knuckles. Valeria's eyes fluttered open. She met Patricia's gaze, and a slow smile spread across her face. Her hand tightened over Patricia's.

Lucho's muttered chant increased, the words catching Patricia's heartbeat and causing it to flutter in time, a tap dancer cut loose from rhythm.

Marco built up against her breastbone in rising waves, causing an unbearable prickling sensation, as though her torso had fallen asleep and was just now regaining feeling. Patricia curled her spine around the burn.

Valeria gripped her hand harder, and now she did see the faintest curl of smoke drifting from between their clasped palms.

She could feel Marco building like a charge, ready to crest, to break free and flood toward her fingertips, toward Valeria, toward—

Lucho snapped, and the candles quenched as one.

Patricia screamed, an agony like fire coursing through her bones. She tore her hand free from Valeria. Blinding white light seared her eyes as she hit the boundary of the chalk circle, and she slid to the floor.

She curled, trembling, against the coolness of the concrete as the pain slowly ebbed away.

Things came back to her in pieces. Valeria's voice, distant. Lucho's cursing. A knock on the basement door: "Mama?" Isidro standing—he'd been kneeling beside Patricia—to answer the knock. Lucho's calloused hands cradling her head. Marco, lying spent and trembling in his spot below her sternum.

"What happened?" she whispered.

Patricia huddled on the couch in the living room under a pile of fleece blankets, shivering despite the heat. Valeria had taken Ava to the kitchen to make some hot tea—Patricia could hear their voices coming soft and low and Isabella's deep, rich laugh as Ava told a story.

Her fingers were beginning to thaw; she clenched her hands experimentally. They'd been numb claws when she'd been brought upstairs. She breathed a sigh of relief.

But the heat hadn't reached Marco. He was balled inside her, static and icy. When Patricia's family had moved to Seattle—she was eleven—they had taken a winter trip into the mountains, where the girls had seen their first icicles spiked and glittering from the rooftops of the ski lodge. Patricia had swallowed a chunk of one on a dare from Valeria, and it had burned inside her stomach, numbing her from the inside out as it melted, excruciatingly slow.

It had been in almost that same spot, she thought. Just below her sternum.

Marco showed no signs of melting.

Isidro was rubbing his shells together in his palms, the rasping click of their polished husks muffled in his big hands. He let them clatter to the table, frowned at the results, then cast again. Marco flinched, and Patricia caught her breath. Lucho glanced over.

"The dead are unhappy here," Isidro said. "The natural way of things has been disturbed."

"By raising Marco?" Patricia asked.

Isidro shook his head. "By whoever used Palo to kill Marco, and is still using it against him."

"But who—" Patricia caught Lucho's sharp look and glanced back toward the kitchen. Ava was walking through the doorway, attention focused on the mugs of tea she carried. She set them on the coffee table, then burrowed into the blankets with her mother, tracing the tip of a wolf's nose with her finger.

Patricia sniffed the tea. "What's in this one?" she asked.

"Mint," said Valeria. "From a bag. That's it."

Patricia held it in her hands, tucked just between her breasts as though the heat of it from there could reach Marco. The warm steam drifted up to fog her glasses.

"Can we go home now, Mom?"

"In a minute, honey."

Valeria still stood in the doorway, looking troubled. "It's Chente," she said quietly. Isabella looked at her, disapproving. It was clear she didn't need to ask who Chente was.

"Is Chente getting into Palo?" asked Isidro.

Lucho frowned at Ava, thinking through his words. "That doesn't seem like him. It doesn't seem up his alley, all the mumbo jumbo."

Isabella glared at him. Lucho winked at her.

"I'm just saying it doesn't sound like Chente, is all. He likes a sure thing, not the worry that you have to line up all these little pieces in order to get a gh — ah, your prenda happy. He wouldn't like to lose that control."

Isidro shrugged. "A man like that might be scratched into Palo," he said, thumbing the cross scars on his own hands. "But he wouldn't become a Tata. You need discipline for that."

The heat of the tea and the sharp scent of the mint had begun thawing away the rest of the shock, and a tiny tickle was beginning to emerge at the back of her mind.

:have: Marco stirred slightly, burrowing into her breastbone.

Have what?

:haver:

Patricia frowned into her tea, trying to decipher what he was trying to tell her. What did she have that would help?

:morning haver haver havyer havi: Marco thrashed once, then lapsed into silence, exhausted.

Have? Oh!—Patricia let out a little gasp, and everyone looked over at her. "Javier," she said.

Valeria gave her a murderous look. "What is it?"

"Javier. He came by today and—" She stopped at the look on Valeria's face. "You still haven't called him back, have you? Anyway, he said something about a, ah, about something like what I've got 'bossing around the boss man.'"

Ava shot her a look that was, disconcertingly, equal parts curious child and bad cop. "Could that happen?"

No one answered. Isabella and Isidro seemed to be deferring to Lucho, but he sat silent, watching Valeria. Valeria was staring at her tea. Finally, she cleared her throat. "We've been bringing things back for the past year or so. When I've gone down to Nicaragua"—a glance at Ava—"sometimes I've brought things back for Chente. Nothing bad. I meet with a woman and she gives me little bundles to put in my carry-on bag. Once it was coins, a few times it's been dirt. Scraps of fabric. Sticks. Nothing really suspicious, just weird. I never asked about it."

Isabella was looking pensive. "He could have been collecting ingredients for a *prenda*, that could be what... what was in the car. If he'd made a *prenda* but the *nfumbe* was angry for being disturbed, maybe it went after the one who disturbed it? That could be."

Isidro nodded. "Lucero can be angry sometimes. Lucero can be vindictive if he feels like he hasn't been respected, or if a mood strikes."

"Who's Lucero?" asked Ava, stirring at Patricia's side.

Isabella drew in a sharp breath. "He's a naughty child," she said. "Who likes to see if he can get away with things, and wishes to always push the boundaries of his keepers. It takes a strong Tata or Yaya Nganga to keep a Lucero, but certain types of, what do we say, *businessmen*"—she spat out the word—"like him because he clears pathways and smooths roads. It is stupid to try if you aren't clever with Palo."

"Lucero can spoil if not ruled with a strong hand," Isidro agreed. "One can become ruled by his *nfumbe*, instead of the other way around."

Lucho frowned, rubbing his palms together in thought. "Val, go call Javier. Meet with him, see what he knows, and leave me out of this for now." His face darkened. "And you and me? We talk later. Go."

Chapter Twenty

VALERIA REJOINED THE group with a resigned expression, and news: Javier would meet her in the parking lot behind Bartell's in half an hour. She said this without looking at Lucho.

He nodded to her, then stretched himself out of his chair. "You good, Pati? You wanna stay here or go home?"

"Home," Patricia said. Ava snuggled in closer. Home was what she needed.

"Here." Isabella pressed something into Patricia's palm: a small medallion stamped with a saint Patricia didn't recognize. "Keep this on you. It will help keep the *nfumbe* from noticing you quite so much." Patricia slipped it into her pocket, where it clinked against the agate. She was gathering quite the collection of magic charms.

Lucho patted her arm. "Let Val take you home, *profe*. We'll figure things out on this end, and let you know. We'll get you back to normal as soon as possible."

Ava cocked her head, but said nothing. She'd been quiet this entire time, probably sensing that if she asked too many questions she'd be banished back to the game room and miss out on all the good intrigue. Patricia was dreading the conversation they would have when they got home.

Valeria snuffed out her cigarette as they got to the car, tossing the butt into the gutter. "You should stop smoking," Ava told her.

"I know, kiddo. But not tonight."

They rolled through the streets—they were relatively busy; it wasn't that late. Patricia checked her phone. Only eight thirty. She still had an hour to wash up and relax before Adrian got home from his game. Probably most of that time would be spent trying to think up a good story for Ava. *Mom, why were you screaming in Mr. Lucho's basement? What's that mark on your hand? Why do you smell like dead goats?*

Patricia sighed deeply, filling her rib cage and letting her vertebrae expand. Valeria glanced over at her. Patricia tried to smile, failed.

Do I tell Ava about you? she asked Marco, but he didn't answer. He was still curled up in shock, though he had melted a bit, starting to soften around the edges and regain a bit of his usual fluidity.

As they pulled up into their street, Valeria let out a curse. Patricia, who was turned to check on Ava, looked up. "What's... oh."

A hulking red F250 pickup sat in front of Patricia's house. She frowned. "I thought you said Bartell's."

"I did," said Valeria. She pulled up behind the pickup. "Maybe he changed his mind, knew we'd be coming here first? I don't know. Take Ava in. I'll go see what's up with Javi."

The window to his truck was halfway down, a curl of cigarette smoke drifting out the window.

The rain had stopped for the moment, and the clouds were pulled back like curtains to reveal inky night sky. There were no streetlights on Patricia's street, and few porch lights, so a handful of stars shouldered through the ambient city light to glint dully. If she tried, Patricia could just barely make them out.

The departed clouds left a bite to the air, too. Patricia tugged her sweater cuffs down, balling them in her fists, shoved fists deep into her coat pockets for warmth. Her breath puffed out white, obliterating the stars. "C'mon, Ava-bean. Tía Valeria just needs to talk to her friend, and then she'll come in, too."

Ava hopped out of the Subaru, slinging her backpack over one shoulder. "Are you staying here tonight, Tía?"

Valeria smiled, though obviously distracted. "Sorry, no. I'm going home tonight."

Patricia could hear Valeria's voice as she unlocked the front door. "Javi, it's me," Valeria said. "Javi?" A rapping of knuckles on glass. Patricia glanced over her shoulder. Javier hadn't moved. Panic was rising in Valeria's voice. "Javier?"

A sharp spike of fear pierced Patricia's heart. "Get inside and lock the door," she whispered to Ava. "Then go to your room. I'll be right back."

She reached Valeria just as she opened the pickup door. A cloud of cigarette smoke poured out, and Javier's hand slid off the armrest, the cigarette tumbling out of his slack fingertips to smolder on the ground. He slumped forward against his seat belt.

In the dim light, Patricia almost didn't see the bullet hole in his temple, just below his hairline. Blood trickled down his hollow cheek, spidering over the tattoos on his neck. Valeria cried out and stepped back, straight into Patricia.

Javier's earring glinted; that crooked smile had half-formed, in a look that seemed despairing, resigned, finished. Patricia stared. Who had...

:smokesmokesmoke: Marco was screaming at her, pointing her to... Javier's last cigarette was still smoldering on the ground. "Val," Patricia hissed, gripping her sister's shoulder. "Val, we have to get away from here."

A footstep crunched in the gravel of her driveway, and Patricia spun to see a shadow there—two—and she yanked Valeria away from the pickup. *To the car? Or to the house, with Ava?*

Valeria tripped on the curb behind her. "Get to Ava," she gasped, tearing her arm out of Patricia's grip.

Patricia hesitated, but Valeria was already running to her Subaru. Someone yelled—one of the men in the driveway, Patricia thought, but no, the shout came from closer. A man tackled Valeria from behind her car. Patricia could hear more shouting coming from down the street, see the dull glint of a gun's barrel at Valeria's temple. "Get to Ava!" Valeria screamed, and Patricia whirled to run.

A heavy blow caught her across the face, blazing light searing through her vision as she fell to her knees. She blinked, rubbed a hand over her eyes—her glasses were gone—and saw blood smeared on her palm. Her vision focused on the black sneakers standing on the walk in front of her. A mechanical click cracked in the silence, and cold metal touched her forehead. Patricia tasted blood.

"The Ramos sisters," she heard someone say behind her. The same cigarette-raw voice from the cemetery, those same shifting footsteps. "Valium, baby," he said. "You have something I need."

Chapter Twenty-One

GRAVEL BIT AT her knees through the damp fabric of her jeans, like she was kneeling on the razor's edge of the night itself, which had already spilled blood and would not hesitate to take another life.

Behind her, Valeria cried out in pain. "Valium, baby," a man said, his voice rough. "Where is he?" Patricia heard him move, but could see only a pair of black sneakers on the gravel in front of her, blurred without her glasses. The sneakers shifted, and a sharp mechanical click split the silence. Patricia froze.

"Marco?" Valeria whispered.

"So she suddenly gets smart. I should have put a gun to your sister's head sooner." Steps shifted on gravel. Patricia tried to stop herself from shivering, but the effort just made her tremble even more.

"What do you want with him?" Valeria asked, a note of defiance beneath the fear.

"That's none of your business. What was your business was to stay out of mine." The voice lowered. "You don't know it, but you fucked up, Marco," he said. "And I got somebody wants to meet you." Terror thrilled through Patricia's spine, but she realized that he wasn't talking to her. Wasn't even near her. She took a quick breath, realizing: Javier hadn't told them.

"I'm sorry," Valeria sobbed. "I—" She cried out, and Patricia flinched.

Do something, Patricia willed herself, but her muscles were useless, frozen in place by the gun's barrel and the knowledge of Ava waiting inside the house. Tears burned tracks down her cheeks.

"I don't give a shit if you're sorry," the man said. Patricia heard the scrabbling of feet against gravel and another cry of pain from Valeria, this one muffled.

Marco raged at that, coursing through her body like lightning, and Patricia, without moving, shoved him sharply, angrily back into his place. He stayed there, quivering against her will.

Don't you dare, Patricia screamed at him, every bow-taut muscle straining with the effort to control him. *Don't you dare give yourself away.* "Val—"

The gun against Patricia's forehead pressed forward sharply, wrenching back her neck. "Shut up, bitch."

A car door slammed. The black sneakers in front of Patricia shifted. "Boss?" The cold steel pressed even harder against her forehead. Patricia couldn't breathe. She struggled to find words in her frantic mind for a prayer.

The silence stretched on, sirens in the distance playing a trick on the mind —were they coming or going? *Oh, Lord...*

"Leave her." The pressure on her forehead disappeared, and Patricia collapsed to the rain-soaked earth as though that point had been the only thing keeping her spine erect. "I bet Valium here will be a bit more cooperative if she knows we're watching her sister and that lovely little girl."

"*Pati!*" Valeria screamed a last time. Car doors slammed, tires screeched, and Marco thrashed with fury against Patricia's rib cage.

She fought to contain his frantic struggle, the moment stretching into an agony that could have been ribs pulled from sternum, ever-expanding breath and lungs bursting, and Patricia breathed out, hard, felt her ribs collapsing back into place.

Patricia lost her battle with her own willpower and vomited in the grass.

When the shuddering nausea had passed, Patricia felt for her glasses. The earpiece was badly bent, but otherwise they were intact. She put them back on with shaking hands.

Whatever Javier had known about Patricia hosting Marco, he obviously hadn't told anyone. But it was only a matter of time before Los Ciegos realized Valeria didn't have Marco.

:then what?: Marco was raging. *:kill:*

Did he want to kill them? Or was he worried they would kill Valeria?

"No one's going to hurt her," Patricia said out loud. "There's no way in hell we'll let that happen."

She stood tenderly, surveying the damage. Porch lights were coming on around her. The distant sirens were closer now, screaming down Roxbury, just a few blocks away. Javier's truck was still parked in front of her house, his body still slumped over the steering wheel, his cigarette butt still smoldering in the gutter.

Her own house was dark; Ava hadn't turned any lights on. Oh, God, how much had she seen?

"Pati? Are you all right?"

Patricia whirled faster than she'd thought possible, felt Marco surge a little, and frowned. It was her neighbor, Shirley, an older black woman who went to Patricia's church. Shirley hugged her, and Patricia went rigid. "Sweetheart, you're so cold, your skin feels like ice."

Ice? Patricia felt like she was burning up. "I need to get to Ava," she said, pushing Shirley back with clumsy hands.

"I called 911," said Shirley. "They should be here any minute." She bustled Patricia up the front steps.

"Ava?" Patricia pounded on the door. She couldn't find her keys. *in grass:* Marco said, but she didn't turn to look for them. "Ava, it's me, it's safe."

Ava finally cracked the door, with the chain latch still on. "I'm opening the door," Patricia heard her say. "It's just my mother, the men are gone."

Ava undid the chain and flung open the door. The phone was still to her ear, but she let Patricia gather her up. Patricia squeezed her tight, fighting back a flood of tears. "It's 911," Ava whispered. "Yes, they're gone," she said into the phone. "They drove to the north, but I didn't see which way they turned, but probably right because otherwise it's a dead end. I think they took my aunt. And there's a..." Ava's voice trailed off, her face going ashen as she looked over Patricia's shoulder. "A deceased Latino male. Yes. OK. Here she is. Mom, the dispatcher wants to talk to you."

Ava held the phone out to Patricia, a dazed look on her face. Patricia took it, then held her tight once more. "Honey, are you all right?"

"They're coming," Ava said, her voice level and calm. "The police, she said they're on the way."

Patricia could hear sirens from Roxbury, turning toward them and closing in. The cavalry was arriving too late for Javier, though, too late for Valeria. Maybe. Patricia fought down a wave of panic. They wouldn't kill Val, not if they thought she still had Marco. In her hand, the handset was chirping for her attention, a tinny voice calling, "Ma'am? Ma'am, are you there?"

Patricia thumbed it off.

"Mom!" Ava snatched the handset back. "You're supposed to stay on the line."

"It's fine," Patricia said quietly. "They're almost here."

Shirley laid a calloused hand on her shoulder, and Patricia flinched, having almost forgotten the old woman was there. "You two come over to my house and we'll wait for the police." She smiled at Ava. "I'll make you some hot chocolate."

"What all did you see?" Patricia asked. To Shirley, or to Ava—she wasn't entirely sure.

It was Shirley who answered. "I was watching my show, and I heard voices. You know there's been a lot more kids looking for trouble coming through here lately, so I took a peek out the window, and I saw"—her gaze cut to Ava—"well, never you mind what I saw. So I called the police."

"Thank you."

Other front doors were opening, curious neighbors coming out to gather around Javier's body at a safe distance. The thin white woman from across the street joined Shirley on the stoop, arms wrapped around herself and shivering in yoga capris, flip-flops, and a WSU hoodie. Patricia couldn't remember her name. "Ohmygod, are you all right?" the woman said. "Shirley, did you call the cops? I thought you must have; they said they were already on the way when I called. I would have called sooner, but my dumbass ex-boyfriend was texting me, and—hon, are you all right?"

"They took my sister," Patricia snapped, too harshly, and the woman recoiled. Patricia scooped up Ava, then walked to where her keys glinted in the dark grass.

She turned Ava's head away from Javier's body as they passed, but Ava looked back. "Who was he?" she asked.

Patricia clenched her jaw. "A bad man who didn't deserve to die like that."

"Did he kill Tío Marco?"

Patricia started to say no, then realized she had no idea. "I don't know, Ava-bean," she said. Back in his spot, Marco shrugged.

Ava's expression was serious, a flicker of something alien and adult shading her child's features. "We should call the detective," she said. "I can do it if you're not ready."

Patricia frowned, caught by that fleeting glimpse of the future in her daughter's face: *Let me take care of you, Mom.* She hugged Ava close, noticing for not the first time how slender she was, how fragile her bones, how thin her skin. She buried her face in her daughter's hair, breathed in the scent. "I'll call him, sweetheart."

She deposited Ava on the couch, then pulled out her phone. *They took val think she has m,* she typed to Lucho. *I'm home with ava, we're ok.*

Detective Bayer picked up after the first ring.

"Detective? It's Patricia Ramos-Waites." She took a deep breath. "They've taken Valeria."

Chapter Twenty-Two

PATRICIA SAT THROUGH a battery of questions from a serious-looking woman officer while others cordoned off her front yard and Javier's F250 with yellow tape. An ambulance idled in the street, lights flickering over the scene, but they hadn't yet moved his body.

Lucho's return text had been brief: *Stay im coming.*

Patricia answered the insinuating questions about her own involvement, her sons, her sister, with as much neutrality as she could muster. "I'm just gathering information," the officer said defensively when Patricia balked at answering whether she or her sister "knew Javier Mejía intimately."

Marco paced like a panther below her sternum, the rhythm of his movements a nerve-racking tattoo just below the edge of her consciousness.

She was answering the same question—How do you know these men?—for the third time in a different way when she heard a commotion outside, voices yelling for someone to stop.

Hope flared—had they found Valeria?—and Patricia broke away from the officer to see Adrian's car in the driveway. He was nowhere in sight, but a cluster of police had gathered by the car with guns drawn. Patricia pushed past the one taking her statement. The woman tried to grab her arm, but adrenaline pulled Patricia free; she heard the officer stumble and fall with a curse behind her.

"My son!" Patricia shouted, running. "That's my son."

She tore through the crowd to find Adrian face down on the ground, a pair of officers pinning him there as he fought against them. She shoved one aside and pulled Adrian to her, clutching him fiercely. Anger crackled like static on her skin. Adrian clung to her.

"He's my son," she hissed at the nearest police officer, who took a step back. The flashing lights on the nearest police car stuttered and flickered out.

:pati chill cops:

Marco tugged at the edge of her consciousness, and she became vaguely aware of the thicket of bodies surrounding her, uniforms prickling with handguns, some drawn, some pointed.

Patricia helped Adrian to his feet, calmer than she'd been in months. Years, maybe.

"Excuse us," she said coldly. She led her son through the crowd and across the sodden grass to the pool of light that marked their front door. Past the officer who had been taking her statement. "Detective Bayer should be here in a few minutes," Patricia said to the woman. "I'll finish giving my statement to him. Thank you."

The woman looked flustered. "Ma'am, I just have—"

"I'll talk to Detective Bayer," Patricia said. She shut the door in the officer's face.

Inside, Ava was sitting with her face pressed to the glass, and Patricia's heart lurched. Twice in an hour she'd seen a gun pointed at her mother's head. Patricia flicked the curtains shut.

Adrian had collapsed on the couch, hands shaking, tracksuit stained with mud. "What the hell is going on, Mom?"

Patricia paced the kitchen, afraid she might disintegrate into a haze of nervous, terrified energy if she stopped moving. "Go change out of those wet clothes," she heard herself say. "You'll catch cold."

"You're covered in mud," Adrian answered. "And you're bleeding." He looked past her to the front door. "Was it those fucking cops, I'll—"

"*Adrian Peter Waites.*"

He froze in place on the couch.

Patricia touched her cheek, felt blood there from the cut below her eye. A medic had dressed it, but the dressing had come off during her tussle with the policemen who had Adrian. She stared at the blood on her fingers, momentarily lost for what to do next.

:paper towel:

Patricia blinked and grabbed for the roll.

"We were at Mr. Carrera's house, he's friends with Tía Valeria," Ava said into the silence, her voice sounding years younger than she had on the phone with the dispatcher. Younger, and full of tremors. "We—" She glanced at her mother, and Patricia saw her file the strange things she'd seen away to think about later. "We had dinner and then we came home," said Ava instead. "There was the pickup outside, and Mom told me to go inside. But then men came with guns, and they took Tía Valeria."

"Who's the ambulance for?" Adrian asked.

"Jav— The man in the pickup," said Patricia.

"What happened to him?"

"He's... dead."

Adrian went pale. "I thought Shirley had had a heart attack or something." He cracked his knuckles one by one, bones snapping in the silence. "What happened to Tía Valeria?"

Patricia's hands began to shake again. She turned the kitchen faucet on as hot as it would go and plunged them underneath.

:truth: whispered Marco.

The whole truth?

:course not me:

Of course not. Patricia took a deep breath. "Your *tía* is involved with some bad people."

"Like the Russian mafia?" said Ava, a hint of her old vigor coming back into her voice.

Adrian rolled his eyes. "Like a gang," he told her. "Which one?"

"I don't know," Patricia lied. "I just know she's gotten in trouble with them. The man in the pickup was a friend who was trying to help her, but the people she's in trouble with..." Patricia fought back a wave of panic. What would Los Ciegos do when they realized Valeria didn't have Marco? And how long did they have before they realized the truth? She took a deep breath, turned off the faucet. "They took her."

"What will they do to her?" Ava whispered.

"I don't know," said Patricia.

All three of them jumped at the knock on the door. "Ms. Ramos-Waites? It's Detective Bayer." Adrian swore under his breath. Patricia shot him a look.

"Adrian, look after your sister. I'll be right back." She stepped back out into the night, hugging herself close against the November chill.

Bayer stood on the doorstep, the scene behind him much as she had left it: police tape and a huddle of uniforms, everything bathed in the strobing light of the patrol cars. They hadn't moved Javier's body yet, presumably waiting for Bayer, and the medics lounged against the side of the ambulance. She could see one of Javier's thin arms sprawled out the open car door, his face turned away from her at a grotesque angle.

Bayer said something, and it took Patricia a moment to realize he was talking to her. She tore her gaze away from Javier's body.

"What?"

"Are you injured?"

Patricia shook her head.

"You have a cut on your face."

"Oh. Right." Patricia touched it lightly; it seemed to have stopped bleeding again. "They looked at it already. They said I'm fine."

"That's good, Patricia. But I'd like to have you talk to the medics again once I'm through, just to make sure. Will you do that for me?"

Patricia nodded. Her gaze wandered back to Javier's red F250, and Bayer took her arm, gently shifting her so her back was to the pickup.

"Good. I was told that someone was killed, and your sister was kidnapped. Is that true? OK. Patricia, do you know who the man in the pickup is?"

Patricia swallowed. "Javier Mejía," she said quietly. "He has two kids and a girlfriend, I think."

"Do you remember, I asked you about the gang Los Ciegos?"

"He was in Los Ciegos," Patricia said, and Bayer's expression turned from professional worry to purely professional. He suspected her, she realized. Of covering for her sister at least. She was done covering for Valeria, though.

She'd already decided to tell Bayer everything she knew about Valeria, if that would get her sister through this alive.

You could visit a sister in jail. She'd done it before.

"Does your sister have any connection with Los Ciegos?"

Patricia nodded. "She worked with them to run ghosts back down to Central America, to visit their families," she said. "At least that's what I gather she did. I just found it out. And I still don't think Marco had any connection to them, except that he was dating her."

"Did she work alone?"

"I guess so?" There was no way she'd bring Lucho into this, not if she could help it.

"Was it Los Ciegos who took Valeria?"

"Yes." Patricia frowned. "I think so, from what they said. I didn't see them. It was dark, and it all happened so fast."

"You and Valeria were just coming home from somewhere, is that right?"

Patricia hesitated a heartbeat too long, saw Bayer catch it. "From a friend's house. Ava was with us. Valeria had told us she was supposed to meet Javier, but then we saw his pickup here."

"Why was she going to meet him?"

Patricia's mind raced, as she realized she hadn't truly thought through the delicate dance of telling all she knew about Valeria without implicating Lucho. Or herself. "He said he knew something about Marco," she said, and Bayer nodded. "She thought she could trust him."

"You knew him?"

"I met him once—no, twice. Once with Valeria... he came over to her place while I was there. Then once he came here looking for her." A tension line appeared taut in his jaw at that, but he said nothing.

Patricia told him everything she remembered about the attack, just as she'd told the police officer before him, trying to describe voices when she was unable to give physical descriptions. "They seemed to think she's hosting Marco's ghost," Patricia said. It might be something he needed to know.

"Is she?"

"No." Patricia frowned, then let a dab of doubt creep into her voice. "I mean, I don't think so. I've never been around her when she was hosting. Would I be able to tell?"

"It depends on the host," Bayer said gently. "Your sister is a professional; you might not have known."

He collected a few more innocuous details from her, then led her back to the medics, carefully ferrying her to avoid any sight of Javier's body. "Do you feel comfortable staying here tonight?" asked Bayer. "I can have an officer stay with you if you like, or, if you have someone else you'd like to stay with...?"

Patricia shook her head. "They wanted Valeria," she said. "Do you think they would come back?" She couldn't have an officer watching, not if Lucho—

"I called my uncle," she said quickly. "He's coming over to be with us." She described Lucho to him while a medic re-dressed the cut on her cheek and checked her pupils.

Bayer left her with the medics to arrange a watch, and Patricia endured their ministrations as long as she could before pulling away. "I promise I'll stay awake and call you if I get dizzy," she told them. She touched the bandage on her cheek. "And I promise this will stay on this time, so long as no one else tries to lay a hand on my family."

Chapter Twenty-Three

PATRICIA SHUT THE door on the world for the second time that night.

She could see the flickering police lights still through the thin curtains on the kitchen window, but she ignored them. The police could do nothing. They didn't know where Valeria had been taken, even if they did know who she'd been taken by. And they would never get to her in time.

Patricia would fare no better on her own. Lucho was the only person she knew who had a direct line to Valeria's captors, and who would have even the slightest idea of how to talk to them. Until he got here, she could do nothing.

Patricia could hear Ava in her room as she collapsed on the couch next to Adrian, who was texting with shoulders hunched. The phone's screen lit his face with an eerie glow in the dark room, making him look ages older than his seventeen years.

She turned on the lamp and the effect vanished, leaving only her son sitting on the couch in grass-stained gym clothes. He looked up from his phone.

"You should put ice on your eye," he said. Patricia nodded wearily. "Hold on." Adrian stood and went to the kitchen. She heard the freezer open, and he returned with one of his sports ice packs wrapped in a kitchen towel.

Patricia pressed it gingerly to her temple. She hadn't bothered to check how bad it looked, but it felt terrible.

Adrian looked terrible, too. Still in shock, maybe. "Adrian..."

"Mom, can I talk for a minute?" His phone lit with a text message, but he flicked it onto silent and shoved it in his pocket. He cracked his thumbs in unison. "This probably isn't a good time, but I promised her I'd tell you tonight."

Patricia nodded, not trusting anything she might say. Adrian was as delicate as Valeria had ever been, she knew, and the wrong word would send him scuttling back to the safety of secrets and silence. Marco shifted ever so slightly; she guessed he meant it to be reassuring. Patricia was grateful, but she didn't need reassurance. There was nothing more that could rattle her already shattered night.

Adrian stared at his hands. "I—" he choked, then took a deep breath. "Lucy—she's pregnant."

Her stomach sank, falling away as she floated above the scene, impassive, watching two heads leaned together, mother and son almost touching. She wondered what the mother would say.

"Oh," said Patricia.

Adrian was crying now, quiet, trying not to let her see. *Do something, Pati—* but for the second time that night, her muscles refused to move. She took a deep breath, then reached out and gathered him close. He melted into her. "How long have you known?"

"Three weeks."

"Oh," said Patricia again. She didn't have to ask why it had taken him this long to tell her. "And what is Lucy... what are you going to do?" She heard the refrigerator kick on in the silence, muffled calls from the front yard. "Is Lucy going to keep it?"

"Yes," Adrian said, his voice muffled against her shoulder. "I promised her I'd tell you tonight, but I still didn't want to." He sat up and sniffed, pushing back the sleeves of his sweatshirt. "But then I was lying there with the cops and thinking this kid would never have a dad, and—" The words came out in a rush, like they'd been bottled for days. Tears brimmed his lower lids. He let Patricia pull him back into a hug. "I'm so sorry, Mom. I'm so sorry."

"It's OK, honey." Patricia kissed the top of his head, mind racing. "Everything's going to be fine." Except that her son was going to be a father through his last two years of high school instead of just a kid, and that Lucy—

oh, poor, sweet Lucy. "Has Lucy told her parents yet?" She felt him nod. "And how... how are they?"

She dreaded the answer to that. She knew Lucy's parents too well.

"They kicked her out."

"What?" Patricia pushed him back to look in his face. "Adrian, when?"

"Last week."

Oh, God, this whole week she'd been self-absorbed with her own problems, while her son and his girlfriend were... "Where is she?"

"Staying with Ms. Gomez. The volleyball coach."

Patricia shook her head. "Call her. She'll stay with us. She can... have Ava's room? Ava can sleep with me. Or you can sleep on the couch, or..." She shook her head. "Until her parents come around. Or..." Would they ever come around? Or until... Patricia had no idea.

She felt Marco stir. :*congrats gramma*:

Something else stirred, too, the first tiny kindle of joy she'd felt all week. She was going to be a grandmother. Not the way she'd hoped, and Lord, at age forty-two...

"I'm awfully young to be a grandmother," she said out loud, and Adrian looked devastated. "Honey, I didn't mean it like that. I just don't even have grey hair. Grandmas have grey hair." *And I still have a nine-year-old.* Patricia shook the thought aside. She gave Adrian a fierce hug. "Adrian Peter Waites, you call Lucy and tell her she'll stay with us. Not tonight, not with the police, and... but after. And don't—" Patricia sighed. "Adrian, I love you."

His return hug was just as fierce. "I love you too, Mom," he said into her shoulder. Patricia was acutely aware of him: his lean, strong arms around her neck, the cords of muscles running across his back. Those fast, fleeting years of childhood rubbed away to reveal a young man with his own cares, who no longer needed to cling to his mother. Patricia breathed her son in, then let him go.

The voices outside had changed, she realized, and the lights flickering over the kitchen curtains were less frantic. She could hear Bayer talking to someone, and although she couldn't make out the words, the cadence and accent were familiar. Lucho.

She smiled wearily at Adrian. He was staring down at his hands. "I thought you were going to really flip," he said eventually, sitting back against the arm of the couch and meeting her gaze.

Patricia thought about this. "I don't have a lot of energy left to flip right now."

Adrian sniffed and gave her a sad smile. "I guess I had good timing then."

"Adrian..." Patricia sighed. Lord. Where did her children get such black humor?

A knock sounded at the door. "*Profe*, it's just me," came Lucho's voice through the door. Patricia took a deep breath and went to open it, ruffling Adrian's hair as she passed.

The whole night felt surreal; even the throbbing pain in her face seemed distant and numbed, like she was watching it happen to someone else. She couldn't decide which event had been more out of the blue tonight: her sister being kidnapped, or finding out that Adrian had... She edited herself. That Adrian was going to be a father.

:opening?:

What?

Another knock sounded on the door, and Patricia realized she was standing there with her hand on the knob. Oh. *At least you're still normal,* Patricia thought, and she felt Marco laugh. At least he still felt real to her, as absurd as that sounded.

Lucho took her in in one hard look, from the grass-stained jeans to the bandaged face, the ice pack still in her hand. "Ava?" he asked.

"She's fine. She was in the house."

He nodded curtly and pushed past her, taking the door from her and locking it. "Who you staying with tonight?"

"I'm coming with you."

Lucho raised an eyebrow. "And where do you think I'm going? I got Lindsay at her mom's and the girls staying with friends instead of at their dorms. I need you somewhere safe, too."

"Why?" The question came from Adrian, who rose from the couch, arms folded across his chest. Patricia's heart skipped a beat—in this light, with that expression, he looked just like Joe had.

"Adrian, this is Lucho. Lucho, this is my son."

Lucho's flinty gaze raked over Adrian. "What happened to you?"

"The police," Patricia said. "They thought—"

Lucho cut her off with a shake of his hand. "Pati, you gotta take your kids and get somewhere safe. I'm not writing an advice column, I'm telling you an order."

"You didn't answer me," said Adrian, walking to join them in the kitchen. "Why?"

"Kiddo, your *tía's* a mess, and these men think she has something they want. When they find out she doesn't, they may come looking here."

"And who are you?"

"Her babysitter," Lucho said sharply. "Now—"

"Is this about a ghost?"

In the silence that followed, the thin, reedy whine of the heater kicking on sounded like a jet plane.

Patricia's jaw worked silently, but Lucho recovered first. "Why the hell you think that?" he barked, but there was no hiding how surprised they'd both been. While what Lucho and Valeria did for the courts was legal, it was also fairly controversial, and Patricia and Valeria had agreed early on not to tell the children.

Adrian just shrugged. "I know Tía Valeria worked as a host." He looked at Lucho. "Are you a resurrectionist?"

Lucho scowled. "I am. And she does." He narrowed his eyes. "Or at least she did. If she lives through this, she's fired. She tell you this?"

Adrian shook his head. "Tío Marco did."

"Oh, did he?" Patricia asked the question out loud, but its intended target cringed beneath her sternum. :*thought he knew sorry meant to tell you*: Patricia sighed. "That's fine," she said, and Lucho shot her a sharp look.

"Your tía's in some trouble, and Lucho and I are going to get her out of it," Patricia told Adrian. Lucho shot her a dark look. "Will you go check on Ava while I tell Lucho what happened?"

Adrian gave them both a measured stare, adding a special dose of toughness for Lucho, then nodded.

Lucho watched him leave. "Good kid," he said after Adrian was out of sight. "Fierce."

"He's—" A tangled knot of emotions wound itself through Patricia's gut, and for a minute she wasn't sure what to say. "He's a good kid," she said eventually. "What's your plan for Valeria?"

"What do you mean, plan?"

"How are we going to get her back?"

"We aren't doing nothing."

"We are. I'm coming with you."

"And where do you think I'm going?"

"To see Chente. To talk to him."

Lucho raised an eyebrow. "You think I wanna let your sister get me killed?"

"I think you're the only one who can talk to them right now. The police can't do anything. I can't do anything. And once they find out she doesn't have"—she checked over her shoulder and lowered her voice—"Marco, what do you think they're going to do to her? Or to me?"

"*Profe*—"

"And what about the other ghost? Isabella and Isidro thought there could be a rogue something, I don't know what, but a bad ghost controlling Chente. Javier thought so, too. Are you just going to ignore that?"

"You don't know what I'm going to do."

"Yes, I do. You're going to go see Chente and try to stop him, but you don't want me to come."

Lucho scowled at her, and she knew she was right. "You take these kids of yours, and you find someplace to stay, right, *profe*?"

"I can help."

"Help with what?" Lucho cocked his head and looked at her, but she had no answer for him. He knew that.

"She's my sister," Patricia said. "I need to help her."

Lucho considered for a long moment. "We get these kids somewhere safe, and you can sit in the car. Fair?"

"Fair."

"Fine." He snapped his gnarled fingers twice. "Let's go, then."

Patricia called Bayer, who'd gone back to the station, telling him she felt safer staying with her uncle, and that he could call off the police guard at her house. Then, heart in her throat, she went to tell Ava and Adrian. They were in their separate rooms; she knocked on Adrian's door first.

He opened the door with phone in hand—"I'll call you back in a minute, I love you, too"—still wearing the same grass-stained clothes.

"Lucy?" Patricia asked. Adrian nodded. "How is she?"

"She's OK. Happy that we talked." He swallowed. "How are you?"

Patricia tried to smile. "I've been better. Adrian, I need you to take Ava and go stay with Gabe tonight."

"What are you doing?"

"Trying to help your *tía.*"

"No."

"Adrian, I promise I'll be fine. I'll be with the police," she lied. It came easily. "With that detective. He thinks they know where she is, and I want to be there for her."

She watched his face, the easiness of the lie overstaying its welcome and working knots of anxiety into her gut. Eventually he nodded. "Did you call Gabe?"

"No, will you? He might be out at a party or something."

Adrian rolled his eyes. "I think you mean he's probably in his room doing his homework," he said. "You could have gave me normal siblings." It was an old joke, said out of habit, and tonight it felt halfhearted in light of Adrian's news. He cleared his throat and jerked his chin at the shared wall with Ava's bedroom. "Ava's been talking to herself all night. I can hear her through the wall. She's probably playing detective again. I went in yesterday and she had dolls tied up everywhere. That girl's bizarre. We need to get her into a sport."

"Maybe Lucy can teach her volleyball," Patricia said, and Adrian shrugged noncommittally.

"I think she's a lost cause." He tried to smile.

"Get changed, honey. I'll go talk to Ava."

Ava was indeed talking to herself; Patricia could hear her asking questions as she tapped on the door. "Ava?"

Ava went silent, and Patricia felt a quiver in her gut. Just Marco; he shifted nervously as she opened the door. Ava was sitting on her bed reading.

"Honey, you and Adrian are going to stay with Gabe tonight."

Ava looked at her quizzically. "Really?"

"It'll be fun."

Ava looked uncertain. "Gabe's not really fun."

"Gabe's fine, honey. I know he lets you watch TV shows I won't."

"Are you coming?"

"No, Ava-bean, I need to help the police find your *tía*." The lie came easier a second time.

"OK."

"OK. Pick out some clothes, and I'll go get your toothbrush."

Patricia smiled at her, but Ava frowned. "Mom? Are ghosts real?"

Patricia was beyond surprises tonight. She sighed wearily. Had Ava found her library book? Or, had Isabella told her something while the rest of them had been downstairs in the basement?

"Yes," she said simply. "But you don't have to be afraid of them. They only come back if a judge says they can, and then they're kept separate from other people." Her throat tightened. "You probably won't ever see one," she lied.

"Oh." Ava gave a little shrug, and tossed her book onto the floor. "OK."

"Pick out some clothes, honey. I'll be right back." She started to turn away, then stopped, a feeling of unease spreading through her. "Ava?" she asked. "Why did you ask about ghosts?"

Ava shrugged. "Cuz I saw Tío Marco."

Patricia felt a chill. "What?" *Marco?* He shrank away from her.

Ava pointed at the foot of her bed. "He sat right there and told me that he loved me, and that everything was going to be OK. And then I read him some of my story. I think it made him happy."

"Just right now?" Ava nodded, and Patricia swallowed hard. "I'm sure it's true. He does love you. But that's not how ghosts work, honey. You just imagined him." *Didn't she?*

:wanted to talk:

Patricia's mind reeled. All that time she hadn't felt Marco, had he been...
No. That wasn't even a possibility. She knew how this worked, and he couldn't
just walk away from her. Ghosts didn't just wander untethered around the
earth. They were hosted, or apparently, they could sometimes be tethered in
pots. Or, apparently, they were part of a greater Sea of the Dead that
surrounded everyone in the living world.

It depended on what you believed, if you believed Lucho, but the one
thing Patricia couldn't believe was that Marco had been sitting here talking
with Ava.

She knelt to give Ava a hug. "You just imagined that," she told her firmly.
"People do that sometimes, when they really miss someone. Now you pick out
some clothes, and Adrian will drive you to Gabe's. You're going to have fun
tonight, and I promise nothing will happen to you, or us."

"Call us when you get home."

The seriousness in her voice caught Patricia off guard. "Yes, Mom," she
said with a smile.

Lucho appeared in the doorway behind her. "Hey, Pati, you ready?"

Patricia kissed her daughter and stood. "I just need to use the bathroom,"
she said. Inside the bathroom, with the door shut behind her, she studied her
face for signs of Marco. "What did you do?" she whispered.

He whorled below her sternum. :slipped:

"Like, slipped out of me? On purpose?"

He shrugged. :wanted to see her:

"Can you—" Patricia frowned. "Can you do it now?"

:pati:

"Try, Marco."

She could feel him concentrating. One of the vanity bulbs popped and
went dark, just as the patrol car lights had when she'd gone out to find Adrian.
In the dim light, the mirror seemed to shimmer and bend in the place right
beside her, but when she turned to look she could see nothing unusual. She
turned back to the mirror. The shimmering spot waved.

Patricia waved back.

The mirror returned to normal. :hard: Marco told her, quivering with the exertion.

"But you did it." Which meant that... Patricia shook her head. She had no idea what it meant.

:don't tell:

"Seriously?"

Marco whirled nervously. *:not yet no more potions spells making it worse:*

"I have to tell him eventually."

:fine just wait pati please:

Marco was right. So far, Lucho's spells and potions had only succeeded in making things worse. Patricia could tell Lucho no, but Marco was being tugged around like a rag doll with no say in the matter. "I'll wait," she whispered.

She ran the faucet, splashing water gingerly over her face, avoiding the neat bandage the medics had applied to her cheek. She studied her eye— Adrian was right, it would definitely need more ice.

A brief, warm curl of air brushed her cheek, tucking a strand of hair behind her ear. *:so sorry:*

Patricia sighed. "None of this is your fault." She toweled off her hands and opened the door.

Lucho was waiting for her in the kitchen. He frowned, studying her. "Is everything all right?"

"Yes," she lied calmly. "We're fine."

181

Chapter Twenty-Four

SHE WATCHED ADRIAN drive off with Ava, then climbed into the passenger seat of Lucho's new Subaru Outback.

Lucho's phone beeped and he read the message, face grave. "We can go," he said to Patricia. He looked at her, serious. "I didn't say anything about you. You don't want to come, you don't have to."

Patricia wanted to gather her children to herself on her couch, to never leave them, to turn on one of Ava's cartoons and watch Adrian roll his eyes at the cheesy dialogue and ape the characters to make his little sister laugh.

Adrian's taillights disappeared at the end of her street.

"I have to," she said, stomach flipping with nerves.

Lucho shrugged. "OK, then. Marco Polo, you gotta lay low, capisce? Things might look bad in there, you aren't gonna like what you see. Val might be hurt, you understand? You gotta let me handle this my way."

"He understands."

"She knows what's smart for her, she's pretending to be hosting you. She's making it as realistic as possible. What we gotta do, we gotta play cool until we know what's going on."

"Do you think we'll make it out?" Patricia asked quietly, nervously.

Lucho flashed her a smile, but there was no cheer in it, and he didn't answer. He turned the key, and the Outback purred to life.

Patricia fastened her seat belt. "We're ready."

Lucho shot her a glance. "'We'? That tea was supposed to weaken your bond with our Marco Polo here. It coming back?"

"Yes." Patricia adjusted a vent to blow away from her face. "Lucho, what's going on with us? He—"

Marco squirmed frantically. *:not yet wait please pati wait:*

"He what?"

"He's just strong. It sounds like he's stronger than other ghosts."

His face went serious. "*Profe*, I don't know. Nothing went right at any stage of this. Val called Marco with a modified spell. You weren't the target host. I never seen a ghost this strong, or one that communicated so well with its host, and then whatever all this is with a *palero nfumbe*—I don't even want to know all that. What I'm saying is, this has been outta hand since day one, and it's been outta my league since you got slapped in the face by that *firma*."

"Then, you mean..."

"I don't know what the hell to do with you." Lucho shrugged and turned onto Roxbury Street, gunning it to get around a bus. "But even though you're the biggest supernatural problem I've ever seen, your sister's managing to steal the show at the moment."

Patricia searched for a joke in response, even halfhearted, but nothing came out. He was right, and every minute they spent discussing her current situation was time that Chente could find out that Valeria didn't have Marco—and Patricia had no idea what would happen after that.

Patricia pushed herself deeper into her seat. Lucho's radio was playing in the background, the quiet voices of NPR babbling to themselves inaudibly under the thwapping of the windshield wipers, just a hiss and a murmur whenever they stopped at a light. *I have to tell Lucho about what happened with Ava,* she thought to Marco, staring past her reflection in the window at the night: blinding glare of headlights, streetlights glossy on puddles.

:not yet just wait:

For what?

She felt Marco shrug. *:want to know first think I could go:*

Go?

:back:

Go back where?

:when outside you think I could just cross if I wanted:

He thought he could just... cross over? Patricia bit her lip. Could he just leave any time he wanted to, now? He hadn't had any agency this whole time, shuttled around in Patricia's mind, drugged and magicked and shoved around. She may have felt trapped in this, but at least she had a voice that wasn't speaking through someone else. She felt suddenly guilty for taking on the role of his jailor, no matter how inadvertently.

:don't feel bad just:

Just what?

:just sucks:

Patricia smiled weakly. *Understatement of the year.*

:stupid words:

Marco? Patricia wasn't sure how to ask, but since no one ever had, she thought she probably should. *Before, we tried to transfer you to Valeria. Did you want to go?*

He went still, as though considering—or as though simply not wanting to give her the answer. Then, finally, he pulsed weakly in his spot below her breastbone. *:no:*

Patricia felt another stab of guilt. *You don't have to. We'll do whatever you want.*

Marco pulsed again, more fiercely. *:don't know her:*

Marco—

:don't know her don't want to:

That's not true, Patricia thought, but in her mind she knew it was.

If it weren't for Valeria, Marco would still be alive. Patricia would—be fine. She would always be fine. But Marco would still be alive.

:wish I never knew her:

"You don't mean that," Patricia whispered. But she knew it was true, and it broke her heart.

Somewhere in the universe, something had shifted. Something luminous had lost its luster, just a touch, like a landscape painting missing something vital. It was as if she stood on Alki Beach staring at the Seattle skyline, but key buildings were missing, and she couldn't remember which ones—or what it had looked like before.

The night was dark with perils, swaths of gloom cut by blinding knife-flashes of light off puddles, fracturing off the wet cement.

Lucho charged through it, and Patricia wished they could keep driving, follow that trail of streetlights that blazed away from the city, south through darkening hills, just keep driving until the world ended at the shores of the Pacific, lapping in inky blackness at gravelly beaches, sand dunes collapsing cliffs into the violent waves while craggy rocks gnawed like teeth, and leave behind whatever darkness lurked beneath the blinding static of the night.

The ghostly lights of SeaTac airport bloomed beside the highway, a jet hanging low in the sky as it hurled itself off the edge of the runway and over the car, the rush of its engines drowning out the sound of Patricia's thoughts for a moment. She craned her neck to watch it pass overhead. Off to somewhere else, she thought, tourists traveling back home, or locals leaving Seattle for good, off to sunnier skies and unknotted entanglements. Women like Valeria, soaring to parts unknown with murky intentions, leaving behind them a trail of collapsing relationships and bewildered friends wondering what they'd done wrong.

Lucho threaded his way over I-5, took the exit toward Southcenter Mall, but didn't follow the hordes of cars there even now, trying to beat the pre-Christmas rush or catching a movie. He turned north, winding through unfamiliar roads, along a river—the Green River, Patricia thought it might be—meandering beside, its surface a slick of streetlights and its invisible depths pockmarked by the smattering rain. It seemed only fitting to be here, overlooking a rain-swollen river made famous by a serial killer, muddy-black with sediment and God only knew what else from the industry upstream now flowing out into the crystalline Sound. The toxic black vein flowing beneath Seattle's emerald surface.

Lucho cut up into the hills on a twisting, steep road hedged in by looming trees, the only light the dim glow of the city soaking the sky a sickly pewter. He pulled into a driveway. The sign beside it was faded and cracked down the center; it had once read Skyline Cement. Lucho typed a code into the call box. "It's Lucho," he said, and the gate rolled open for them.

They were surrounded by city, Patricia reminded herself, but it didn't feel that way. This was one of those spots never regraded and still overgrown with trees, with thickets too steep to landscape and so left to grow wild. Pockets of impassible wilderness were scattered throughout the city, like the one she and Valeria had escaped into so long ago—earlier this week?—sullied only by English ivy and the occasional lawless homeless encampment.

This wilderness had been claimed by a different sort of lawless set.

Lucho turned off the ignition, and the Outback shuddered into a silence broken only by little ticks of cooling metal and an irregular ping as fat drops of rain loosed themselves from the branches above to splash down on the roof.

"*Profe*, you wanna wait here?" he asked.

Yes, yes, yes, with all her might Patricia wanted to wait here. The idea that she could stay curled promisingly in her ear, a seductive note.

"I go talk to these guys, and I come get you if we need you." Lucho cocked his head at her. "We could do it that way. If you want."

Patricia let that promise linger another warm, weighted moment, then let it fall aside. "You need us."

"I don't think I do. And you don't know shit about what you're getting into."

Patricia met his gaze, her own resolve tight now. Whatever he saw there made Lucho frown. "She's my sister," Patricia said simply. He nodded, once, and with a crack that sounded in the silence like a gunshot, opened his door.

"You just let me do the talking, *profe*," he said. "We're gonna get your sister outta this." He held open the door for Patricia. "And then I'm gonna kill her myself."

Chapter Twenty-Five

WALKING INTO THE grove, Patricia felt something quick and strange slipping across the face of the night. A thin, secretive drizzle blurred the edges between mist and rain. Patricia wondered if Lucho could hear her heart punching against her breastbone, jostling places with Marco, who had gone still as a shadow.

They had seen no one—Patricia had no way of knowing if this was a good or a bad sign. Lucho seemed on edge, but that was to be expected.

What Patricia hadn't expected was that she would feel so light on her own feet, so slippery. The tension that had been winding its way into her stomach for the last few days was no longer binding her in its coils—now it was a spring wound with power, something ready to loose itself and take out whatever had been in her path.

This must be how the mouse trap feels, Patricia thought, holding back a wild, inappropriate giggle.

:pati hold together: Marco shifted nervously in his spot. A cold flush of sobriety; he was right. Patricia was losing the plot.

They'd gone past the shuttered main offices of the cement plant, down a trail behind that was paved with broken cement and slippery with moss and rain—Patricia lost her balance once and her hand shot out to steady herself on the jagged foundations of the office building, came away with palm scuffed and stinging.

Patricia nearly screamed when a floodlight opened up on them. Lucho held up a gnarled hand to shield his eyes, but didn't flinch. "*Buenas noches, muchachos,*" he said pleasantly. "*Soy yo, y la hermana.*" Patricia could see only the silhouette of two men against the blinding light, one lanky, one stout. Both blatantly armed. She wondered if one of them had pulled the trigger to end Javier's life.

"That her?" said the stout one.

"I'm Valeria's sister," said Patricia, tired of being answered for. "I want to see her."

Lucho shot her an annoyed look, but the man ignored her. "Chente wants to see you, *abuelito,*" he said to Lucho. Grandpa. Patricia was surprised at the word, but now she could see the change in Lucho's usually easygoing demeanor. He'd gone stiff-necked and grandfatherly in the last few minutes, rousing memories of the friendly-but-formal, strict-yet-loving old man Patricia remembered from her childhood in Nicaragua. Crisp slacks and a warm, old parchment smell that lingered for hours along with his cologne every time he hugged her good-bye.

The men nodded to Lucho respectfully and escorted them inside. It was a shed that had apparently been used for machinery repairs; it still smelled of diesel, and the cement floor was tie-dyed with engine oil in varying monochromatic shades, a morbid hippie's color scheme. The corners were blurred with dust, giving the room a soft feel, like the first color films, life painted painstakingly, frame by frame, to give it a nostalgic wash.

After the floodlight, it took Patricia's eyes time to adjust. The glow was created by candles, dozens of pillar candles in makeshift sconces throughout the room, guttering on ledges and cascading wax down workbenches. It wasn't the first time candles had been lit here, but the fuzzy dust from the shed's corners hadn't collected on the old wax. It was still bright white and new as a manufactured haunted house.

There were four other people in the room, in the back where the light was brightest. Three stood barefoot: a lanky old black man who stood head and shoulders over Lucho, a fat man in an expensive-looking coat, and a younger man with a gun shoved in his waistband under his track jacket.

Valeria was tied to a chair between them. Her back was to Patricia, her head drooping, a gag tangling through her wild hair. It was impossible to tell if she was injured. Marco whirled once, then went still. She could feel his fury humming just below her sternum, but it was controlled now, as patient as an owl at hunt. We wait. The thought could have been either of theirs.

Their arrival sent a shudder through the candles—a draft, Patricia thought; it swirled around the room fast as a blink, leaving the candles closest to Patricia snuffed out and smoking.

The fat man turned to study them. "*Abuelito*," he said to Lucho. The cigarette-rasped voice from the parking lot, from the cemetery. Chente. "There's someone here I've been wanting you to meet. Then maybe you can help us with our little Valium problem. Seems she's got a ghost she don't want us to find."

So Valeria was still alive—she had to be if they were still trying to get Marco out of her. Patricia felt a thrill of hope. She stepped around Lucho to see her sister, but did not dare approach. Valeria's eyes were wide with fear, but she seemed uninjured except for a scrape on her cheek and bloodied knuckles. Patricia took a deep, full breath to calm both herself and Marco.

The room smelled metallic, earthy, like fear and sweet-sour wine blended with cigar smoke. From her new vantage point, she could see now what the group was gathered around.

On a low platform built of bricks and earth sat a small cauldron, a row of evenly cut sticks running around its mouth to contain a collection of unidentifiable objects within. The whole cauldron was glossy and bright; a dark, brassy pool soaked slowly into the earth around it. Like engine oil, that same viscosity, but Patricia knew from the smell that it wasn't oil. Her heart skipped a beat, then she realized with relief that a black rooster lay at the cauldron's pegged feet, its head torn off.

An enormous conch shell plastered with torn feathers protruded from the center of the cauldron, the mouth of the shell sealed with a black wax that had an uneven hue, like it had been mixed with dirt. Or blood. Something glittered in the center of the wax: a shard of mirror that stared at her like an eye from the depths of the conch shell.

It winked, and the candles flickered again in a vast swath, shuddering out around Patricia. Patricia clutched her head as a headache split through her skull. She dropped to her knees with a cry.

The voice she'd first heard that night at Loretta's echoed through her thoughts: invading, angry, curious, triumphant.

Ahhhh, it sighed. *Hello, Marco.*

Patricia opened her eyes and the room was empty. Lucho was gone. The old priest and Chente and the guard were gone. Valeria was gone, the chair she'd been tied to overturned in the corner. Fear spiked through Patricia's heart, and she was about to cry out her sister's name when sense stopped her. She didn't know where they were or what was going on, and she needed to figure that out before she started screaming.

Marco?

:here:

He was wound tight inside her, but his voice didn't come from within. It echoed faintly off the distant walls. Patricia whipped around, expecting to see him standing there with a sheepish smile and hands in his pockets.

She saw no one.

The little altar was still there, the earthy smell mingling with pungent grease and candle smoke. Patricia took a step closer, and the aroma got stronger, dense and humid and secret, like the Managua of her childhood after heavy rains, like dirt floors and flooded root cellars, hollow, dark places burrowed into the earth. Someone had relit all the candles.

She heard a child's laughter behind her.

Slowly, she turned around.

The boy looked like Gabe had in elementary school, all ungainly angles and unruly hair after an awkward growth spurt—none of Adrian's already compact athleticism. He sat on the ground, feet tucked close and knees drawn up, not protectively, just comfortably. His elbows hooked around his legs, and one hand was clasped loosely around the other wrist. Brown hair and brown eyes, and a perfect Cupid's bow mouth drawn into a frown. He tilted his head to look at her.

Patricia forced herself to step forward two paces and sit down in front of the boy, mimicking his pose. Ankles crossed, knees pulled up. Her heart thrashed against her rib cage. She took a shaky breath. "What's your name?" she asked.

The boy frowned at her. "I want to talk to Marco."

"Why?"

"Marco?"

Marco shifted, tentative. *:tell I'm here:*

Patricia puzzled at that, grasping for what to do next. Was it a command? A plea? Had he meant to say "don't"?

Before she could say anything, the boy rolled his eyes. "I know you're here," he said. "Obviously."

:what want:

"How did you get in her?"

:long story:

Patricia's mind raced. She was speaking with the ghost from Chente's altar. The child ghost in the iron pot. Was this real? She couldn't hear anything else around them. Maybe they weren't in the same room, from real life, after all. Maybe she was dreaming. "What's your name?" asked Patricia.

The boy blinked coolly at her, a thousand-year-old expression on his young face.

"My name's Patricia," she said. "And I have a little girl that's just about your age." That blank expression didn't change. "What's your name?"

"How is Marco in you?" the boy asked again.

"Why are you curious about Marco?"

"He moved me. You're not supposed to do that."

How did one talk to a ghost child? Patricia went for the same way she'd talk to any other child. "Did that make you angry?"

A fierce little shrug. The answer was yes.

"Is this where you live?"

Another shrug. "It's OK."

Patricia looked around. She certainly wouldn't call the dank room OK.

"Do you ever get to go outside?" she asked.

That fierce look kindled once more in his eyes. "Will you take me?"

Warning bells clanged in Patricia's mind. She realized she had no idea what the boy was asking, what it would entail, and whether or not she would survive it. She tried to shift the conversation onto safer ground, but every topic she could think of seemed slippery and perilous, wreathed with double meanings that she had no way of guessing at.

"Where are you from?" she asked instead.

Another shrug, just as fierce. The boy wasn't interested in talking about it —or he didn't know. That angry petulance in lieu of an answer: fear. Patricia tried another tactic.

"How long have you been here?"

The boy got to his feet, one swift, jaguar-like move that belied his ungainly form. Patricia checked herself. She'd been seeing clumsy Gabe there in his awkward angles, but this boy was no human child, not anymore. She had no idea what he was capable of.

He crossed by the iron pot on the altar, not giving it a second look, and knelt down to pick something up off the floor. Patricia shifted but didn't stand, ready to jump to her feet if she needed to. He turned back to her, hands cupped around a spider. "Here," he said, though he didn't try to give it to her. "They get in, sometimes."

:what want:

The boy looked directly at Patricia for the first time, his gaze penetrating and cold. "I want to go outside." He set the spider inside the mouth of the iron pot; it skittered up the side, lost its purchase and fell. It tried again. "I want to go outside like you do."

Patricia frowned. "Like I do?"

"Shut up, I'm talking to Marco."

An adult response froze on Patricia's tongue, petrified there by the incredible venom in that small, flute-thin voice.

:we don't talk to adults like that:

The boy sneered. "You think I'm just a kid? You're all the same. Everyone thinks I'm just a kid, and my parents—" He broke off with a frown. Patricia wondered what he was remembering, or not remembering. "How did you get in her?" he demanded instead.

"We came with Lucho," said Patricia, finally finding her voice.

"No. No! Her. How did *Marco* get in *her*."

:called I was they called: Marco shifted uncomfortably. :didn't want:

Patricia frowned. She remembered Valeria saying that she'd asked Marco, that he wanted to come back. Marco twisted unhappily. A movement caught Patricia's eye: the spider trying and failing to climb out of the mouth of the pot. It reared back on its hind legs, stretching miserably for the rim, tumbling back down.

The boy frowned. "Why wouldn't you want that? You get a new body, You can do whatever you want."

:not my body:

"It could be." The boy's haughty gaze raked down Patricia, appraising. "Haven't you tried?"

"Now listen to me—"

"I said shut up!" the boy screamed at her, fists clenched and eyes blazing. "I don't want to talk to you."

"I don't care how old you are, or who you think you are, we—"

"You're stupid, you b—"

"Don't talk like that to anyone, not adults, not—"

:take you outside or no:

The boy stopped screaming at her midsentence, gaze focused intently just behind her. Patricia felt something brush her arm; the hair raised there, but she was too afraid to turn away from the boy to look. She slipped her hand into her pocket to feel her agate smooth against her fingertips. For a moment, the sulphur of the guttering candles smelled like sun-baked kelp and salt breeze.

"You'll take me," the boy said quietly, glaring at the spot behind Patricia.

:not with that attitude:

"You think you can control me?"

:don't think anything don't care yelling like that:

Fury flushed the boy's unnaturally pale face. "You think you can control me?" He shouted it now, grabbing the chair Valeria had been tied in and bashing it against the cauldron. The cauldron didn't budge, though the contents shifted and the conch shell toppled, trapping the struggling spider underneath. Patricia could see one leg trembling.

"No one can control me!" He flung the chair past Patricia, where Marco had been. It shattered against the wall.

"That man who put me in that stupid bucket, he thought he could control me," the boy said, eyes flickering in the candlelight. "And my parents, always 'Boy, hey Max, he—'" He blinked, caught for a second by what he'd said. Then he screamed in fury and launched himself at her.

Patricia scrambled to her feet, not sure what would happen if he touched her. He flew past her and caught himself quick as a cat, coiling for another spring. She tried to dodge, but he had her cornered. He reached toward her with both hands, leering.

Pati, Pati—

She heard her name being called, once, twice, and then she closed her eyes—this was a dream, she knew it.

She opened them to see the boy.

He grabbed both her wrists in his hands, wrenching her toward him with a grip so much stronger than she had expected. He grinned, eyes blank and yellow. Marco shrieked as he roiled within, dissolving from her. She could feel him draining.

With a scream of agony, Patricia pulled on the faded memory of a self-defense class the women's group at her church had done, drove her forearms out and around from the elbows, wrenching free of his grip. The boy stumbled forward with a hiss, and Patricia slipped back, stars in her eyes as the back of her head smacked into a wall too close to her.

She got her hand around the agate again as she kicked back against the boy, catching him in the gut. He doubled over, his yowl of pain the thin cry of a seagull dampened by the crash of waves, and bright salt spray stung Patricia's face—

She opened her eyes to see Lucho, frowning. He gripped her arms. "Pati, you OK? I thought you were gonna faint for a second."

Patricia's heart was racing. *Marco?*

:here:

She took a deep breath. "How long was I out?"

Lucho looked puzzled. "You weren't. You just looked dizzy and I caught you. I said your name a couple of times, and you came back. You OK?"

She nodded. At the front of the room, the iron pot glistened dark with blood. Valeria whimpered.

Chente gave Patricia a dismissive look, then turned back to Lucho. "Bitch can't handle herself, you shoulda left her at home, *abuelito*." He looked back at Valeria. "Now. Where were we?"

Chapter Twenty-Six

"Your lovely assistant has been causing us troubles," Chente said with a nod at Valeria's back. Patricia could see her shoulders moving jerkily in rhythm with her breathing.

Lucho nodded tensely. "Raising Marco was a stupid thing to do, but our Val isn't always very bright. Shouldn't have been your problem, though." His gaze flicked to the dark, beanpole-thin man, who unfurled himself from his crouch near the cauldron like a praying mantis, his movements deliberate, giving the impression not of slowness, but rather of someone trying hard not to startle people by moving too quickly. Alien movements that hid tremendous speed and grace.

"*Abuelito*, I'd like you to meet the Tata Nganga Enrique. Lucho here is our resurrectionist."

The black man nodded his head slowly, and Lucho gave him a sharp nod in return, both carrying the same level of wariness and respect. "*Encantado*," said Lucho, with a lift of his eyebrow and a tone that said he was definitely less than enchanted by this encounter.

"Likewise," said Enrique. His voice was low and soft, scarred by cigar smoke and rumbling through Patricia like a distant train. He glanced at her briefly, then returned his attention to Lucho. Marco shivered.

"You're old friends, then, huh?"

Enrique spared the briefest of glances at Chente, dismissing him. "I am also a contractor, Resurrectionist. I was asked to help in this... situation."

"So Val raised her boyfriend's ghost like an idiot," said Lucho. "And now she's tied up in front of a *prenda* with chicken sacrifices and candles. I think I missed the part of the movie where we called in the witch doctor. No offense, man," he said to Enrique. "I just wanna know what's going on."

Enrique smiled, gracious as an annoyed king who's decided not to behead someone just yet. "None taken. We walk different paths, you and I."

Lucho pursed his lips. "Yep." He glanced back and forth between Chente and the priest, as though trying to decide who he should focus his questions on. "So what's Marco got to do with any of this?" he asked generally to the room, no decision made.

It was Enrique who answered. "He was an enemy of Lucero Mundo," he said, tilting his chin to the cauldron for a moment before locking his gaze back with Lucho's. The cauldron was as it had been before Patricia's... vision, or dream. She wasn't sure what to call it. Candlelight glanced off the glistening pools of blood inside it, tracing gleaming rivulets that were still drying glossy on the outside. The motion of the candlelight made it seem alive, malevolent, dancing and shifting even when she looked straight at it.

She was standing so she couldn't see the mirror—or so it couldn't see her, maybe—but she still felt the haughty gaze of the little boy.

"You ever meet Marco?" Lucho said. "He was maybe the enemy of mosquitoes. Or the environment, because of all those muscle cars he liked. He was a good kid."

"He moved the *nfumbe*," said Enrique.

"You le—" Patricia felt Marco clamp down on her vocal cords before another word came out. She clenched her fist around the agate and his grip released instantly, but she was grateful for his intervention. She'd been about to say You left the *nfumbe* in a car!—but she wasn't supposed to know that. Her knees went watery as she realized how close she'd come to giving them away. "What's an *nfumbe*?" she asked instead.

"It's the spirit of the dead," answered Lucho, sparing her a glare and then returning his attention to Enrique. "The Palo priest strikes a pact to care for it, and the spirit acts as the priest's medium to converse with the dead."

"The hand of the living reaching out for the hand of the dead," said

Enrique with a grim smile. "Both pulling each other to a higher plane. You know your Palo."

"I have friends," said Lucho. "Don't tell them I been paying attention, though. They'll think they're converting me."

The child's bones Marco had moved, Patricia understood, now nestled deep within the cauldron.

"Marco moved the *nfumbe* without its permission," said Enrique, and for one terrified moment Patricia was sure he'd overheard her thoughts. If Marco spoke to her, would it echo through the room like it had in the vision? Marco shifted within her in acknowledgment. He was afraid of that, too.

"And so you killed him?" Lucho asked conversationally, but there were cords of steel beneath the words.

"Lucero commanded it," said Chente, and the tall priest shot him a disturbed look that Chente missed and Patricia didn't understand.

Valeria shifted in her bonds, and the entire focus of the room moved to her. "What do you want with my apprentice?" said Lucho. "She's no one's enemy except her own."

"She has her own *nfumbe* hosted inside," said the priest. "Lucero wants to meet him." His nostrils flared. "And we were just in the midst of introducing them." He nodded to the armed young man, who pulled out his gun and trained it on Lucho and Patricia. "You're welcome to watch if you don't make any noise."

"Do you need help?" Lucho asked. "With the ghost. It's my style of magic put it in. I don't know how much experience you have getting them out of people, but I do it for a living."

"Stay out of this, *abuelito*," said Chente, but the old priest only regarded Lucho quietly, then nodded.

"I would welcome your expertise," he said. Lucho stepped forward, holding up a hand for Patricia to stay back. She and the armed thug stood together in the back of the room; his gun hand shook, and she realized he looked as nervous as she felt.

Enrique stopped Lucho before he joined the circle, grabbing first one hand, then the other, to mark with chalk. He scrawled symbols on Lucho's forehead, too, and had him take off his shoes and socks to mark his bare feet. He didn't explain, and Lucho didn't protest.

Lucho stepped up beside Valeria, bending quickly to say something to her. Seemingly satisfied that she was unhurt, he straightened. "The way we do things, the ghost lives in the host, or he goes back to his afterlife in a different plane. The host stands on the border between planes, she makes herself the doorway for the ghost to come through into this world, but he can't set foot inside, he can only stand in the frame. Strong ghosts can speak more clearly, but weak ones only give impressions to their hosts."

He lay a hand on Valeria's shoulder. "Marco is an unusually strong ghost," he said. "I wondered why, until I learned his death was unnatural. You worked his death, so it's possible you could work him out of Val. But if your Lucero only wants to meet him, I think we should do it our way."

Enrique was humming under his breath, a low, chanting tune that deepened into song, though Patricia didn't recognize the language.

Patricia wondered if he was planning to answer Lucho, or if he would just ignore Lucho's suggestion. He dropped into a squat before the altar, drawing a small gourd from near the base and sipping from it. He blew the liquid over the cauldron, a fine mist that eddied in the candlelight. He relit a stubby cigar and tapped the ash onto the cement floor, then inverted it, placing its glowing end in his mouth. Blowing through the cigar, he sent out a plume of smoke that filled the cauldron and poured out its mouth like dry ice.

This done, he sat back on his heels, head bowed as though studying what he saw there in the smoke. His shoulder blades knifed through the thin material of his T-shirt. No one moved until the last of the smoke had dissipated.

Enrique began to chant again, reaching below his wooden stool for a little clay bowl filled with water. From its depths he scooped out four shells, the same type that Isidro had thrown at Lucho's house.

"What does Lucero want of Marco?" asked Lucho again, and the priest gave him a look under hooded eyes.

"What does any *prenda* want? It wants to grow. It wants to become more, to be greater. A young *prenda*, well." He straightened to his full height, and pulled a knife from the waistband of his pants. "The dead tell me that if Marco is possessing this woman, he is in her blood."

Patricia gasped, and the guard shot her a look that, along with his gun, kept her frozen firmly in place. Lucho stepped forward so he was between Valeria and the priest. "Nope," he said simply.

"You are here to help," said Enrique, "but this is not a discussion." He bowed his head in respect. "I have no intention of harming this woman, Resurrectionist."

Lucho didn't move. "That's an awfully sharp knife."

"For making very precise cuts," answered Enrique. The blade flashed in the candlelight. "In being drawn out of her, her blood becomes a version of the dead, to be filtered through them, and known by them. Lucero will know her, and Marco if he is truly in her." He stepped past Lucho, who was watching him with steel in his gaze.

"And what will happen if your Lucero tastes my apprentice's blood?" asked Lucho. "I'm not sure I'm so comfortable with that. She's already been linked with me."

"Through blood?" Lucho shook his head and the priest raised a skeptical eyebrow. "Well," Enrique said. And that was all. He paused, knife in hand. It lingered over Valeria's forearm, catching the light of the candles and the warm mahogany glow of Valeria's flesh, and for a moment there was an unexpected likeness between the sharpened steel and soft flesh. Patricia's breath caught.

Enrique tilted his head as though listening, one half of his face in shadow, the other catching the light of the candles on his softly lined cheeks. Patricia saw Valeria tense as the knife's edge rested on her forearm, but she made no motion.

"How do you deal with spirit possession?" Enrique asked Lucho, a note of curiosity in his voice. With a dancer's grace he rocked back to squat over his thick, calloused heels, the knife in one hand, dangling from his knee with the tip pointing at the ground. Patricia expected to see blood dripping there, but the blade was clean. Valeria's shoulders relaxed, slightly.

"I wouldn't call this spirit possession," said Lucho. "A spirit possession is when someone has been taken by a ghost unwillingly. Valeria is a host."

"And should the dead one inside her leave, he would join Kalunga. The sea of the dead."

Lucho shrugged. "Sure," he said skeptically. "I mean, I have no idea. You got me, güey."

Patricia winced at the cavalier attitude, but the old priest just smiled.

"You guys gonna get on with things? Or just talk philosophy all night?" Chente was looking equal parts anxious and angry. Enrique shot him a murderous glare, which Chente caught this time. "I ain't got all night," Chente snapped.

"I believe this situation is different than I was led to believe," said Enrique, and Patricia frowned. Led to believe? Had he not made the altar in the first place?

"Look, Chente, what are you trying to do?" Lucho asked. "You wanna talk to Marco, you know how to do that with a host."

Chente's nostrils flared. "Lucero wants to talk to Marco."

"So let him talk," Lucho said. Enrique gave him a sharp look. "Look, all I know is you're dabbling in something serious, and I'd guess you don't know the first thing about what you're doing." He cocked his head to Enrique. "Not you, güey, you look like you know your shit for sure. Just, Chente, I been with you for how long? And you got any supernatural problems, you been coming to me. And now?" He waved a hand toward the cauldron. "What are you doing?"

"We're not talking about ghosts anymore, *abuelito*. I got a ghost problem, I know you can help me. But now we're talking about fate. Can you help me with that?"

"Fate," said Lucho quietly.

"Fate. That's why I built a Lucero Mundo. To unblock paths and guard crossroads. Gets you unstuck and moving. Keeps you out of trouble."

Lucho raised an eyebrow. "*You* built?"

"I had it built," said Chente impatiently.

A stony look from Enrique. It hadn't been built by him, then. Patricia was oddly pleased by this. He didn't seem the sort to leave his skeletons hanging out in cars.

Enrique met the gang leader's gaze with disdain. "I will consult the dead before we go any further." Chente let out an exasperated sigh, but Enrique just returned to his bench and pulled out his shells. "Unlike some, I'm not in the habit of getting myself killed by angry *ngangas.*"

Patricia remembered what the boy from her vision had said: "That man who put me in that stupid bucket, he thought he could control me."

And what had happened to that man?

Enrique rattled the shells in his fist, then tossed them before the altar with a flick of his lanky wrist. He frowned. He pursed his lips at them, tried another chant, blew more cigar smoke. He threw them again.

Each shell fell face down.

"*Muerte parado,*" he whispered. The dead at a stop. He looked up sharply. "*¿Quién quiere hablar?*"

Who wants to speak?

The room was silent but for the patter of rain on the roof. It had picked up, and Patricia could hear wet branches slapping against the roof. The armed guard beside her had tucked his gun back into his waistband, and his hand was there now, arm flexed and eyes searching the room. Chente frowned at the cauldron.

Lucho stepped closer to Valeria, a protective hand on her shoulder. Valeria's spine straightened, either because of Lucho, or because of the electric, terrifying air that now crackled through the room. Patricia could feel it, too, a wild and careless spirit, like the wind that threatened to pull you off a cliff and into the wild Pacific during a storm, like the first scent of a fire that would consume your home.

Patricia felt the hair rise on the nape of her neck, as though someone was standing too close behind her, the faintest of breaths on the back of her neck, like Joe would before he would lean in to kiss—

Patricia remembered to breathe.

"*¿Quién quiere hablar?*" Enrique said again, quietly this time, respectfully.

"I want to," said Marco, and a chill, sharp as a needle, pierced Patricia's spine. She stumbled, catching herself on the ledge lined with candles. Wax poured over her hand as one knocked over. She barely felt it.

She clapped her unburned hand over her mouth, but the words hadn't come from her, and they weren't echoing inside her head. The armed guard beside her was ashen, staring at the doorway. Patricia turned to look.

Marco stood there, flickering like a bad signal sometimes to full strength, sometimes barely visible. He gave her a faint smile. "I've got something to say."

Chapter Twenty-Seven

CHENTE LET OUT a string of profanity. The priest unfurled himself to his full height and stood there like a warrior about to go into battle. Lucho turned so he could see Marco, but didn't put his back to the altar.

Valeria wrenched herself against her bonds to turn the chair, the wooden legs scraping against the cement floor. Her eyes were wide, with fear or grief, Patricia couldn't tell. Her jaw worked against the gag, but no sound came out.

"Marco?"

Patricia realized she was the one who said it. Enrique raised an eyebrow—he hadn't known to recognize Marco—and the armed guard beside her looked like he was about to throw up.

"I'm not a pawn in your game," Marco said to the room at large. "You can't call me up and tug me around, just to see what happens. You can tell that to your bratty little boy. I can't tell if he can hear me."

Patricia could feel the cauldron seething at her, and when she looked closely she thought she could see the spider from her vision, struggling to escape. She blinked, and nothing there moved. Where was the little boy? Max?

She hadn't realized she'd said it aloud until everyone looked at her. She straightened, mortified.

"What little boy?" asked Lucho, exchanging a glance with Enrique.

"The—" She looked back at the doorway, but Marco was gone. What had just happened? Was it another of the strange visions, another—she looked around, and realized that everything was the same as it had been. There was no Marco standing in the doorway, just as there had been no little boy. Good Lord, she was going crazy, wasn't she?

Patricia peeled wax off her scalded hand while everyone stared at her.

"Pati, you need to wait in the car?" Lucho asked.

"No," she said.

Lucho's expression hardened. "Pati—"

She swallowed back fear. "*Marco quiere hablar,*" she said, looking at Enrique. "He's the one that wants to speak to your Lucero."

Valeria let out a scream of frustration against the gag.

"Fuck," said Chente, staring wide-eyed at Patricia.

Enrique just smiled. "And what does your Marco want to say to my Lucero?" he asked.

In the cauldron, the shard of mirror glinted like a wink. Patricia closed her eyes to focus on listening. Marco purred inside her.

"He wants to say that he understands Lucero is angry, and he apologizes for any part he played in disturbing his bones. He didn't mean it maliciously." She took a step forward, and felt more than saw the armed guard move at her side. "And he wants to say that for his part, he's not angry at what happened." She took another step forward, laid her hand gently on her sister's shoulder. "At anyone."

She felt Valeria shivering beneath her touch.

:and what more sonovbitch want:

"And he'd like to know, now that Lucero has taken his life and his family, what else he wants with us."

Enrique nodded slowly, then dropped into a squat before the altar and began to hum. Patricia felt her pulse start to pick up with the rhythm. She squeezed Valeria's shoulder, and her sister tilted her head to press her cheek into her hand.

Enrique must have been asking Lucero the question. Patricia could sense it in the way he bobbed his head with the chanting, a serpentine motion at once quizzical and rhythmic. Frowning, Enrique took sips from the gourd beside him, aspirating the liquid over the cauldron. Patricia's eyes began to water, and Lucho coughed as the heat of the liquid hit the air, like the time the cap had come off the bottle of white pepper when Joe was cooking and the entire contents fell into the hot frying pan.

The old priest turned to his coconut shells once more, singing to them, casting them, and frowning at the results. Playing twenty questions with the dead, Patricia started to realize, as she caught hints of Spanish in with words from other languages, phrases like "Do you want?" and "What do you need?"

Patricia flinched at the scream of anguish that split the room, looking first to her sister. No one else had moved, though Lucho gave her a concerned look at the way she'd jumped. Enrique was still murmuring over the shells.

The scream came again, resolving into the wail of a petulant child who hasn't gotten what he wanted. In the depths of the cauldron, the mirror shard shone bright.

Can't even talk to him, yesnoyesno, it's a dumb game. Patricia pressed her hands to her temples as the words split through her skull.

"Pati?" She could feel Lucho's calloused hand on her elbow. Enrique had stopped his muttering.

:*what want*:

The voice laughed. *I want what you have. I want a host. Get out and see the world again.*

:*still trapped*:

Really? You think you're trapped? Let's trade and you can see how it feels.

Patricia saw a glimpse of movement, one rush of shadow coalescing briefly into the shape of an outstretched hand. She gasped and jumped back, crashing into Lucho. He stumbled, caught her. "Pati, what's happening."

"The boy," she said. "He's in my head."

Enrique's eyes went wide. "Lucero Mundo is speaking to you?" he asked, sounding equal parts intrigued and jealous. *There's your host,* Patricia thought to the boy, but she wasn't sure if he was still around to listen.

"He wants me. He wants a host, like Marco has," she said. "I think that's what this whole thing is about. He saw that Marco was called back into a host, and that he can go out in the world. That's what Lucero wants. To go out in the world." She closed her eyes, listening for him. "That's what he told me earlier."

"Earlier?"

"When I almost fainted when we came in. He was talking to me—it was like a vision, with everyone else gone from the room. He asked me to take him outside."

Enrique looked furious. He turned to Chente. "You've created a monstrous thing," he said. "An *nfumbe* that answers to no one, without the proper bonds and respect it should have had between *prenda* and *tata nganga*. Whoever built this prenda for you was a fool who got himself killed, and you were a fool to trust him."

Blotches of color appeared on Chente's cheeks, and Patricia took a step away from him. What would Enrique gain by provoking the gang leader like that?

"And was I a fool to hire you?" Chente growled.

"I was a fool to say yes," spat Enrique. "But would I sit by and let arrogant braggarts make a mockery of my practice? No. You're worse even than this one," he said, jabbing a finger at Valeria. "She brings back her boyfriend because she's sad. You disturb the dead without knowledge because you want to get richer and fatter."

Chente let out a string of Spanish swear words, reaching inside his jacket and pulling out a handgun. The guard beside Patricia tugged his own gun out of the waistband of his pants. Chente leveled his weapon on Enrique. "You wanna tell me who you're working for right now?"

Lucho raised his hands. "Hey, hey," he said. "We're all cool here, we just need to talk this through. Chente—"

He stopped midsentence as Chente swung his weapon straight at Lucho's chest. "*Abuelito.* You wanna tell this *pendejo* who he works for? And, by the way, who you work for?" He paused, gun steady and chest heaving with anger. Slowly, he let his arm drop until the weapon was aimed at the back of Valeria's head. "And who our little Valium works for?"

He considered her a moment. "She doesn't have Marco shoved up inside her anyway, does she?" he said contemplatively. A sharp click split the silence as he cocked the gun.

"No!" screamed Patricia, launching herself at him before she even thought what she was doing. She slammed against the bigger man's side, feeling only solid muscle beneath the suit. She screamed as he flung her back, heard a gunshot go off—one? two?—and her body slammed against the floor.

She looked up to see Enrique crouched with catlike grace near the cauldron, and Lucho scrabbling with Chente as he tackled the bigger, younger man, his old body surprisingly strong.

The armed guard was on the floor, his arm bent at a horrible angle behind him, his weapon spinning away. Patricia hadn't seen what happened, but she could see the look of terror on the man's face, and the faintest of shimmers in the air. "Marco?" she asked.

:valeria: was all he said.

Valeria was slumped against her bonds, deep, rich blood blooming from the back of her blouse.

The angle of the bullet had spattered blood in front of her, and Patricia could see droplets of it glistening fresh on the cauldron. The candles around the room began to sputter. A warm, satisfied thrumming began low and soft from the center of the room. "Enrique?" she called, and the old priest, who had been helping Lucho with Chente, looked up. Not at Valeria, but at the cauldron, eyes wide.

With a deft gesture he clocked Chente in the temple with his own gun, and the fat man collapsed. Enrique hurried back to the cauldron. "Lucero is feasting on human blood," he murmured. "This may be very, very dangerous."

He relit his cigar and puffed at it a moment, handing Patricia the ceremonial knife. He mimed a sawing motion at his wrist. She looked at him in horror, and he took the cigar from his lips to blow smoke over the altar. "*Suéltala, pues,*" he barked impatiently.

Free her. Relieved, Patricia cut Valeria's bonds, the ceremonial knife sliding easily through the rope. Lucho was there at her side, helping to steady Valeria in the chair. "Let's get her back," he said, and together they dragged her away from the cauldron.

Valeria was breathing in shallow, racking breaths that each pumped more blood out of the wound. The front of her shirt was soaked in it. Patricia tore off her jacket and packed it over the wound, pressing hard. "Call 911," she said to Lucho, who already had his phone out of his pocket.

Behind them, Patricia could hear Enrique singing, strength in his voice. Chente was lying motionless. The armed thug was gone, having run while Patricia was focused on her sister.

Valeria gasped for another breath. "Pati, I'm so sorry. Tell, tell Marco—" She let out a cry of pain, but it was weak. Patricia's blood chilled.

Patricia pressed her jacket harder against the wound. "You can't die, Val. We need you." *And Marco may not be ready to see you,* Patricia thought, but did not say. She couldn't feel him now, and she didn't try to search for him. She could hear Lucho behind her, giving what sounded like directions over the phone.

"We have to get her up to the parking lot," he hissed to Patricia. "We can't have them here." He looked past her, to where Enrique was working, sweat beading off his brow as though in a battle of wills.

The old priest gritted his teeth, wreathed in cigar smoke and song. He glanced over his shoulder to see them watching. "Go," he snapped. "I'll make sure she's safe." But then he cried out, arching back as though seized from behind, his spine torsioned unnaturally. His jaw worked soundlessly as he tried to speak.

Valeria moaned, eyelids fluttering. Patricia could hear the faintest of laughs, a child's self-satisfied giggle.

"Max!" Patricia shouted. She dug her hand into her pocket, curling her fingers around the agate. Whatever she believed it could or couldn't do, having it in her hand still gave her the feeling of being centered and protected. "Max, this isn't a game. You let them go right now, or so help me I'll—"

A gust of wind blew open the door, sweeping around the room to extinguish all the candles at once. You'll what? said a knife-sharp voice.

In the pitch black, Patricia could see only the bluish glow of Lucho's iPhone screen, illuminating his face in a ghastly halo. "What the hell, Pati, I—"

The light went out.

All was silent.

Chapter Twenty-Eight

THE ONLY SOUND was faint rain. Patricia could feel warm blood seeping through her coat, sticky on her hands. Enrique's screams of anguish had vanished with the light, and even the storm raging outside seemed to have lulled for the moment.

"Lucho?" she called.

He didn't answer.

Patricia fumbled in her pocket for her phone, thumbing on the screen as a flashlight. Behind her, footsteps sounded slow and steady. "Hello?" she called, turning to shine her phone's light, heart racing. She kept her other hand pressing hard to stop her sister's bleeding.

She could see nothing in the darkness, just the dull gloom of grease-stained cement, the room's ceiling too far above to see, the chair Valeria had been tied to tipped once more in the corner. Enrique and Lucho were gone.

"Is this how you do it?" a young voice asked over her shoulder. Patricia whirled back to see the boy sitting beside her sister's head, liquid brown eyes glinting gold in the light of her phone just before the screen winked into energy-saving mode. She thumbed it back on.

The boy reached out to touch Valeria's cheek, where blood had been splattered. He smeared his finger through it and lifted it to contemplate a moment. "Is this how Marco got in you?" he asked, and brought the finger to his lips.

"No!" Patricia shouted. She dropped her phone, clattering dark to the ground, to catch the boy's wrist. She felt cold flesh, brittle bones, then nothing but smoke as his wrist disappeared from her grasp and she tumbled forward across Valeria's body.

She checked the pressure on her sister's wound, but blood didn't appear to still be coming out. She fumbled with her free hand for Valeria's neck. The flesh was warm, but she couldn't feel a pulse. This is a dream, she told herself. This is—

"You think you're just dreaming me?" the boy said. "You're as stupid as all of them, as that man who first made me." In the darkness, Patricia couldn't tell where his voice was coming from.

"What happened to him?" she asked.

"Died, I guess."

"You guess?"

"I think he did something wrong."

"What makes you think that?"

The boy didn't answer at first. "I didn't really mean to do anything to him," he said after a moment. "But I don't think he was very smart." His voice was swirling around the room now, like he was pacing, but impossibly fast. Patricia's fingers finally brushed against her fallen phone. She thumbed at the screen.

Nothing happened.

Panic rising, she hit the button again—on the third time the screen lit up and revealed the boy's face, only inches from her own.

Patricia screamed and jerked backward, the phone falling from her hand and landing this time with a sickening crunch that could only mean it was done. The boy laughed.

One by one, candles began to bloom in the darkness. The boy was sitting back by Valeria's head, the corner of his Cupid's bow mouth smeared with blood.

"What are you doing?" Patricia asked.

He shrugged. "Trying."

"Trying to get Valeria to host you?" Patricia fought down a wave of panic. That couldn't work, could it?

He frowned. "I don't feel anything."

Was that good? "Well, for the record, that's not how Marco got in me." Where was he?

:here beach:

She looked up at the boy, but he didn't react to Marco's voice. Beach? She turned back to the boy. "Max, do you understand that if I don't get my sister help, she could die?" Patricia tried to keep her voice level, but failed at the end.

The boy just shrugged. He daubed his finger in blood once more and licked it off. "She doesn't have much left."

"Blood?"

"Time. How did Marco get in you?"

Patricia's heart caught in her throat, and she reached again for her sister's pulse. She still felt nothing, but she told herself again, this was a dream, just a vision. Just a flash in time so brief it might pass in the blink of an eye. She prayed she was right.

The boy sighed impatiently. "How did Marco get in you?" he asked again.

"She called him back," Patricia said. "She did a spell of some sort."

The boy looked worried for a moment. "Can only she do this?"

Patricia considered lying, but the moment the thought crossed her mind the boy just rolled his eyes. "I can *hear* you," he said with irritation. "The old man can, can't he? Not the cigar guy, he doesn't know how. But the one you came with." Patricia nodded. "Then ask him."

"Ask him what?"

"To put me in you."

"I can only host one ghost at a time," she said, though she had no idea if that was true.

"What about her?" He poked his finger into a pool of Valeria's blood once more.

"Stop that."

"Can't she host me?"

"Not if she's dead."

The boy considered that for a moment. "I don't want the cigar man," he said. "Or the fat man."

"Then will you help me get her out of here?"

The boy frowned. "Won't you just leave, though?" Patricia slipped her free hand around the agate. She caught a whiff of salt breeze; she looked up, and so did the boy. He sprang to his feet. "You'll just leave, I know you will. I can't trust you!"

"I can't promise that my sister will host you."

"It doesn't seem hard. You're not even that smart."

"Now, listen, young man. That's not—"

:pati beach:

The candles guttered out for a brief moment, then flickered back on to reveal Marco sitting on the other side of Valeria. He gave Patricia a flash of a smile, then leaned over Valeria to brush her hair off her face. He kissed her forehead gently, bent to whisper something in her ear. Patricia saw his lips moving but couldn't hear what he was saying, an odd feeling after having him invading her head for so many days. She looked away, feeling like a voyeur.

The boy watched them impassively.

From somewhere far away she heard the sound of crashing waves, and she gripped the agate harder, remembering. Sand in between her toes, feet plunged into waves so cold her bones ached, but with life, life so free and razor sharp like the tide pool rocks slicing into palms of hands as she reached a tentative finger to stroke the rough skin of the giant purple starfish, to brush against the sticky petals of the anemone and watch them flinch away...

Marco kissed Valeria sweetly on her unmoving lips, hazy sunlight glimmering on the first of the silver strands in his black hair, the breeze throwing eddies of sand up around them. A wave crashed, and Patricia felt freezing water wash over her feet and knees. She shivered, and not just from the cold. It was a good-bye kiss. Marco thought he could cross over on his own if he wasn't tethered to Patricia. Was he about to try?

The boy stood, turning in wonder. "Where are we?" he asked.

Patricia craned her neck to look around. Haystack Rock loomed just beyond them, its base frothy with winter-storm seas. A gull cried out, swooping through grey skies overhead. "Cannon Beach," Patricia said, surprised. They were in the exact spot she'd first found the agate, she realized, which now lay warm in her palm. "You wanted to go outside, so I took you to one of my favorite places."

"It's really cold," the boy said, but he didn't seem upset by it. He bent down to trace a finger through the damp sand, then danced back as another wave fanned over around them, erasing his line and leaving a crust of dirty foam at its farthest edge. Patricia felt it soak through her shoes. The tide was coming in.

"Oregon beaches are cold." It was Marco who spoke, as clear as he ever had in life. Patricia caught her breath. Marco brushed his fingers once more over Valeria's cheek, then got stiffly to his feet. "What are beaches like where you're from?"

"Warm," said the boy promptly. "We used to go swimming a lot. But they were flat for miles, not like this." He pointed at Haystack Rock. "That's really cool."

"Have you ever seen a starfish?" Patricia asked.

Marco smiled at her, and she saw understanding in his gaze. If he planned to cross back over, could he take someone else along? "They're everywhere out in the tide pools," he said. "You wanna go look?"

The boy's eyes widened, then he looked back at Valeria's body. Another wave washed up around them, leaving foam traced pink with Valeria's blood. "They'll just leave us."

"They can't," said Marco. "You think they haven't tried to leave me? I'll show you how." He met Patricia's gaze, then smiled at her sadly, and in a wild moment, Patricia realized that this, finally, was good-bye.

"Marco..." She started to reach for him, but caught herself and pressed down on Valeria's wound.

He leaned over and kissed her on the cheek. "Thank you, Pati." His lips were cold and dry as paper.

"Marco," she said, finally finding her voice. "Good luck."

He smiled brightly. "Thanks," he said, that twinkle back in his eye. "See ya on the other side."

The boy had been watching this, and now sat up. "So, if you're going, then can I take that one?" He pointed a finger at Patricia.

Marco shrugged. "Sure thing, kid. After we look at the starfish. They can't go anywhere." He held out a hand, and the boy took it eagerly. The expression on his face changed rapidly from excited to terrified.

"What—" He tried to pull away, but Marco tugged him closer, wrapping his arms around the boy. The boy was screaming. Marco locked eyes with Patricia and smiled, fading into nothing as she watched. *:bye pati bye tell val love:*

The hazy sunshine faded to black.

Chapter Twenty-Nine

THE ROOM REEKED of cigar smoke and white pepper fumes, and the acrid remnants of dozens of guttering candles. Patricia's fingers sought frantically for Valeria's throat, and she was rewarded by the faintest of pulses there, tiny wings fluttering beneath the cool surface of her skin. "Val," she whispered, and Valeria whispered something in return, though Patricia couldn't make it out.

Lucho cursed at his phone. "It's dead," he said, slipping it back in his pocket. "But they know where to find us. In the parking lot, at least." He knelt beside Valeria. "We need to move her up there."

"We shouldn't move her," she said. "She's not strong enough."

"They can't find her here," snapped Enrique. He was standing again, face grey beneath his dark complexion, but with none of the anguish he'd displayed earlier. She wondered if that had been part of her vision, too. He was relighting candles around the little altar; coils of smoke wound through their golden glow. "I have to do something about this *prenda*. It would be very dangerous for it to fall into the wrong hands."

"The boy's gone," said Patricia. Enrique frowned at her. "Max. The... *nfumbe*. Or whatever he was. He's gone."

"How?" Lucho was staring at her; Enrique was staring quizzically at the cauldron. The iron glistened with blood, Valeria's among it, but the mirror shard no longer glinted even as candles were relit.

Patricia had no idea how to even begin explaining. "Marco, he did it." She felt a wave of grief. "Marco's gone, too. Somehow they went together."

"We'll have some story time later, *profe*," Lucho said. "Plan B." He jabbed a crooked finger toward Enrique. "If your Lucero's powered down, can we move it?" Enrique nodded. "Then you and I, we get that thing out of here to keep headlines about death cults and human sacrifices out of the news."

Enrique glared at him. "Palo isn't a death cult."

Lucho gave him a thumbs-up. "And Pati, don't you dare move."

Lucho grabbed a pair of burlap sacks from a pile in the corner, and they used them to wrap the cauldron. The two old men grunted and struggled to move the altar through the back door. In the gloom of the candles, Patricia realized she could hear another rasping coming over Valeria's labored breathing. A groan, a shift.

Chente, she realized. He was starting to sit up now and still looking dazed.

She recovered first, and lunged for the gun Enrique had used to knock him out. She aimed it at him while slowly scooting back across the floor to where Valeria lay, hating being on this side of the weapon as much or more than she had being on the other side. "Don't move," she said. "I'll shoot." He started to stand. "My sister is dying," she said. "You want to bet your life that I'm not angry enough to shoot you?"

His laugh was harsh as sandpaper. "I'd definitely bet you never shot one of those things before."

Patricia's hand tightened on the grip, and with an effort she moved her index finger to cover the trigger. It felt cold as ice and curved like a fang. Deadly. Beside her, Valeria moaned. "This close, it doesn't matter if I'm a good aim," she said.

Chente shrugged. "No, it don't, because you still got the safety on. Gimme that—"

He lunged at her, and Patricia flung the weapon with all her might before his body slammed into hers. Her head cracked against the floor and her arm twisted close to popping behind her as her grip on Valeria's wound slipped.

She drove her knee up and felt it connect with soft flesh. Chente yowled and raised back his fist to strike.

A shot rang out and he froze.

"Get up." Lucho's voice sounded from the doorway. The gun was in his hand now, and the furious expression on his face said he truly knew what he was doing with it. Chente got gingerly to his feet.

Valeria's face was ashen, her eyelids fluttering and lips moving silently. "Val?" Patricia asked, but she didn't respond. Patricia could hear sirens getting closer for the second time that night. She prayed that these would be in time.

"Tie him up," Lucho snapped at Enrique, who took the lengths of rope that had been holding Valeria and began an expert series of knots to bind Chente's arms and legs. When it was done, Lucho handed Enrique the gun, then ran up to the parking lot to find the medics.

Once he had left, Enrique dropped into a crouch beside Patricia. He began humming again, sketching on the bloodstained, oil-stained cement with a piece of white chalk. A *firma*, arrows pointing in multiple directions, curving toward and veering away from Valeria.

"What are you doing?" Patricia asked, trying to keep the fear out of her voice.

"Helping," he said simply, and went about his work.

Patricia lay her free hand on her sister's cheek and began helping in the only way she knew how. "Father in Heaven," she whispered, tears running down her cheeks. She sought words for a prayer, feeling her sister's cool skin, the ripe, brassy smell of blood, her own anguish as she struggled to give control away, to rest whatever happened in celestial hands more capable than her own, more knowing, more understanding of mysteries and able to perform miracles.

Patricia watched her sister's face. Or able to withhold miracles, if that was what he saw fit, if that was part of the plan that Patricia was far too small to know.

"Valeria," she whispered. "I love you."

"Love you, too." A whisper.

"You can't die, Val. You're going to be an aunt. A great-aunt, I mean."

Valeria's eyes fluttered open, and she frowned, swore weakly. "Adrian?" Patricia nodded. "Knocked Lucy up? Stupid kid."

Patricia sighed. "Not their brightest moment."

Valeria coughed, blood speckling her lips. "You don't want me around the baby."

Patricia brushed her sister's hair back from her forehead. "You're my sister. Of course I want you around." She fought back tears. "Marco said to tell you he loves you."

"I know," Valeria whispered. "I saw him. I saw what you did, Pati. You're amazing."

"Don't start saying nice things just because..." Patricia couldn't bring herself to finish the sentence. "Nothing is going to happen. You're going to be fine."

Voices neared. Valeria closed her eyes, her hand falling away from Patricia's as the door burst open, and Patricia felt herself gently pulled back, medical uniforms swarming around her sister and strong old arms around her shoulders. She smelled Old Spice and mud and sweat: Lucho. Somewhere deep inside she noticed how hard they were working, these medics, their flurry of activity around Valeria, their haste, and it rekindled hope.

The soles of their shoes and canvas-clad knees scrubbed at the chalk *firma* Enrique had drawn, and she realized with a start that he was no longer here. He must have slipped out the back while she'd been talking with Valeria.

Bayer was there, too, in the corner with Chente and handcuffs, but Lucho steered her toward the door to follow Valeria's stretcher up the mossy, slippery steps and into the parking lot. It's not my blood, Patricia told medic after medic —I'm fine, I'm fine, only the black eye and cut on her face from earlier in the evening.

She made herself small in the ambulance, squeezing Valeria's hand tight while a web of tubes to blood bags and monitors were inserted into her sister's arms. She felt the tiniest of squeezes in return.

She scooted back as a medic reached across her to connect yet another machine, and realized her phone was back in her pocket, unshattered. She'd missed a text from Adrian. *Gabe says hi we're watching him play video games. Call me when you find tia V even if its late, Gabe's doing a raid all night, whatever that means. We need to get him a life. Love you mom.*

She looked up to see Valeria watching her, a hint of her old spark returning to her eyes. "Is it that hot basketball coach?" she asked weakly.

"Adrian. I sent him and Ava to stay with Gabe tonight."

Her eyelids fluttered briefly, then reopened. "But you're still going on that date next week, right?"

"Not if you die," Patricia said.

Valeria coughed. One of the machines beeped a warning, then went back about its business. "Don't be silly," Valeria said.

"And not with this black eye."

"It shows you have adventures. Men like a woman with a good story."

"I don't think I'll tell him all of it."

Valeria smiled weakly.

She certainly couldn't tell anyone about the way her body felt, scooped out and half-empty, the spot beneath her sternum nothing but a void. Nothing beating but her heart.

God bless you, Marco. She sent the thought out to wherever he might be, but she had no idea if he could still hear the indistinct murmurs of the living, or if it would matter to him if he could, anymore.

One of the medics bent between them to take Valeria's pulse. "Ma'am, I need you to buckle in," she said, and Patricia scooted back into her chair, working the seat belt with one hand without letting go of Valeria's hand with her other. She squeezed her sister's hand tight.

God bless you.

Acknowledgments

THANK YOU TO my husband, Robert Kittilson, for all the support, encouragement, and reminders to take care of myself as I've shambled after this dream. I couldn't ask for a better partner than you.

Thank you to my family: to Mom for teaching me a love of literature, and for catching so many of my typos over the years; to Dad for teaching me that stories can be found anywhere; and to Lacey for being the best sister a gal could ask for.

I'd especially like to thank the people who helped this specific novel come to life:

Thank you to Jeffrey Ford, who instructed our class at the Richard Hugo House to "Follow a character for a while and see what they do." I wrote the first chapter of this book in that class, and when I read it aloud, Mr. Ford told me if I didn't turn it into a novel, he would write it himself. It took me a while, sir, but here it is.

Thank you to Ken Scholes and the good people at Cascade Writers for giving me feedback on the first chapter during that wonderful retreat on the shores of the Pacific Ocean.

Thank you to the Four Windows team—Christine, Andy, Alisha, and Ian —for workshopping this novel into existence. Much depth was added and many ridiculous scenarios averted thanks to your incredibly insightful feedback.

And finally, thank you to Kyra Freestar for the amazing editorial work.

Your edits and comments gave this book just the shine it needed.

Also from Razorgirl Press

NeuTraffic by Andrew Gaines

John Graham, Thought Commuter License 178, has a simple mission: deliver a message. In a near-future, post-revolution Seattle, he and the other underground messengers are the only tenuous threads that keep the fledgling New Cascadian Order from falling back into chaos. Careful, paranoid planning and incredible luck can only take the young Nation-State so far — and now even the Thought Commuter network's secret intelligence can't save them from a devastating air raid.

His route home destroyed, John is forced on an odyssey through the bizarre new environment of his changed city. Seattle is boiling under the threat of renewed chaos, and the new society's structures are threatening to dissolve...but that's the least of John's problems. Because as John journeys through the mental landscape of his past, he's beginning to suspect that society isn't the only thing unravelling. His own sanity might be coming spectacularly undone.

School of Sight by Alisha A. Knaff

There is a world not everyone can see: a world of fairies and witches, shapeshifters and vampires. A world that co-exists with everyday life. When a young sibyl gets a first glimpse of that world, reality seems to crumble and everything becomes one big question mark.

The world of the supernatural proves to be deeper and wider than the young sibyl could ever have guessed as the local sybil community is threatened and the young sybil is drawn into a dangerous game between powers too old to be understood. It is more important now than ever to have friends at your back, but in a world this secret, enemies and friends look just alike.

Brass & Glass Book One: The Cask of Cranglimmering by Dawn Vogel

When Svetlana Tereshchenko, captain of the airship The Silent Monsoon, catches wind that a cask of mythical Cranglimmering whiskey has been stolen, she and her renegade crew of outcasts fly off in search of it. With the promise of a reward worthy of the cask's legendary lineage from both the Heliopolis Port Authority and the head of the Kavisoli crime family, Svetlana and her crew embark on a breathless chase that takes The Silent Monsoon from one end of the Republic to the other.

What Svetlana assumes will be an easy search and recover mission quickly becomes more complicated as each step she takes uncovers secrets and lies about the cask and its contents. Now, with an ethereal Ghost Ship haunting their path, friends reveal themselves as enemies and alliances develop with the most unlikely associates. The lives of her crew hang in the balance as Svetlana makes the crucial choice of whom she can trust and whom she should fear.

Trace by Ian M. Smith

Joanne Shaughnessy needs a job, and bad, which explains why in the course of 24 hours she has joined a shady medical study on the chi of amputees with a questionable physician at its helm, and agreed to buy antiques for an eccentric Chinese woman who seems to think Joanne has a supernatural affinity for it. She might just be taking advantage of two easy marks' open pocketbooks, but when she stumbles into a cache of mysterious letters, she starts to wonder if Ming is right, and if she can actually hear the voices of the dead.

To complicate matters more, she's being followed by a band of monocle wearing tech-heads desperate to harness her mysterious powers into unbelievable technological advancement.

63757917R00135

Made in the USA
Lexington, KY
17 May 2017